Fire and Brimstone

Chaos of the Covenant, Book Two

M.R. Forbes

Published by Quirky Algorithms

Seattle, Washington

Cover illustration by Tom Edwards

tomedwardsdesign.com

CHAPTER ONE

GLORITANT SALVIG THRAVEN LOWERED HIS head.

Only for a moment. A single, brief instant to respectfully acknowledge the passing of his finest Evolent. Trinity. It was a shame she had to die.

When he raised it again, he smiled.

"Is this how it begins?" he said to himself. The Great Return. The promise of the Covenant. A new Evolent in the making, perhaps the strongest of them all. "Perhaps stronger than me?"

He laughed at the idea. He was a Gloritant of the Nephilim. He had survived the wars. He had seen civilizations rise and fall. He had been in the Extant for millennia, tending to his flock, preparing them for the future when the promise of the Father would be fulfilled. A promise born of the cycle of all things. Chaos. Strife. Death. Power. Control. The Outworlds, the Republic. They were labels. Two shards of a broken whole, but only two shards. He would unify them, as he had been ordained to unify the Extant. He would harvest them, as the Father had promised the harvest.

Nine hundred planets. Twenty-two species of advanced intelligence. The most successful evolutions to arise from the countless seeds that his kind had helped God sew across this universe.

Until the rebellion. Until his demise at the hands of the Father, when the Nephilim no longer followed his commands or accepted his rule. When his technology became their technology. When his blood was filtered to become their Gift.

It had been left in ruin. Primordial. Basic. It had taken time to start over. They had waited in the Extant for the crops to grow. They had been patient, as their Father told them to be patient. Their civilization rose and fell and rose again, and he remained above it all. He never forgot the Covenant. He never lost hope. It was promised to them, and the Father didn't break promises.

He stood up and walked over to the transparency, through which he could monitor the construction of his fleet. Ninety-nine ships rested across the plains of Kell. The *Fire* was the largest. It sat at the head of the group. Peaceful. Calm. Patient. It was proof that the ways of the past, the technology of the first Nephilim would see them rise once more. He would be the uniter. He would bring his flock back where they belonged, never to flee again.

He had taken a risk putting the *Brimstone* into the field, dangling it in front of the Republic so brazenly. He had taken a bigger risk allowing the imbecile Ursan Gall to go to Drune with the hopes of rescuing his wife. He had never expected the Outworlder to be sensitive enough to feel the change in her Gift. While Ursan had accepted it, he didn't believe in it. He wasn't capable of believing in it. His mind was so filled with vengeful hate that he couldn't see how the power of the Gift could carry his potential beyond his emotions. He had taken it because Trinity had asked him to. Whether that decision would transform him or devour him was still to be determined. Thraven had known his Evolent would revive after her first mortal wound. He also knew she wouldn't revive after the second. Abigail Cage, an unlikely Potential, had taken her head.

Would she take Ursan's as well?

He laughed at that thought, too. With the *Fire* under his control, the *Brimstone* was expendable to serve a greater purpose. With Trinity's death, a new force would rise.

By the time it did, his fleet would be completed, the war machine of the Nephilim revived once more, the promise set to be fulfilled.

The harvest was nearly ready.

CHAPTER TWO

ABBEY SAT UP. SHE BLINKED a few times. She turned her head toward the medical bot standing beside her, staring at her.

"I'm not dead," she said.

"No," the medical bot agreed.

"I should have been dead."

"Yes."

"Why am I not dead?"

"I do not know. I am currently in recovery mode due to a systems fault. I am unable to diagnose."

Abbey looked down at herself. Bits and pieces of her hellsuit rested across her flesh and on the table, expelled from her body as it knitted itself back together. The suit was still intact on her feet and calves and missing from her upper torso where she had taken the most damage. Dried blood was caked across her skin, marking her everywhere. When she thought about it, she could still feel the bullets hitting her. She could still feel the pain of the mutilation.

And that was what had happened. She hadn't just been shot. She had been mutilated. Torn up by the collective firepower of an entire platoon of soldiers, most of them in battlesuits. Where had that shuttle come from? And who the hell was the asshole that ordered them to kill her?

She reached up and rubbed her face, picking some of the blood away. She held it between her fingers, staring at it. The Blood of Life. That was what Thraven's killer, Trin, had called it. The Gift that had made her somewhat bulletproof, and now, seemingly immortal.

"You only have half," she remembered Trin saying to her. Half of the Gift. Half of the power.

What could she do with the rest? Set herself on fire?

Benhil called her the Demon Queen. That didn't mean she wanted to be one for real.

That wasn't right. She wasn't immortal. As far as she knew, she had never stopped breathing. She had never stopped living. She had come as close to the edge as anyone would ever want to be, but she hadn't gone over. There was a distinct difference. Somehow, her team had gotten her out of there. Somehow, she had survived.

She leaned over, pulling the scraps of her hellsuit off her body.

"Do you have a robe?" she asked the bot.

It walked over to a nearby shelf and retrieved a thin white cover, holding it out to her.

"Thank you," she said as she took it and slipped it on. "I'll send Gant back in to reset you. If I have time later, I'll see if I can update your programming to accept miracles as a potential cure."

And that's what it was, wasn't it? A fragging miracle.

She wished it were that simple. She was afraid of what it really meant. The only things she knew about Gloritant Thraven scared the shit out of her. He had access to a power unlike anything she had ever seen or heard of before, something a part of her wanted to call magic, while the other part wouldn't believe such a thing existed. He was building an army that included any number of warships. He had control over the *Fire* and the *Brimstone*, the two most powerful starships the Republic had ever made. Oh yeah, and some of the soldiers in that army could only be stopped by removing their heads.

What. The. Frag?

"I will look forward to that," the bot said. It used an appendage to reach into a cabinet behind it and retrieve two pills, holding them out to her. Another limb produced a cup of water. "Take these."

"Painkillers?" Abbey said.

"Yes."

She smiled. "I'm not in pain."

It froze for a moment, clearly trying to process the statement. Then it put the pills and water back.

"I will prepare your discharge report. You are free to go."

"Thank you," she said, not that she needed the bot's permission to leave. She hopped off the table, looking back at the mess she had left behind. "Are you able to sterilize the room in recovery mode?"

"Yes. I will clean up."

She didn't envy the bot. There was blood everywhere. Only the Gift had saved her. She wished it felt like a gift. She couldn't help but think it was more like a curse.

She opened the hatch, stepping out into the dim corridor of the *Faust*. The air smelled heavy. Burned. She wasn't surprised they had been forced to fight their way out. A simple mission to make contact with a single Skink, and it had gone to hell. Completely to hell. They had been led right into the middle of something that stank worse than she did right now.

Trin had told her the *Fire* and the *Brimstone* were inconsequential in comparison to the bigger picture, and she couldn't find an argument to counter that statement. She had been up for less than two minutes, and she was already on her third terrifying thought.

She needed to talk to Captain Mann, to update him on what had happened and to find out what he knew. She was willing to bet that it was more than he had let on. He wouldn't have been a very good HSOC if it wasn't.

She made her way from Medical back toward the ladder that would lead up into the rest of the starship. She was surprised Gant hadn't been waiting for her outside the clinic, his fingers working feverishly on some bit of metal or another in an effort to keep himself calm. The absence forced her to consider that he hadn't made it off Drune. That he had been killed.

Scary thought number four.

She heard voices as she neared the ladder, feeling a small sense of relief that she wasn't alone on the *Faust*, even though she knew the idea was ridiculous to begin with. Someone had carried her back here. Someone had flown them out.

"I'm telling you, it's fragging suicide," Benhil said. "You saw what happened to Queenie. That woman that attacked her, you saw what she was capable of doing. She was on fire, for shit's sake. And did I mention those soldiers? They were burned to a fragging crisp, and they were still coming at us. What the hell was that? Damn, we needed all the collective luck we had left to make it out of there alive. I don't know about you, but I'm done. Let Mann drop me, seriously. You hear me, Ruby? Tell him to flip the switch, because this isn't fun. I'd rather die easy than go back out there and get thrown around like the invisible hand of God is bitch-slapping me or get taken out by a fragging piece of toast."

"It was always ninety-nine percent suicide, Jester," Airi said. "Do you think rotting in Hell is better?"

"I think anything is better. Whatever the frag is happening out here, it isn't normal. It isn't even human."

"Neither am I," Pik said.

"That's not what I mean. It's - I don't know. It's like a horror stream. Demons, you know. For real. Monsters. Nightmares. Shit."

"Can you just cool it for a minute," Bastion said. "Ruby, don't tell Mann to kill Benhil just yet."

"I have no intention to," Ruby replied. "Yet. I may be synthetic, but I still understand emotions."

"Jester, the mission is to recover the *Fire* and the *Brimstone*. We do that and we're free and clear. We don't have to fight the bogeymen; we just have to get the ships back."

"And how the frag are we supposed to do that? We ran away, which means we don't even know where the hell they are. Which means we're back to square one."

"Your whining is giving me a headache," Pik said.

"Frag you, Pik," Benhil said. "Seriously, Bastion. Our only lead was on Drune, and even if he isn't dead, there's no way we're going back there. Gant is missing. Queenie is dead. We're screwed, even if none of you want to admit it. I don't want to die, but letting Mann do it is a hell of a lot less painful than what's in store otherwise."

Abbey decided she had heard enough. She could feel herself getting more and more angry, the sensation of motion beneath her skin beginning to return as she did. She wanted to shower and change, to get back into a suit and have the familiar pressure on her flesh again. She was glad to hear the others standing up for one another and the mission. Or maybe it was self-preservation and denial? It didn't matter. They weren't quitting, and they certainly weren't letting Captain Mann shut them down. Especially not now.

She started climbing the ladder.

"Frag me?" Pik said. "Why don't you come over here and say that to my face?"

"Number one, because your face is too ugly for me to look at," Benhil replied. "Number two. Oh, there is no number two. It's because you're ugly."

"That's it," Pik said. "You want to die? I can take care of that."

"Pik, wait," Airi said.

"Move, Fury, or I'll move you."

"Do you think because you're bigger and stronger you can just tell me what to do?" Airi asked.

"Pretty much," Pik replied.

Abbey reached the top of the ladder. The others were assembled around it. The only one who noticed her was Ruby, and while a smile played at the synthetic's face, she didn't say anything. Abbey turned her head, finding Airi in the middle of pulling a knife from a belt at her waist, while Pik advanced toward her. Benhil was behind them, wearing an angry, frightened expression, while Bastion was leaning against the bulkhead, waiting for the whole thing to play out.

"Enough," Abbey snapped, sharply enough that she could see the muscles on Pik's back tighten as he froze. "I want you Rejects at attention, right now."

She glanced over at Ruby. She had a full smile now as she snapped to attention. So did Airi and Pik. Benhil glowered for a couple of seconds before joining them.

"Nice dress," Bastion said.

Abbey glared at him. He was smiling, too.

"How much did you hear?" Benhil asked.

"I heard enough to know you're on my shit list, Jester," she replied. "You could have at least waited to be sure I was dead before you started your bitching."

Benhil looked at the floor. "Shit, Queenie. Did you get a look at yourself?"

"I can't believe you healed from that," Bastion said. "I mean, I was hoping you would. We all were, in our own way, even Bennie, but damn. Whatever they gave you, I want some."

"No, you don't," Abbey said. "This isn't a gift, no matter what that bitch called it. It's uncomfortable as hell, and it's fueled by anger and hate."

"I don't mind a little anger and hate," Airi said. "That's my natural state of being."

"Yeah, you're not really dissuading me with that argument," Bastion said. "Three hours ago you looked like you got stepped on by a mech. Now you're back in one piece. And I repeat, nice dress."

Abbey realized the back of the gown had slipped open. She grabbed it and tugged it closed. "That's two."

Bastion laughed in reply. "You have nothing to be ass-hamed of."

"Oh, you didn't," Pik said.

"That was bad," Benhil agreed. "Really bad."

"Okay, enough jokes," Abbey said, having to force back her smile. They didn't know how much she needed a dose of levity at the moment. "I need a debrief. Start by telling me what happened to Gant."

"Dunno," Pik said. "He went apeshit when he saw you were getting hit."

"Gantshit," Benhil said.

"He was on a rampage," Airi said. "He killed four of their soldiers, and it looked like their commander tried to use his magic on him, and he just shrugged it off like it was nothing."

"It isn't magic," Ruby said.

"Then what is it?"

"Inconclusive. Magic doesn't exist. Therefore it isn't magic."

"Magic is any science we don't understand," Abbey said. "FTL used to be considered impossible, and the properties of disterium were called magic. In that sense, magic does exist."

"True," Ruby agreed.

"Then let's call it magic for now," Bastion suggested. "It'll make it easicr to talk about it."

"We could always settle on fragged-up-demon-shit," Benhil said.

"That's a mouthful," Bastion replied.

"Get back to the point," Abbey said. "Where is Gant?"

"Back on Drune?" Bastion said. "I looked for the little freak-monkey. I couldn't find him, and we had to blow off the planet."

"You left him behind?" Abbey said. "I assumed he was dead."

"He could be?" Bastion said.

"You don't know for sure?"

"No."

Abbey stepped toward him, and he pressed himself against the wall in response.

"Queenie, wait. Come on, that's not being fair. You were dead. The whole place was a war zone. I had to get airborne, or we would have all been dead with you, and we don't heal."

"He's right," Benhil said. "We all looked for Gant. If we had seen him, we would have tried to grab him."

Abbey turned around again, looking at each of the Rejects. "Airi, Pik, do you agree?"

"Yes," Airi said.

Pik nodded. "Sorry, Queenie. I know you two were friends. The good news is that the little guy may still be alive."

Abbey decided to drop it. She hoped Gant was still down there, hiding out somewhere. She imagined he would send a message their way if he was.

"Where are we now?" she asked.

"Outworlds," Bastion said. "About four hundred light years away from Drune. We dropped out of FTL to do some easy repairs and get our shit together."

"You said three hours?"

"Yup."

"Ruby, have you tried to contact Captain Mann?"

"Not yet, Queenie."

"Queenie," Bastion said. "The *Brimstone* was in orbit when we bailed."

"And you outmaneuvered it?" Abbey said, surprised and impressed.

"I wish. It had a torpedo lock on us. Then the craziest thing happened. The shot went low."

"What?"

"It missed and hit the other enemy battleship, the one we saw off Orunel, instead. Blew the fragger right up."

Abbey stared at Bastion, trying to make sense of it. "How can that be possible?"

"It shouldn't be. I don't know."

"I guess we don't know where it went after that?"

"No. Back to Thraven, I guess."

"Okay," Abbey said. "Jester, you're right about being back to square one."

"I told you so."

"Shut up and deal with it. No more shit about letting Mann kill you. I need you to come up with another way to track down the ships and Thraven. You can only die when I do."

Benhil looked like he was going to argue, but he decided against it. "Yes, ma'am."

"Ruby, get Captain Mann on the line. I need to discuss this with him."

"Yes, Queenie."

"Fury, you're about my size. Where's your hellsuit?"

"In our quarters," Fury replied. "But it's coded to me."

"You'll have to suit me up for now, then. Meet me up there in five. I'm going to get cleaned up first." She whirled on Bastion as his mouth started moving. "That's three."

"I didn't even say anything," Bastion said.

"You were about to."

"You don't know what I was going to say."

"Stow it and get a course plotted for the nearest planet that isn't a nearly deserted, waterless shithole. Preferably closer to the Fringe."

"Yes, ma'am."

"What should I do?" Pik asked.

"Go take inventory of the armory. I want to know what we've used and what we have left."

"Okay."

Abbey turned and headed back to the ladder, grabbing it to climb to the top level of the ship.

"Queenie," Bastion said as she gained the first rung.

"What?" Abbey replied.

"It's good to have you back."

CHAPTER THREE

"NEPHILIM?" CAPTAIN OLUS MANN SAID, his mouth barely able to move. How was she holding him like this? He tried to shift his arms and failed. "Like fallen angels?"

"Time has a way of disorganizing facts," Emily replied. "History would have you believe that the Seraphim were some kind of mystical beings. That's what humans turned them into, but that isn't what they were."

"Then what were they?"

"We were an intelligent species. The first intelligent species. The crew of a starship, believe it or not."

"I don't believe it."

"I don't care. I don't need you to believe the truth to know it is the truth. I've seen the Covenant. Look at the cover again, Olus. Do you think that's paper?"

Olus found his head was suddenly free. He turned it to look at the projection again. "It looks like paper to me."

"The discoloration is from data loss. My version is a copy, of course, a duplicate of the original carried from this part of the Galaxy nearly ten-thousand years ago."

"That's a long time."

"It is. Sadly, the original was damaged, too, or none of this subterfuge would be necessary. A casualty of war. Do you believe there were intelligent races that long ago? Do you believe there were starships?"

"Does it matter?"

"No. Is your mind that small that you can't believe? And Gloritant Thraven speaks of you with such respect. You should be honored by his caution."

"For all the good it's done me. How did you know I was here?"

"I could smell you."

"I saw your lifestream. I know what you were doing in there."

"Did you enjoy it? Mars is old, but her body is in good condition."

"Why do you drink her blood?"

"I enjoy it."

"You enjoy it? That's all?"

"It's a long story, going all the way back to the origin of the Nephilim. Sorry, Olus. I don't have time to tell it to you."

She moved to him, leaning past and reaching to where he had placed the extender. She pulled it off, dropping it onto his lap. She smiled as she grabbed his helmet and lifted it off his head, throwing it into the corner of the room. Then she ran her hands over the terminal's controls.

"Gloritant Thraven," she said. She glanced at Olus. "Let us see if the Gloritant has the same idea of what to do with you as I do."

"I can't wait," Olus said.

It took a few uncomfortable minutes of silence for Thraven to respond, his form projecting into the empty space ahead of the desk. He was resplendent in a crisp black uniform, handsome in a way that Olus couldn't quite put a finger on. He smiled as soon as he saw the prisoner. To Olus, it was the smile of a snake.

"Captain Mann," Thraven said. His attention turned to Emily. "Venerant Alloran. I assume you have a good reason for this?"

Olus was surprised. Thraven didn't sound happy.

"Gloritant," Emily said. "I caught Captain Mann searching through my secured terminal. He knows about the *Fire* and the *Brimstone*, and about my involvement."

"I told you to be cautious," Thraven snapped. Emily reacted immediately, falling forward on her knees, choking. "Is this your idea of cautious? There are reasons I've allowed Captain Mann his freedom so far, despite the damage he's managed to do. Or do you think I'm incapable?"

"Gloritant?" Emily said, barely able to breathe. "No. I'm sorry. I thought-"

"That was your first mistake, Alloran. I give you orders. You follow them. You don't think for yourself."

"Should I have let him take the data?" she asked.

The furor in Thraven's eyes cooled, and Emily was able to get back to her feet.

"You should have anticipated that he would try to retrieve it and taken greater care to remove the evidence. You were careless. You've created another complication. Be thankful I still have need of you." His eyes shifted back to Olus. "You've created a complication of your own."

"Glad I could help," Olus said.

Thraven smiled. "Lieutenant Cage is quite a handful, isn't she? Did you know she killed my best assassin? I knew you were brilliant, Captain. You outdid yourself with her."

"If your tool Lurin hadn't been such an idiot, I might not have even known she was valuable," Olus replied.

"That is why Lurin is dead," Thraven replied. "Of course, you already know the prison was cleansed."

"Who are you," Olus asked. "What is it you're after?"

"Only what was promised many, many years before you existed."

"An ancient spacefaring race," Olus said. "I got that part of the story already."

"More than spacefaring, Captain. More than ancient. You have no idea."

"Care to fill me in?"

"I have more important matters to deal with."

"Like Cage?"

Thraven's smile vanished. "I would prefer that you were still in play, Captain. As long as you were investigating the disappearance of the ships, the Republic was willing to sit on the sidelines and wait for your reports, to give you time to handle the matter quietly."

"With the help of your plants on the Committee, I'm sure. Like Omsala."

"I'm not quite ready to go to war with the Republic just yet. The *Fire* and the *Brimstone* are powerful, but even they wouldn't survive a joint assault by multiple fleets."

Olus felt a chill as he realized what Thraven was suggesting. "You're building more of them."

The smile returned. "Many more," he said. "We didn't have the resources for all of the research and development that went into the prototypes. The specifications were damaged, and time also erased portions of the data. Now that the technologies have been reintroduced and reintegrated, it is simply a matter of time before we fulfill the promise of the Covenant and make our Great Return."

"Return to where? Earth?"

"No," Thraven said. "Though the path leads through Earth, through the worlds of your charted universe, and through the beings of the one you call God. We intend to return home, Captain. Our true home. We intend to finish what we started here and free our brothers and sisters from the yoke of control they've been under for countless ages. We killed one Shard of God, and we will not rest until we've killed them all, along with the Source."

Olus continued to feel the cold chill wash over his body. He had no doubt about Thraven's seriousness, even if he wasn't quite sure of his sanity. Then again, the fact that he was being held paralyzed by nothing at all did lend weight to the man's statement, as outlandish as it seemed. In the end, it didn't matter if what Thraven believed was true or not. The Gloritant still wanted to do harm to the Republic, and that meant he had a responsibility to do everything in his power to stop him.

Which wasn't looking like very much at the moment.

"Gloritant," Emily said. "What do you want me to do with him?"

Thraven stared at Olus for a minute, still and silent. Olus stared back at the man, trying to get a look at the backdrop behind him. The comm projection blurred it intentionally to keep focus on the subject, but maybe he could spot something that would give him an idea where he was preparing his assault.

"I need time, Venerant. Time to finish preparing the fleet. I will inform General Omsala of Captain Mann's condition, but I expect we'll need more than that to convince the rest of the Republic Council that the Director is part of the problem and not part of the solution."

"You want to frame me?" Olus said.

"I can't simply kill you," Thraven replied. "Or I would have beforehand. Your position and reputation require a more delicate touch. Venerant Alloran, you are personally responsible for Captain Mann."

"What do you want me to do with him? I had thought to convert him."

"In time, perhaps. For now, ensure that he does not escape Feru."

Olus stared at the image. There was nothing there he could use. The background seemed to be a transparency of some kind, with a flat plain spread behind it. He could make out the shape of starships there, confirming Thraven's statement that he had a fleet in production. So what? They could have been on any one of hundreds of planets.

"That's all?" Emily said. "You want me to hold him prisoner?"

"Yes. That's all."

The link was broken, the projection vanishing. Olus looked into the empty space for a few more seconds. He knew exactly what Thraven intended.

Even worse?

He had created the conditions for him to do it.

CHAPTER FOUR

ABBEY WATCHED THE DRIED BLOOD fall off her, the cleanser pulling it away as it rained down from overhead. Slightly thicker than water, the gel captured dirt and grime and dead skin, sloughing it off as it fell to the floor, sinking into a tube where it would be carried to recycling and treated for another use. It only took a minute for it to get her completely clean, and she stepped out of the stall and grabbed the robe the medical bot had given her, wearing it as she crossed the short open space to the quarters she shared with Airi.

Airi was already waiting there, having placed her hellsuit on Abbey's mattress in anticipation of her return. She was sitting on her own bed, legs folded and head straight, eyes closed.

Abbey removed the robe and picked up the hellsuit. The feeling of the Gift beneath her skin had only intensified as the blood washed away, and she found that she was hungry again. She began pulling the suit on, thankful that Airi was close enough to her size that it would stretch to fit her.

"Queenie," Airi said, opening her eyes, noticing her movement. She turned her head, her expression changing slightly before she caught herself. "Let me help you." She moved in front of Abbey, reaching under the edges of the hellsuit and pulling it together. "There you are."

"Thank you," Abbey replied, feeling comforted by the pressure of the material against her skin, though slightly discomforted by the way Airi had looked at her half-dressed body. She knew why the former Master Chief had been sent to Hell. Other than that, she didn't know much about her at all. "I'll see if I can figure out how to clear the security settings later, or maybe getting a new suit from somewhere. I hope you don't mind helping me gear up until then?"

"Not at all," Airi said.

"I noticed the way you were looking at me," Abbey said, deciding to be blunt.

Airi's pale skin started to redden, and she looked at the ground. "My apologies. I was staring. I'm sorry. Please don't get the wrong idea. It's just, you healed from critical injuries, and there's no sign of any scarring."

Abbey felt relieved and embarrassed. "Oh. Right. Now I feel like an idiot. I thought you were checking me out."

Airi laughed. "You have a very nice body. I would have to be blind not to see that. But I wasn't looking at you that way." She paused, letting the smile fade before speaking again. "Do you know why I was in Hell?"

"You murdered your commanding officer. Cut his throat while he was sleeping. Premeditated."

"Yes. But the Republic doesn't care about reasons. They care about outcomes. My commander was an asshole, and he was a worse criminal than me by far. You're only a criminal when you get caught. Or when you don't know the right people."

"You tried to get off on an insanity plea."

"And got sunk deeper into Hell when the psychologists told them I was unstable."

"Are you unstable?"

"I think I can be. I think anyone would be if they had been treated the way I was treated. I couldn't take it anymore, and I won't take it anymore. Not from anybody. Pik thinks he can control me because he's bigger? No. He can't. He won't."

"I'll handle Pik," Abbey said. "We're all crazy in our own way, aren't we?"

"Bastion told me you think you were set up."

"I know I was set up. That doesn't make me not crazy. Not now. I've got something inside me that's still changing me. And I don't want it."

"I do."

"No, you don't," Abbey said again. "I know you're angry. I know you're hurt. I think if you had this so-called Gift, it would destroy you."

"Maybe. Maybe not. I'd like to see for myself."

"Even if I knew how to share it, I wouldn't. My job is to get us out of this alive and intact, as best I can."

"Understood," Airi said.

"You can help me, though. I got lucky with the sword. I still don't know what I'm doing. It seems like it might be a handy tool to have on my belt, especially if we run into more assholes with the Gift, considering they can stop bullets."

"And deflect lasers," Airi said. "You didn't see the one that came off the shuttle. He took the blue-haired woman's head."

"Just her head?" Abbey asked.

Airi nodded.

"What the hell for?"

"I don't know. He took it and ran away."

"I don't know if I like the sound of that."

"I can teach you," Airi said. "I recovered the sword from Drune, but we don't have another."

"Maybe Captain Mann can get me one."

"Yes."

Abbey put her hand on the hellsuit. "Thank you again for this. I'm going to go eat. I can't believe how hungry I feel."

"I'm sure you used a lot of energy recovering from your wounds."

"That's probably it, but I don't know. Something about it doesn't feel natural." She shrugged. "There's nothing I can do about that now. We already have enough to deal with."

"Queenie," Ruby said, her voice filling the room through the ship's loudspeakers. "Can you please come to the CIC immediately? We have a situation."

"Another one?" Abbey said, looking at Airi. "We have a CIC?"

"That's what Ruby has started to call the common area behind the cockpit," Airi said.

"I guess that's as good a label as any." The speakers were unidirectional, and she hadn't replaced her lost ear communicator yet. She would have to head down to see what the latest problem was, though her stomach was begging her to let her wait a minute.

"I can get a few food bars for you," Airi said.

"Okay. Thank you."

Airi bowed slightly as Abbey fled the room, heading down the ladder into the common area. Ruby was there with Bastion.

"Queenie," Ruby said. "I'm picking up an emergency beacon from Captain Mann."

"A beacon?" Abbey said. "From where."

"Feru," Ruby replied.

"Inside Republic space," Bastion said.

"I know where Feru is," Abbey said. "I assume the beacon means he's in trouble. Who else might be receiving?"

"This isn't a standard military beacon. This one is keyed directly to me."

"So, nobody else."

Airi slipped down the ladder, carrying a handful of food bars. She handed them toward Abbey, who took one and tore it open.

"Hungry?" Bastion asked.

"Starving."

"What about Captain Mann?" Ruby asked.

"What about him?" Bastion said. "He got himself in trouble; he'll get himself out."

"Ruby, set a new course for Feru," Abbey said between bites.

"What?" Bastion said. "Queenie, I know you got beat up a bit, but I'm hoping you still have some small measure of sanity left. We can't go to Feru."

"Why not?"

"We're in an unmarked, Outworld ship for one. Which is all fine and dandy when you're on the Fringe or in the Outworlds, but Feru is deep inside Republic space. For another, this is our best chance to get out of this shitty deal."

"What do you mean?"

Bastion smiled. "Think about it. If Mann is dead, he can't send the signal to unleash the hounds. We're home free. You can go back to Earth and your kid, and I can go back to, well, wherever the frag I want to go."

"He has a point," Benhil said, appearing from the lower deck. Pik came up right behind him.

"What's going on?" Pik asked.

"Captain Mann is up the comet," Bastion said. "Queenie here wants to go rescue him. I say frag it, let him die."

"You were on Drune, weren't you?" Abbey asked. "Whatever is happening is bigger than two stolen starships. It's bigger than our freedom."

"No it isn't," Pik said. "We've got another way out, and we should take it."

"What the hell good is freedom if some nutjob is just going to come along and take it all away?" Abbey asked. "We need to stop him, not make things easier for him."

"I vote to let him die," Bastion said.

"This isn't a democracy," Abbey said. She was starting to get angry again. She could feel the Gift responding.

"It sort of is," Pik said. "You're outnumbered four to one."

"Four to two," Ruby said, moving to stand beside Abbey.

"So you assholes are going to mutiny over this? Trying to save a man's life? He got you out of Hell, whether you like the terms or not."

"I only ask myself one question," Benhil said. "What's in it for me?"

"I won't kill you," Abbey replied.

"Go ahead and try," Pik said. "You can't take us all at once."

Abbey looked at each of the Rejects. She could feel her body shaking with anger. She had nearly fragging died for them, and this was how they were going to pay her back?

"You all deserved to be in Hell, didn't you?" she spat. "The only way we aren't going to Feru is over my dead body."

The others froze, trying to decide what to do. Abbey raised her hands, ready to attempt to use the Gift, even if she wasn't sure it would work. It didn't feel the same as it had before. It was present, but it seemed weaker.

"I can't do it," Pik said, backing down. "You came back for Airi and me on Drune. I owe you for that."

"Me, too," Airi said.

Abbey glanced at Bastion and Benhil. Bastion shrugged and walked away, going back to the cockpit.

"I look like an asshole for the second time today, don't I?" Benhil said. "Feru it is, I guess."

He started climbing the ladder.

"Here, Queenie," Airi said, handing her another bar. Abbey took it eagerly, tearing the wrapping off and taking a bite. "I just want to go home," she said. "My parents think I'm dead."

"You will," Abbey said.

"Queenie, there's something you should know," Ruby said.

"What is it?"

"I thought it might be helpful to see how the crew reacted to the news. There is a complication." She paused, biting her lower lip. The way she did it, it was clear the move was designed to be enticing. "The kill signal is on a timer. If Captain Mann doesn't reset it, the clock will hit zero, and the transmission will go out."

"What?" Airi said.

"If Captain Mann dies, you all die," Ruby replied.

CHAPTER FIVE

GANT REMAINED SITTING AGAINST THE blast door inside the *Brimstone's* engine room for a few minutes, trying to calm himself down. He pulled a small piece of metal wire from his lightsuit, manipulating it in one hand, bending it into the shape of a Gantean Suzeen, a three-dimensional, twelve-pointed star.

He had been planning to sabotage the ship, to break the engines and leave it stranded so that Abbey could come and find them. He had been expecting a standard disterium conversion reactor, a device he knew well.

Instead, he had been treated to a split-second look at a fragging monstrosity. A fragging nightmare.

He closed his eyes, and it was the only thing he could see. Bodies. Terran bodies, pressed against the walls of the compartment and hanging from the ceiling, held aloft by a dark material that was wrapped around their arms and legs. They had tubes running into and out of them. One was carrying a nearly clear material to them. Water? Nutrients? The other tubes were blood red and connected to a machine in the center.

The Terrans were alive, their eyes open, their chests moving slightly up and down as they breathed. There were at least one hundred of them, though he was sure it was more. He couldn't see all the way to the back of the space.

The device in the middle was tech of some kind. It was made of alloy, matte black like the starship that had been in orbit around Orunel, the one that belonged to the assholes that attacked the planet. It had the connectors sticking into it, and a transparency in the back that showed both the current level of the collected blood and other pipes and tubes that revealed the plasma swirling through it. The blood that moved through the machine was darker in color, and it looked thicker. It reminded him of the blood that had poured out of blue-hair's neck when Abbey chopped her head off.

He had no idea how it worked, and he hoped he never needed to learn. Whatever this was, it wasn't right. It wasn't sane. How could the Republic have created something like this? How could they approve of it?

He didn't have a high opinion of the masters he had once served, but he was pretty sure they wouldn't have. That meant Eagan Heavyworks knew what this ship was. And if that were true, didn't it also mean they had helped Thraven steal it?

And what the hell was the ship? How could he even define it? It was using Terrans as some kind of horrible fuel source? What might it be using for weaponry? Fragging fetuses?

The idea made him nauseous. His fingers worked more quickly, folding the metal into a Suzeen. He had to do something, but what? Obviously, his original plan wasn't going to work.

If he could get in, could he save the poor bastards inside? Could he at least put them out of their misery? What if life support was dependent on the reactor? He would be killing himself, and while it might get one of the ships out of Thraven's control, it would make it harder for Abbey to find out where they had taken the other one.

"Plan B," he said to himself, swallowing his fear. "Get the beacon up. Let Abbey figure out what to do with this horror show."

He pulled himself up on shaky legs, making his way over to the terminal on this side of the blast doors. He activated it, hopeful that the system wouldn't report its use. It didn't matter. It was secured. He would need the command key to get in. He backed away from it. The comm systems were likely a different story. They would be using those systems, and he doubted they would lock up every time they were finished.

He returned to the external hatch, opening it and peering out into the corridor. It was clear. He ducked out of the engine room and hurried down the hall. He would have to head closer to the bridge, closer to the enemy, to find an open terminal. He was an engineer, not a ninja, but hopefully, his size would make it easier not to get caught.

It took close to ten minutes, but he finally found himself closing in on the occupied part of the starship. He moved more cautiously when he did, keeping out of sight of the assholes, hugging the walls and slipping behind frame supports whenever he spotted one that might have spotted him.

He opened the nearby hatches in turn, seeking out living quarters and terminals. He found a few, checking them quickly. Locked. It seemed the ship had little more than a skeleton crew. He kept going, losing track of time in the pattern of hiding and running, opening doors and closing them, activating terminals and abandoning them. Finally, he opened one of the hatches and found himself in larger, more plush quarters. The terminal in the corner had a secondary terminal hooked into it, one that looked a lot less fancy but a lot more damage resistant, a worn and beaten mobile box. He hurried over to it, examining the wiring. It was primitive but functional. He moved to settle in ahead of it when he heard a noise to his right. He ducked beneath the terminal, looking back in the direction of the sound. It had come from a closed door, another room in the suite.

He wasn't alone.

He decided he would find another terminal. He began to retreat from the room, making it a few meters before the door swung open. He dove back under the terminal, pressing himself into the back corner. He wished he still had his gun.

A pair of boots appeared a moment later, coming his way. He remained still while their owner sat down at the terminal, slumping back into the seat. Gant risked lowering his head slightly to get a better angle to see the soldier. He drew back when he recognized the one who had ordered Abbey's death. He felt his anger building, tempted to jump the man right there. He forced himself to stay restrained. He couldn't help Abbey that way, and maybe he could learn something useful.

"General Thraven," the man said, activating the comm.

CHAPTER SIX

URSAN STARED AT HIS WIFE'S head, resting on the bed in the quarters he had claimed on board the *Brimstone*. He still wasn't quite able to accept what he was seeing. He was still surprised at himself for what he had done.

What else was he supposed to do? He had seen the bitch who had cut off Trin's head. She had the Gift, and she had impossibly outmaneuvered his wife with it. Who was she? What the frag was she doing on Drune? Was she the reason Trin had been there? He didn't have any answers, only questions.

Only pain.

His soldiers had killed her. At least he hoped they had. They had shot her dozens of times, shredded her body to a near pulp. He hadn't gotten to take her head, though. That Gant had shown up, berserking across the field, attacking with a fury he had never seen from the species. He knew the Gant were incredibly loyal to those they took as alphas, but he hadn't expected it to have a resistance to the Gift. That surprise had cost him his kill, and forced him to retreat or risk losing his entire platoon. The head was all he had left of her.

He reached down and stroked her blue hair. Her eyes were frozen in a look of surprise, her mouth slightly open, She had never expected the woman in the red softsuit to get the better of her. She hadn't expected to be torn in half by a Gift-enhanced sword. A fragging sword of all things! Who carried a sword, anyway? Weapons like that had gone out of use thousands of years ago.

Trin was dead, and he wanted to know why.

He reached up and wiped his eyes, clearing the tears from them once more. He had refused to take off his helmet until he had made it back here. He refused to let his crew see him fall apart. He was, though. He was losing it. Had lost it. He had taken her head and carried it back here with him. They were probably whispering to one another about it even now.

He could feel the Gift within him, squirming through his body. He moved his hand from her head down to her neck, where a line of dried blood was resting. He stared at it, hesitant. What he had already done was insane. Would he turn himself into a monster as well? More of the Gift would make him stronger. Would it make him strong enough?

He scraped the blood off with his fingers, bringing it to his lips. He tasted it gingerly before slipping the fingers into his mouth, sucking the blood off and swallowing. He repeated the action a few more times, the tears streaming from his eyes again.

"I'll find her," he said to the head. "If she isn't dead already, I'll find her, and I'll destroy her. I promise."

He stood up, stepping back and looking at Trin's face again. Was there any way to bring her back? He knew some of what the Gift could do. He knew how it could heal. Could it return her to him?

He made his way out of the bedroom, heading for the terminal there. He sat down, slumping in the chair, tired and angry and sad.

"General Thraven," he said, opening a link. Then he leaned back further, wiping away the wetness on his face while he waited.

"Captain Gall," Thraven said, responding a few minutes later.

"She's dead," Ursan said.

"I'm aware."

"Who is she?"

"Who is who?"

"Don't frag with me, General," Ursan said. "The other one. She had the Gift. Who the hell was she?"

"Oh. You mean Lieutenant Cage. Lieutenant Abigail Cage of the Earth Republic."

The Earth Republic? Ursan could feel the Gift burning within him. Hadn't he lost enough to the damned Republic?

"Where did she come from?"

"Hell. She was supposed to be converted. She escaped. I sent Trin to find her."

"You sent Trin to die, you son of a bitch."

Thraven raised a hand, and suddenly Ursan was choking.

"Watch yourself, Captain," Thraven hissed. "I allowed you to make an attempt to save her. Did you arrive too late? The failure is yours, not mine."

He felt his throat clear. "She shouldn't have been there," he said, coughing. "Not alone. I told you we're better as a team. This woman, Cage, wouldn't have been able to stand up to both of us."

"Your wife was the best assassin in the Outworlds, Captain. I had no reason to believe she would fail against a woman who had only been given the Gift days ago."

Ursan put his head in his hands. "I know. I'm sorry, General. I'm not handling this well."

"You're only human, Captain."

"The Gift," Ursan said. "I know if we lose our heads, we can't regenerate. But what if we have the head? Can we bring it back? Maybe attach it to a synth body or something?"

Thraven's eyes narrowed, and he looked disgusted. "Did you take Trin's head, Captain?"

"I might-"

"There's nothing anyone can do. Your wife is decapitated. I'm afraid it's fatal. The Gift isn't magic. It can't do the impossible, only things that seem impossible to those who don't know any better."

Ursan nodded. He had been hopeful. That didn't mean he was going to throw Trin's head out of an airlock. "What about Cage? Do you know if she's still alive? I fired a torpedo at her ship, but it missed."

Thraven's whole face turned dark. "What?"

"It hit the Lahar," Ursan said. "I don't know how. We had a lock."

"You hit the Lahar?"

"Destroyed it, I think. I'm sorry, General. I don't understand it. We couldn't hit that damn ship no matter what we did. All of our shots seemed to go around it."

"I see," Thraven said, his expression turning curious.

Ursan was surprised by that. He should have been furious for the loss of the battleship. He expected to find himself choking again.

He didn't.

"You disobeyed my orders. You destroyed one of my ships. You should be thankful I don't kill you where you stand."

"I know," Ursan said. "Please, General. If Cage is alive, I want to find her. I want to be the one to catch her and kill her."

"Your wife couldn't do it, but you believe you can?"

"I have a lot of motivation."

Thraven smiled. "Return the *Brimstone* as you were ordered, Captain."

"General-"

"Are you resisting me again, Ursan?" Thraven said. "Are you questioning my ability to lead this war again?"

"I want revenge."

"I want the *Brimstone*. That is an order, Captain. Do not disobey me."

Ursan scowled but nodded. "Yes, sir," he said. "We're on our way."

Thraven cut the link, his projection vanishing.

"After Abigail Cage is dead," Ursan said, getting to his feet. "Once I've had her blood, I'll kill you too, you son of a bitch."

CHAPTER SEVEN

"We're almost to Feru," Bastion said, glancing back at Abbey as she entered the *Imp's* cockpit. "I hope Fringe patrol doesn't catch up with us too quickly." He shook his head, still not happy about the idea of trying to rescue Captain Mann. "I hope we can avoid orbital patrols and Planetary Defense, too. The place has to be crawling with Republic assets after what happened here."

"I told you what Ruby said," Abbey replied. "Regardless of what you thought you wanted, and whatever you were willing to do to get it, if we don't make an effort then we're all dead."

"That doesn't mean I have to like it."

"I haven't liked anything since they sent me to Hell. I'm still here. I'm still fighting."

"Better go strap in, Queenie. I have a feeling this is going to be a hell of a ride, and we don't have Gant here to fix our shit if it decides to break."

"You'll get us down. I have faith in you."

She tapped him on the shoulder and then headed to the rear of the shuttle. Pik, Benhil, and Airi were already strapped in, looking almost like a real team in their dark lightsuits. She was the one who stood out. Her softsuit and the HUD Gant had made her were both destroyed on Drune, and they didn't currently have another that would fit her, which meant she was going in unenhanced. It wouldn't be the first time she had made a drop without augmentation. She had done a job in a short dress and high heels once, a mission to get some data from some rich corporate asshole who turned out to be funding a mercenary unit for the Outworlds. The hellsuit was still a step up from that. She just wished she had more pockets, a tactile interface, and some Breaker gear.

Brute forcing her way into anything just wasn't her style.

At least she had an ear communicator, though it was a pretty lousy setup compared to the TCUs the rest of the Rejects were wearing. It was enough to connect her to the network and send orders, but she would be relying on them to do most of the heavy lifting.

"Ruby," she said, contacting the synth. "ETA?"

"Ninety-seven seconds, Queenie," Ruby replied.

Abbey took a seat, pulling the built-in straps over her chest and attaching it between her legs. She glanced over at the others. Pik raised his hand in acknowledgment.

"Speed is key here, Rejects," Abbey said. "Ruby will dump the *Imp* near Feru's orbit and head into FTL again, taking up a position still in sensor range, but hopefully far enough out that PD and any Republic orbital defense will decide to observe and let border patrol deal with the problem. It's not like our space bird is all that imposing, and I think her presence will leave them a bit confused. Meanwhile, we'll have twenty minutes total to find Mann and get him out. We have to make it back into orbit for the rendezvous, or the odds are high that the *Faust* is going to get blown apart by a Republic warship while we're fragging around on the surface. If that happens, none of us go home, and we all die. If Mann dies, we all die. If the *Imp* gets knocked out, we all die."

"Is there any scenario where we don't die?" Benhil said. "Because this is the worst battle cry I've ever fragging heard."

"You want me to hold you while you piss, too, Jester?" Abbey asked. "It's honest. We have to be clean and on point or we're fragged. There's only one way we live, and it's by doing everything right."

"I've got your back, Queenie," Pik said.

"Do you, Okay?" Abbey replied, not letting him off the hook for his earlier resistance.

"Yeah. I'm sorry about before. I just thought we had an easy way out, you know? No offense, but I'm a little claustrophobic riding around in this thing, and Jester smells."

"I smell?" Benhil said. "Try getting a whiff of yourself sometime."

Pik laughed.

"Twenty seconds, Queenie," Ruby said.

"Lucifer, are you set?"

"Roger. Firing her up now."

The *Imp* shuddered for a moment as the reactor came online. Abbey put her hand on her thigh, to the belt wrapped around the hellsuit. A pistol with an extended magazine sat on her left side. A Republic Army standard issue knife rested on her right.

"Ten seconds," Ruby said.

Abbey leaned her head back. Twenty minutes. They had a general idea where on the planet Mann was because of the beacon, but otherwise they were going in blind. What were the odds they could get in, grab him, and get out in twenty minutes?

She didn't want to know, but she was sure they weren't very good.

"Mark," Ruby said as the *Faust* blinked into existence outside of Feru.

"Lucifer, punch it," Abbey said.

"Roger."

Then she was shoved back into her seat as the *Imp's* thrusters fired full-bore, sending them rocketing forward toward the shielded hangar opening. The force field dropped for a split second as they hurtled through, giving them passage out into space. Abbey could see through the *Imp*'s forward canopy from her position, and she felt her jaw clench at the sight of the Republic battleship hovering in orbit ahead of them. Her eyes caught sight of the ship's identifier a moment later. The *Driver*.

"Returning to FTL," Ruby said. "Good hunting, Queenie. Good hunting, Rejects."

"The *Faust* is away," Bastion said. "I'm picking up activity from the surface. It looks like PD is sending units our way. Oh, and we're being hailed."

"We're a shuttle full of escaped convicts," Abbey said. "I have a feeling they won't give us the VIP treatment no matter what we say."

"Aww, Queenie, you're so negative," Pik said.

"I'm getting action from the *Driver* now," Bastion said. "It looks like they're sending an escort."

"Any kind of escort they have, I don't want," Benhil said.

"Can you get around them?" Abbey asked.

"I've got a good vector, but these are starfighters we're talking about. Looks like Rapiers."

"You're telling me this thing can't outrun a Rapier? What kind of crap did Mann give us?"

Bastion laughed. "Approaching orbit. Hold on."

The *Imp* shifted in space, rolling and pointing toward the planet, the view constantly shifting and changing as Bastion adjusted vectors to avoid the fire from the incoming starfighters. Abbey saw a missile go streaking past, missing them by less than a meter and detonating way too close. The shuttle rocked as it crashed through the small burst of quickly vaporized air, and Bastion altered direction, shifting them perpendicular to the planet.

"Here comes PD," he said. "Are those Daggers?" He laughed again. "I don't think I've seen a Dagger in fifteen years. Isn't this where Eagan Heavyworks built their ships? You'd think they could have provided some upgrades. No wonder the Outworlders were able to get in here unnoticed."

The *Imp* shook again, a tone sounding in the cockpit.

"Shit," Bastion said.

"Can you stop talking and concentrate on getting us down?" Abbey said.

"I'm more focused when I'm talking," Bastion replied.

"You just got hit."

"It was a lucky shot. Anyway, what was I saying? Oh yeah. Hold on."

The *Imp* twisted, the inertia pushing Abbey around in her restraints despite the dampeners. A Dagger appeared in front of them, and she watched as a round of fire from the shuttle's forward guns tore into it, blowing it silently apart.

"Lucifer, what the frag?" she shouted. "Those are friendlies."

"What?" Bastion said. "I don't know much about the company you keep. Well, I do, now. Queenie, unless I'm blind, they don't look very friendly to me."

"They're trying to defend their planet. You know, the one that had two orbital stations destroyed along with a Republic fleet? Can you blame them for attacking us?"

"No, but they should expect us to fight back. Hold on."

The *Imp* maneuvered again, shooting past a Rapier as it tried to get an attack vector. The planet was approaching rapidly.

"Anyway, as I was saying, someone on that planet is holding Captain Mann prisoner. That means they're involved in this shit, one way or another. And Mann told us to do whatever it takes to recover the ships. You heard him say it. Kill whoever you have to. Destroy whatever you have to. Just get it done. If you want a chance to get Mann out alive, if you think this really is bigger than two ships, we can't afford to be above killing Republic soldiers and destroying Republic assets. I'm sorry, Queenie, but we can't. It's them or us. You need to make a firm decision and stick with it."

Abbey stared ahead, through the forward viewport as another Dagger flashed past. She knew Bastion could have taken it down if he wanted to. He was giving her a choice, waiting for her orders. Damn him for making a good argument.

"Do what you have to," she said reluctantly. "You're right."

"Thank you, ma'am," Bastion replied.

They sank deeper into the atmosphere, the *Imp* staying smooth as Bastion guided it in, still slipping and jerking and altering course to avoid the fighters giving chase.

"Beacon is six hundred klicks ahead," Bastion said. "Four Rapiers on our six, and I've got visual on two more Daggers incoming. I won't kill them unless I have to."

The *Imp* rolled, sliding to the left and inverting. Tracers skipped by from the Rapiers, narrowly missing the shuttle as Bastion expertly avoided the fire. The Daggers were coming on hard ahead, and he started adjusting to avoid them before canceling the maneuver, triggering the forward gun batteries instead. Heavy slugs pounded the two starfighters, creating a plume of smoke as they both began tumbling away almost in unison.

"I had to," Bastion said, the shuttle blowing through the smoke.

He sounded a little too pleased for Abbey to believe it.

"Two hundred klicks," he said a handful of seconds later. "Prepare for ingress. I'm going to circle around to throw the Rapiers long enough that I can land."

"Roger," Abbey said. "You heard him, Rejects. On your feet."

The others stood, keeping themselves firm to the ground with the magnetic attachments on their lightsuits. She didn't have that luxury, and she kept a tight grip on an overhead beam as she made her way toward the rear of the shuttle.

"I've never been to Feru before," Bastion said, keeping up his dialogue while he avoided the attack. "It seems like a nice enough planet. A little humid, maybe, but all of the greenery is nice. Queenie, did you know my father was a botanist?"

"What?"

"A botanist. Someone who studies plants. He went all over the galaxy helping catalog native plants on worlds with pre-existing ecosystems. I went with him a couple of times. It isn't as dry as it - approaching the beacon. Damn, it looks like it's in the middle of a jungle. Well, a jungle right beside a huge compound. I bet he's in there."

"Did you need a crystal ball to figure that out?" Benhil said.

"Shut up," Bastion said. "Blowing past. Hold on."

The *Imp* shot over the top of the compound, streaking by with the Rapiers still tailing.

"They have to know we're coming," Airi said. "What if they kill Captain Mann before we can get to him?"

"If they were going to kill him they would have done it already,"

Abbey said. "There's no benefit to leading us here."

"Queenie, we've got a problem," Bastion said. "I don't see anywhere to land this thing down there, and even if I did, there wouldn't be enough time to touch down and get airborne before the Republic thruster heads catch up."

"Damn. Give me an option."

"I can slow down over the top. You can jump."

"I'm not wearing an augmented suit," Abbey replied. "I can't jump."

"I can," Airi said.

"Me, too," Pik said. "It's okay if you have to sit this one out, Boss. We'll take care of business for you."

Abbey didn't hesitate. What other choice did they have? "Affirmative. Fury, Okay, Jester, you're up. I'm out. Fury, you have the lead."

"Roger," Airi said.

Abbey leaned over and hit the controls to open the shuttle's rear hatch. She almost fell over as the *Imp* rocked to the side to avoid enemy fire, but Airi reached out and caught her.

"Thanks," she said.

"Anytime," Airi replied.

Abbey looked out behind them, at the three Rapiers still giving pursuit. Then she looked down. They were still almost fifty meters above the landscape, way too far for her to jump, and at the edge of what the lightsuits were rated for.

"Lucifer?" she said.

"On my mark," he said. "I'm going to hard stop. Hold on."

She grabbed the side of the shuttle in anticipation.

"Mark," Bastion said.

The reactor screamed, the thrusters shutting down, the anti-gravity coils going to full power to compensate. They came to a shuddering slow-down, the Rapiers shooting by on both sides, sending a final volley as they did. It pinged into the shuttle on their right, the slugs missing Pik by inches.

"Bastards," Pik said.

"Now," Airi said. Then she was gone, out of the shuttle and headed for the courtyard of the compound below.

"See you soon, Queenie," Pik said. He saluted as he threw himself from the shuttle. "Bombs away."

Benhil watched from the edge for a second and then turned to salute her as he threw himself out.

"Clear your head, we're on the move," Bastion said.

"How the hell are we going to retrieve them?"

"I can outfox those tools in the fighters with my eyes closed. I'll get a better approach set up while they're inside. Watch your head, Queenie. The Rapiers are circling back, and I don't want you to lose it to the hatch."

Abbey watched the falling Rejects extend their arms, the gossamer film between flowing out to slow their descent. She looked to the cockpit, where Bastion was leaning over, looking back at her.

"What's the holdup?" he asked.

"Lose my head?" Abbey said. "Maybe I can make the jump after all."

"I don't think-"

She didn't wait for him to finish.

She threw herself from the shuttle.

CHAPTER EIGHT

SHE DIDN'T THINK ALL THAT much about the fall. After all, it wasn't the fall that would kill her.

Then again, after what had happened on Drune, she was pretty sure the fall wouldn't kill her either.

It would just hurt real bad.

She watched the scene below her. Benhil, Airi, and Pik were almost on the ground. A squad of guards had emerged from one of the doors and was moving into a defensive position, spreading out behind a half wall ahead of the main structure. The Rejects spotted them immediately, finding their own cover and prepping their rifles.

Nobody seemed to notice her.

She could feel the Gift beneath her skin. She reached inward for it, trying to use it to help break her fall, even if she wasn't sure how. She didn't feel it burning. She didn't feel it responding. She only had a few seconds. She knew there was one thing that had seemed to cause it to react. She needed to get angry.

She turned her thoughts to Hayley. These assholes were trying to keep her from her daughter. They were trying to kill her teammates. They were holding the key to her survival captive. And, if she hit the ground without the damned Gift, she was going to break her damned legs and probably get shot to hell again.

She felt the burning beneath her skin, rising up from her feet and into her ankles, from her ankles to her knees. Gloritant Thraven had given her this. He had hoped to control her, to use her. Mann was using her too, but at least he had good intentions. At least he wanted to help protect people. Thraven had forced her to agree to kill innocent individuals. He was pushing her toward a place she didn't want to be, whether he knew it or not.

The ground came on hard and fast. She hit if feet first, the impact sending out a shockwave that seemed to spread around her, the kinetic energy being pushed outward instead of absorbed into her body. Her knees flexed slightly, and then she was still, standing, and unharmed.

She allowed herself a slight smile. Then she got to work.

"Fury, Okay, I'm down," she said. "We can't afford to get pinned here. We have ten minutes. That's not a lot of time."

"Affirmative," Airi replied.

"Cover me."

"Okay, Boss," Pik said.

Abbey pulled the knife and the pistol as she ran toward the side of the main building, perpendicular to the guards. They still hadn't noticed her, and they were even more distracted when the Rejects started firing on their position. Bullets bit into the wall and the side of the building while the guards hunkered down behind it.

Abbey stayed close to the wall, coming at them from the side, raising her pistol and aiming without the assistance of the TCU. She fired, two bullets for each guard, hitting three of them before they realized they were under attack from their flank. They turned her way, staying low while Benhil, Airi, and Abbey continued to fire. They didn't see Pik running toward them, and he vaulted the wall, grabbing two of the guards and throwing them hard into the side of the building. The remaining soldier stood to run, only to be hit by Airi's assault.

"Clear," Pik said.

Abbey joined him at the door the guards had streamed from. He tapped the controls, but it didn't open.

"Locked," he said.

"I thought you couldn't make the jump," Airi said, reaching them. "But I'm not surprised you changed your mind."

"Or that you survived the fall," Pik said.

"If I had my softsuit and gear I could open this in seconds," Abbey said.

"We'll have to do it the old fashioned way," Pik said. He stepped back and waved his arms. "Get ready. They might have more guards on the other side.

The Rejects leveled their weapons. Pik charged the door, turning to put his shoulder against it. Trovers were big and strong on their own. Augmented by a suit, even a lightsuit, they were massively powerful. The door agreed, bending inward as he slammed into it.

"One more," he said, backing up and ramming it again. It folded under the pressure, breaking off its guides and collapsing loudly into a kitchen. Pik held his arm out toward it. "Ladies first."

"Too kind," Abbey said, moving into the building. She scanned the kitchen. "Clear."

"How do we find Captain Mann in here?" Benhil asked. "This place is huge."

"We don't need to find him," Abbey said. "We just need to find somebody who can take us to him."

"In other words, don't kill anyone else?" Pik said.

"Not yet."

"Okay."

They moved through the kitchen and out the doors, into a large, open space with tables arranged around the edges and clear floor in the center. It was vacant as well, and they followed the doorway into a wide corridor.

"Queenie," Bastion said. "How's it going down there?"

"We're inside, trying to find Mann. How are things with you?"

"Getting a little bored with flying circles around these monkeys. I really want to shoot them down, if only for their incompetence."

"If it buys us time, do it," Abbey said, drawing a look from Pik.

"What? Is there a difference between killing one and killing a thousand? It's still killing."

Pik smiled. "Welcome to my worldview."

Abbey moved out into another hallway, keeping her posture alert and ready. Airi stayed close, her rifle positioned on her left side.

"I'm reading something on IR," she said. "Coming this way."

"How many?"

"Uh, I got something, too," Pik said. "It looks like they're trying to surround us."

"This way," Abbey said, leading them forward at an increased pace. She wished she had a TCU so she could see what they saw. "How far?"

"Fifty meters," Airi replied. "Next hallway after that door." She motioned toward a door ahead of them. It looked like it was made of actual wood.

"It's going to get ugly in here," Pik said, turning around as the first of the squads behind them closed in. He started shooting, backing them off.

"Remind me to kick Mann's ass for getting captured," Abbey said.

"Roger," Airi replied.

They reached the door, standing on either side of it. Abbey looked at Airi, raising her eyebrow.

"They're static, Queenie," Airi said. "Waiting for us."

"While they cut us off," Abbey said. She looked back at Benhil and Pik. They were a few meters behind them, still taking random potshots to keep the other guards honest.

"Queenie," Bastion said again. "You've got PD headed toward the complex."

"Damn," Abbey said. "We're taking too long. Can you slow them down?"

"Why don't I just do everything? I'm on it."

Abbey looked at the door ahead of them. Then she raised her hand toward it, trying to access the Gift. She was already angry, and she thought it would come easily. She could even feel the burning beneath her skin, the power ready to act from wherever it originated. She imagined the door breaking off its hinges, exploding into the soldiers behind it and knocking them down. She wished for it to happen. Then she begged for it to happen.

It was no use.

"I've got it," Pik said. "Cover me."

Abbey stepped aside, prepared to let him knock it down. She couldn't get the Gift to do what she wanted it to. She had it, but she didn't know how to use it. Not completely.

Pik approached the door, while Airi turned to shoot at the soldiers at their backs. Abbey remained beside the Trover, ready to shoot into the next room once the door was out of the way. Pik turned his shoulder, preparing to charge.

"Wait," Abbey said. "I want to try something."

"This isn't the best time to experiment, Boss," Pik said.

"I don't know about that," Abbey said.

Her heart was pounding, her pulse heavy, her body burning. She was angry about being here. Angry about being shot at. Angry about someone wanting to do harm to the Republic, and by extension her family. Anger wasn't enough. There was another ingredient she was missing, the one she had used against Trin on Drune.

Hate.

Plenty of people said it was wrong to hate. They said it led to the wrong side of humanity. The dark side. But at least hate was honest. It wouldn't hold punches, or pretend to be something it wasn't. You knew it when you saw it. You knew it when you felt it.

And Abbey was feeling it. She hated that the guards on the other side of the door were in her way. She hated that they were slowing her down. She hated them for keeping her here while Planetary Defense closed in and time ran out.

She put her hand up again, holding it out. She could feel the energy of the Gift pooling there. She thrust her palm forward, and all of that energy poured out and into the door.

It exploded from its hinges, hurtling backward, slamming into the soldiers behind it and shattering into splinters.

"Oh, shit," Pik said, at the same time he began firing into the group.

"Alive, damn it," Abbey shouted, shoving him without thinking.

Pik stumbled sideways into the wall, knocked off-balance by the blow. He glanced at Abbey with fear and respect in his eyes.

Abbey didn't notice. She charged into the corridor, grabbing one of the guards and slamming him into the wall, jumping up and kicking a second in the head and knocking him down. She took hold of a third, pulling him roughly to the side of the hallway and holding him there, both hands under his helmet and wrapped around his throat.

"Where do you keep prisoners?" she asked.

"What? We don't-"

"Where?" Abbey said, bringing her knee up into his gut. She could hear his ribs crack beneath the blow, and only then did she realize how strong she had become. She let him go, stumbling back, suddenly feeling sick.

Pik caught her, helping her stay on her feet before grabbing the guard.

"Answer the lady, or I'm going to snap your fragging neck," he rumbled.

"That way," the guard said, pointing down the hall. "There's a stairwell down at the end." He started to laugh.

"What's so funny?" Abbey said, recovering from her shock.

"The Venerant is down there. Good luck." He kept laughing.

"Venerant?" Pik said.

"Probably another pain in the ass like that bitch on Drune," Abbey replied. "I'll take care of her. Let's go. Jester, Fury, let's move."

"Roger," Airi said, backing up toward them.

Pik punched the guard in the head before letting him go. He crumpled to the ground and didn't move.

"I like them better that way," he said before joining them in a lumbering sprint toward the end of the hallway.

The rear guards piled into the corridor behind them, sending bullets into the walls and floor around them.

"Go," Abbey said, slowing down and turning. She had seen Trin stop bullets with the Gift. Could she do it, too?

At the moment, she had no shortage of anger. No shortage of hate.

She raised her hand. She couldn't see the rounds, but she could feel the way the Gift burned under her skin, somehow warning her that they were coming. She held her hand out, so furious that she barely noticed how the slugs seemed to strike an invisible wall only centimeters from her hand, the heavy metal rounds flattening and dropping to the ground. The soldiers stopped shooting a few seconds later, realizing that their attack was ineffective. They didn't seek out another way to hurt her.

Instead, they ran.

Abbey smiled as she watched them go. Trin had said she only had half of the Gift. What could she do if she had it all? How much power would she have?

She froze, recognizing the temptation. She was using it to protect her team. To protect herself. That was all.

She turned and ran back to where the others were waiting, clearly shocked.

"Unbelievable," Benhil said.

"Stop wasting time," Abbey replied. The door to the stairwell was open, and she headed into it. "We have work to do."

CHAPTER NINE

THEY HURRIED DOWN THE STEPS, a winding set that dove at least a hundred meters underground. Abbey took the lead, bouncing down them four at a time, with the other Rejects following close at her back. The guards topside didn't follow, preferring to stay away from her after seeing what she could do.

There was a dark metal gate at the bottom of the steps. It looked old, and it separated easily from its moorings beneath Abbey's influence, clattering loudly on the floor as it toppled. Abbey cringed at the noise out of habit. Did it really matter? She was sure the Venerant, whoever that was, already knew they were coming.

The gate fed out into a long stone corridor, lit through spaces in an uneven cobblestone floor. It was an interesting design, unlike anything Abbey had ever seen before. She followed it past a series of doors, all surprisingly made of wood, with small, barred cutouts in the center that allowed them to see in. The spaces were small, carved into stone, and containing only a small mattress and a primitive looking toilet. It reminded her of Hell.

There was a second gate at the end of the corridor. Abbey broke through that one as well, and they emerged into a central area.

A woman was sitting at a simple table, a projection of different parts of the compound floating ahead of her. She was young and wearing only a nightgown that was semi-transparent in the light of the flames that ringed the space. She smiled when they entered, her eyes locking onto Abbey as she turned off the projection.

"The Queen of Hell," she said mockingly.

"And you are?" Abbey asked, accepting the title.

"That depends," she replied. "Some people know me as Emily Eagan, wife of Mars Eagan. Others know me as Venerant Alloran, a servant of the Nephilim. Which do you prefer?"

"I prefer you dead."

She laughed. "You have a taste of the Gift, Lieutenant Cage. You've obviously learned to command it to some extent, a feat which is not achieved lightly. I applaud you for that. I know you killed Evolent Trinity, another success not easily earned. But she was a convert to the cause. A Terran, not a Nephilim. Not like me."

"What's a Nephilim?" Pik asked.

"The future," Emily replied. "And the past."

"And the present," Abbey said. "Your Evolent said the same fragging thing before I cut her head off. I don't have time to bullshit, so either hand over Captain Mann or do something violent so I can do something violent back."

Emily smiled. "I appreciate the no-nonsense attitude, Lieutenant. It's refreshing after all of these years."

She didn't even lift her hand. Airi, Benhil, and Pik grunted as an invisible force pushed them backward, slamming them into the wall and holding them there.

"You have no idea what you've walked into, do you?" Emily asked. "No idea what the Nephilim are, where we came from, or what that means to you and your kind? I understand now why Thraven wanted me to wait here with Olus. He knew you would come for him. He wanted to bring you to me so that I could finish the job that Trinity failed to do. It's his way of allowing me to make up for my error in judgment."

"Are you going to stand there and talk?" Abbey said.

"I can do two things at once," Emily replied.

She flicked her wrist like she was swatting a fly, and Abbey found herself flying back and hitting the wall between Airi and Pik. The impact cracked the stone and her spine, and Abbey fell to the ground, paralyzed.

"Do you think you're strong because you have a piece of the Gift?" Emily asked. "Do you think you know what I'm capable of because you defeated an Evolent?"

She moved her hand again, and Abbey flew across the room, slamming into the far wall. She felt the tears flow from her eyes in response to the pain. What the hell had she just gotten herself into? What the hell had she gotten her team into? She had walked into the room like she owned the compound. When had she gotten so reckless? So stupid?

She was paying for it now. They all were.

"It will heal," Emily said. "Even with only part of the Gift, you're a difficult kill. Well, as long as you keep your head attached, but you already know that. The question is, how quickly will it heal? Have you fed the Gift? Have you kept it strong?"

Abbey lifted her head. Fed the Gift? No wonder she was so damn hungry all the time. She had eaten half their supply of rations on the way to Feru. She could feel her body knitting back together, the Gift burning beneath her skin. She downplayed it, remaining on the floor without moving.

"You don't even know what I'm talking about," Emily said. "The Blood of Life. Why do think we call it that? Blood alone can't give you power. It's a transport mechanism. It's fuel."

"There's something else in it," Abbey said.

"Yes, and that something else requires human plasma to function. As a human, you can convert the food you ingest to fuel. It isn't as efficient, but it works. As a Nephilim, I don't have that option. If I want to keep the Gift I have no choice but to go to the source."

"You're telling me you drink human blood?" Abbey said, disgusted.

"Would you, Lieutenant, if you knew it would give you the strength to kill me?"

She moved her finger, and Airi was thrown from the wall, landing in front of Abbey. Abbey could see how tense Airi's muscles were as she tried to free herself from the invisible hold.

"You have to be fragging kidding me," Abbey said softly, shifting her attention from Emily to Airi and back. "I'm not a monster."

"No? If you don't do it, she's going to die anyway. So are your friends. So are you. You can save her. You can save yourself. All it takes is a little taste."

Abbey wanted to vomit. She'd rather they all die than become something inhuman. "Go frag yourself."

Emily laughed. "Why do I have a feeling you told Evolent Trinity the same thing? Come on, Lieutenant. All it takes is a bite, right here." She leaned her head over and put her fingers to her neck. "There's an artery there. Good flow, and easy to stop the bleeding when you're done. The Gift will thank you for it."

Abbey looked at Airi's neck without thinking. Airi noticed, her eyes growing wider. Was it the worst thing she could do if it saved all of their lives?

"Oh, I can see it, Lieutenant. The temptation. The hesitation. You know there's no other way out of this. No other chance that you and yours survive. Go ahead." She shifted her finger again, and Airi slid a little closer, her head beneath Abbey's, her neck in easy reach. "Once you've done it, the next time is easy."

Abbey looked down at Airi. Her heart was beating so fast her whole body felt like it was shaking. The Gift burned within her, urging her to do as the Venerant suggested.

Take it.

Taste it.

Tears ran from her eyes, dripping onto Airi's face. She clenched her teeth. Who was in control here? Her, or the Gift? What the hell did all of this mean?

Emily started laughing. "You can try to fight it all you want, Lieutenant. The Gift is in you. It's only a matter of time. Thraven wants you, and I'm going to deliver you to him to redeem myself, all prepped and ready for what comes next. He knew you would come. He knew I could convince you. Just one taste, Abigail. Just one-"

Her speech was interrupted by the echoing of gunfire from the entrance, and bullets ripping into and through her body. She turned her head, caught by surprise, thrown backward by the force of the assault.

Bastion stood in the doorway, emptying his rifle's magazine into her. He kept shooting until he was dry and she was a bloody mess on the floor.

"The bad news is, they sent reinforcements," Bastion said. "Like, three squadrons. The good news is, shooting me down means I'm here to help you out."

"They shot you down?" Pik said. He had fallen to the floor when Emily dropped. "Has that ever happened before?"

"Shut up," Bastion said.

Abbey ignored them. She grabbed her knife, rising to her hands and knees. Then she shoved herself forward, launching through the air on the strength of the Gift, headed toward the downed Venerant.

She almost made it. She was only inches from landing on Emily when the woman's hand shot up, and an invisible fist hit her in the gut, knocking her up and over. She hit the floor and rolled to her feet, coming up facing the woman.

"Oh. Frag," Bastion said, releasing the empty magazine and reaching for another.

Emily Eagan stood up, the bullet wounds vanishing as she did.

"Hell, no," Airi said. "This is bullshit."

Emily threw her hands out to both sides. A wave of something spread out in front of them, slamming into the Rejects and knocking them from their feet once more.

All except Abbey. She absorbed the blow, grabbing her knife tighter in her hand. She felt like she was on fire. If anger and hate were the keys to getting the most out of the gift, she was ready to take the fragging kingdom.

She jumped forward, going back at Emily Eagan with even greater speed than before. Emily put up her hand and Abbey felt the Gift trying to slam into her. She matched it with her own, canceling it out. Emily ducked away as the knife came in like a blur, spinning and kicking out, clearly trained to fight.

They engaged one another, moving quickly, hands and feet darting in and out, striking and blocking. Abbey scored a few superficial hits with the knife, able to see how quickly the wounds healed, the gashes closing in seconds. She growled in anger and frustration, the Gift adding its strength to hers.

"You're fast," Emily said. "Well-trained. A true prize for the Gloritant." She threw a series of punches as she spoke, each of them countered with quick blocks.

"Shut up," Abbey replied. She turned the knife over in her hand, slipping it up and in on the woman. Emily stepped back, grabbing the blade to keep it from hitting her chest. It healed before it could bleed.

"Can you feel it?" Emily said. "The anger? The hate?"

"Yeah, I can," Abbey said.

"Do you like it?"

Abbey didn't let up. "Yeah. I do."

Emily laughed. She slapped Abbey's arm away, throwing her other hand out. The Gift slammed into Abbey's chest, knocking her back. Emily used the moment of surprise to burst forward, slipping past Abbey's defenses and getting a hand around her neck.

"Too slow," Emily said.

"Am I?" Abbey replied, even as her fist pummeled Emily's gut and the knife sliced through the outstretched hand, removing it cleanly. The force of the punch tossed Emily back and into the wall. At the same time, the Rejects started shooting again, sending a barrage of bullets into the Venerant, tearing her open as they had before.

Abbey didn't hesitate this time. She grabbed the dismembered hand and threw it to the ground as she charged forward, her feet skipping lightly on the floor, diving into the middle of her team's assault, unwilling to give Emily time to heal. She felt the bullets striking her, slamming her in the back, but she ignored it, coming down on top of the other woman.

She lowered her blade to Emily's neck as the Rejects stopped shooting once more.

Emily was laughing again.

"What's so funny?" Abbey asked. The wounds were already healing. She dug the knife into Emily's neck and left it there.

"Look at all the blood, Lieutenant," the Venerant said.

Abbey glanced down. The nightgown had been shredded, leaving Emily's regenerating body naked and bloody. She felt a sudden urge to lean down into it, to consume the thick red liquid right then and there.

"If you partake of the Blood of Life, your Gift becomes greater," Emily said. "You're already so strong for one so new. Don't you want it, Lieutenant? It's there for the taking. Even after I'm dead."

Abbey licked her lips almost unconsciously. She swallowed hard, fighting the desire. The need. Gloritant Thraven was more powerful than Emily Eagan, and Abbey had only beaten her with the help of her entire squad. As much as she despised the concept, was there any logical reason to resist? She had promised Hayley she would make it home, whatever it took.

"That's right," Emily said. "Nobody can resist. Not once the Git is inside of them. Not forever."

Abbey stared at the blood. She wanted it. She looked into the Venerant's eyes. "Then I guess I should thank you," she said.

Then she pressed down with the knife, more than hard enough to end the fight.

She sat on top of the dead woman's body as the blood oozed from the arteries, so much thicker and darker than normal. She blinked, trying to fight the urge. She turned her head, finding the Rejects behind her, guns still raised and ready for round three. She looked back at the blood, lowering her hand to it. She collected a small sample onto her index finger and raised it to her face, smelling it. It was metallic and heavy. She rubbed it between her fingers. It had a subtle roughness to it. Was there something alive in there? Was that the coarseness she felt? What was it?

She brought it toward her lips.

"Queenie?" Bastion said, putting his hand on her shoulder. "We need to grab Mann and get our asses out of here."

Abbey shivered, her concentration broken, her mind returning to its rightful place. She looked up at Bastion and then held out her other hand. He grabbed it and pulled her to her feet.

"Thanks for the save," she said.

"You won't be thanking me when we get outside. The entire jungle is filling up with Planetary Defense militia, and the Republic's got three squadrons in the air. I have no fragging clue how we're going to survive this."

"We'll do whatever it takes," Abbey said.

"Queenie," Airi shouted from the corridor adjacent to the room. "I found him."

Abbey let Bastion go in front of her, hanging back. When nobody was looking, she brought her fingers to her mouth, letting them enter and sucking Venerant Alloran's blood away.

She shuddered as she swallowed, a sudden fear working its way through her.

What were they turning her into?

What was she allowing herself to become?

CHAPTER TEN

GANT WAITED FOR A WHILE after Ursan left the room, remaining hidden in the shadows of the desk, pressed tight against the corner. It wasn't an uncomfortable position to be in. On Ganemant, his kind had long lived in hollowed out stone and slept in chambers that weren't much larger than where he was now, preferring the cozy warmth of small, dark spaces to the noise and openness of Terran living. Of course, since the Terrans had arrived on their planet, more and more of their construction had been sized to accommodate larger beings, and that part of their history was quickly getting lost.

It was the price of progress. A price he had never minded paying. As one of only a few thousand Gants who had ever left Ganemant, he was proud of his adventurous nature, even if it had cost him everything in the end.

Almost everything. He had a second chance. A new alpha. And now he knew for sure that Abbey was still alive. It had taken all of his will to keep from chittering with excitement at the news, to remain silent while his body vibrated with warmth over the fact. Not that it had calmed his anger against this man, Ursan Gall, or his soldiers much. They had still tried to kill her, and nothing else had changed. He was going to kill them all, one way or another.

The timing was everything.

He slipped out from beneath the table, jumping onto it and kneeling in front of the terminal. He wasn't as good with computers as he was with mechanical parts. The shape of his hands didn't lend itself to working projections, and most software didn't recognize the twin thumb configuration. Even so, he had enough experience that he should at a minimum be able to trace the route back to the main comm link array, and then make his way there to physically frag with it.

He activated the terminal. It wasn't locked. What would be the point? This ship was under Ursan's control and composed of Ursan's soldiers. He had no reason to expect a stowaway. It took some work to navigate through the menus, as he was forced to hold his hands together to mimic the shape of a human hand and then work the whole thing with just that. It was awkward and slow, and he kept looking over his shoulder every ten seconds and pausing to listen for approaching footsteps. He was thankful his hearing was better than a Terran's.

The terminal had no idea where the comm link was located on the ship. Fortunately, he knew enough about Republic Navy Internetworking services to backtrace the physical location based on pings to the specific modules. Any Republic Navy craft in the fleet would have both long and short range comms, as well as quantum filtering for signal processing during FTL. While ping times were in the .00001 millisecond range, the precise reporting had a lot of meaning, especially to an engineer. By also accessing one of the unsecured reactor services, he was able to correlate times to guesstimate distance.

In this case, the comm link was likely a few hundred meters closer to his position than the "engine" room he had come from. He used that term loosely considering what he had seen there. The thought of it still made him nauseous.

Of course, that wasn't much of a definitive position, and it wasn't good enough to know it was closer. Was it up, down, port or starboard? He had another way of determining that, thanks to the organization of Republic Navy networks. Every node on the ship was designated and numbered nearly identically across the board, with codes that stood for relative position in the ship starting from the ass. By pinging each node and checking the time, he could eventually triangulate the location down to a few dozen meters.

Of course, it would take hours to manually ping the nodes. Fortunately, some clever Ensign somewhere had already added a command to do just that, and that command was standard issue on all Republic Navy ships. Gant executed it, watching the numbers output across the projection in a list that seemed almost endless. He eyeballed it quickly, matching the last few digits in the response times against what he had gotten back from the link. It took a few minutes, but he wound up with a general idea of where the frag he was going.

Deck 13, Node 67, about three-quarters of the way down from the central crossbeam. Meaning the link array was in the belly of the ship, and since the *Brimstone* had sixteen decks, that meant it wasn't positioned at the bottom of the hull, either.

Gant motioned with his false hand to clear the list, pausing before he completed the gesture, his ears picking up the sound of feet on the metal floor beyond the room's hatch. He froze momentarily, waiting while the feet stopped in front of the door. Then he jumped off the table, his hand hitting the projector control as he dropped, turning it off. He scurried back to his hiding place, watching as Ursan Gall's boots made their way across the room to the adjacent bedroom. He could only hope the man didn't come to use the terminal. If he had, he would realize immediately that someone had been doing something interesting with it, and that the someone was probably not supposed to be on board.

"I can't do this without you," he heard Ursan say. "I don't want to. We'll figure something out. Dak says he knows an expert on Anvil who may be able to help. Says he does all kinds of augmentation; shit that doesn't seem like it should even be possible. I know Thraven wants the *Brimstone*, but he'll thank me if I can get you back. I'm sure he will."

Gant peered out from the corner of the desk. He could see Ursan now, standing over the bed with a satchel in his hands. He put the satchel on the bed and then lifted the head up, wrapping it in a towel before placing it reverently inside.

"I've seen too many amazing things, done too many things I thought impossible. I don't believe you can't be saved. I won't believe it. Once you're awake, we'll find this Abigail Cage, and we'll do unto her as she did unto you. An eye for an eye. Then we can kill Thraven, and we can take over the war. We'll bring the damn Republic to its knees in the name of the Outworlds, in remembrance of Caliban."

Then Ursan fled the room, carrying his wife's head without sparing a glance toward the terminal. The whole episode left Gant feeling sick once more. Even if Gall could find someone capable of reviving a Terran head, the brain had been deprived of oxygen for hours, and the flesh was already in the process of decomposition.

What the hell would he be bringing back?

He waited until he couldn't hear the hard soles on the floor, and then he scrambled away from the terminal, away from the room as quickly as he could, opening the hatch, checking the corridor, and running opposite Ursan's back.

He needed to get the beacon up and running, and a message out to Abbey. He knew where the *Brimstone* was going, and he expected her to be there soon after it arrived.

CHAPTER ELEVEN

URSAN MADE HIS WAY BACK to the bridge, holding the satchel containing Trinity's head delicately, as though he could damage her with any hint of carelessness.

All eyes were on him as he entered, but he ignored them, returning directly to the command chair and sitting and placing the satchel in his lap.

"Dak, set a course for Anvil," he said, with no hint of hesitation in his voice. The Trover's eyes darted back for a moment, but he followed the order as it was given.

"Aye, Captain. Setting a course for Anvil."

Ursan leaned back, his eyes straight ahead, focused on the viewport as the *Brimstone* adjusted its vector slightly and then made the smooth transition to faster-than-light travel. Anvil was near the far end of the Fringe, home to a major Outworld military hub whose sole job was to prevent the Republic from trying to sneak around to the planets at the outer segment of the unsettled universe. An entire support economy had grown on the planet as a result, providing anything a soldier might want. Augmentations, pleasure bots, Construct gaming, drugs, alcohol, and black market military gear. It was big business, and it attracted traders from all over the Outworlds despite its relatively distant relation to the rest of the non-Republic galaxy. He hadn't been too surprised to hear the name of the planet when Dak had cautiously mentioned knowing someone there who was a master bot-maker. A Plixian named Gorix. He was rumored to have done impressive augmentation work, merging biological with mechanical.

It was only a rumor, but it was also the only chance Ursan had. His heart was broken, his body so filled with anger and hate that he couldn't dismiss the incessant motion of the Gift as it demanded retribution for her slaughter. Cage wouldn't be enough, not nearly enough, but he knew he couldn't get to Thraven without Trin, and he knew Trin would choose him over the General.

"I'm not crazy," he said out loud to the members of his bridge crew. He knew they thought he was. From the moment he had gone forward to take her head, they had been whispering that he had lost himself.

"Nobody said anything, Boss," Dak said.

"You don't need to say it. I know you're all thinking it. Even you. I'm not, though. I'm going to get her back. What's so wrong with that?"

"Nothing, Boss," Dak replied. He was silent for a few seconds before turning to look back at Ursan. "Can I be honest with you, Captain?"

"What is it, my friend?" Ursan said.

"We're all for trying to bring back Trinity. All of us like her a lot. But, we were wondering if maybe we should bring the *Brimstone* back to Thraven first, and take the Triune to Anvil. He's already pretty unhappy with us, and we're not in a position to counter him right now, especially after we destroyed his battleship."

"What do you think Thraven is going to do when we bring back the *Brimstone*?" Ursan asked. "Do you think he's going to let us leave again? Do you think he's going to let any of us out alive?"

"He'll have the ship. Maybe he'll forget about us."

"General Thraven doesn't forget about anything. If he doesn't kill us outright, he'll send us off on some other mission somewhere that's nowhere near where I want to go. I'd rather get there in an unstoppable warship. Wouldn't you?"

"An unstoppable warship won't do shit for us once we're boots on the ground," Dak said.

"That's where you're wrong. Thraven would still need to get a ship in system. He'd still need to drop units to the planet."

"You're suggesting we should intercept them?"

"If that's what it takes."

Ursan caught the nervous murmurs from the rest of the bridge crew. His bridge crew. Or were they?

"He brought this on," Ursan shouted. "He sent Trin to Drune to die. He let us go so we could see it. We've all been through a lot of shit together. Ten years running merc jobs before Trin, two years after, and three years with General Thraven. We've got fifteen years together, most of us. Since when did you all become so afraid?"

"He isn't like other people we've worked for, Ursan," Ligit, the systems officer, said. "We all saw what he did to you and Trin. The stuff that you can do. Anything you can do, he can do it a hundred times better. That's not a man we want to cross, and I don't think you should cross him, either. Not for this."

"To save my wife? You don't think it's worth that?"

Ligit turned away from him without speaking. Nobody was willing to say what he knew they were thinking. What had prompted his outburst in the first place?

"You think she's dead, and she's going to stay dead, don't you?" he asked. "Ligit, damn you. Answer me."

Ligit looked back at him. "Aye, Captain."

Ursan acted before he thought, raising a hand and gesturing toward the man. Instantly, his head jerked downward, slamming into the terminal in front of him. His body rolled off his chair and didn't move.

"Is he?" one of the other crew members said.

Ursan lowered his hand, his whole body shaking. What the hell had he just done?

Dak rushed over to Ligit, putting a hand to his neck. "He's still alive. By how much, I don't know."

"Bring him to medical," Ursan said, his voice uneven. He hadn't meant to react that way. Losing Trin was making him unstable. Unsteady. "I'll apologize to him once he's patched up."

"Aye, Captain," Dak said, lifting the man easily and carrying him from the bridge.

The rest of the crew turned back to their stations. Ursan could sense the sudden fear and tension surrounding them.

Everything would be better once they reached Anvil.

Once Trinity was back in his life.

Once Abigail Cage was dead.

CHAPTER TWELVE

OLUS LOOKED UP WHEN AIRI'S face appeared in the cutout of the door.

"Queenie," she shouted. "I found him."

He cringed at the words. Damn Thraven. He was pushing the pieces precisely, and getting them into a bad place.

"Captain Mann?" Abbey said. "Move away from the door."

Olus pushed himself against the side of the room. There was no sense resisting. It was already too late.

The door exploded inward, flying back and slamming against the wall where he had just been resting, breaking apart and settling across the room.

"Captain," Abbey said, entering the small cell.

"Cage," Olus replied, looking her over. Her hellsuit had a couple of gashes in it, and her head had some dried blood running down the side. "You look like hell."

"You should have seen me on Drune," she said. "This is the second time I've had to rescue you."

"Sorry to burst your bubble, Lieutenant, but it isn't much of a rescue."

"What do you mean?" Bastion asked, moving in behind her.

"Thraven wanted me here," Abbey said. "I know that much. He

thought his Venerant would get me under his control."

"You mean Emily Eagan?" Olus asked. "Where is she?"

"Out there. She got a little overconfident, and wound up losing her head."

"You killed her? How?"

"With the help of the Rejects and the power of the Gift."

"Is that what they call it? Whatever it is that let her hold me in place without lifting a finger?"

"Yeah. Or the Blood of Life. Dumb, right?"

Abbey smiled. Olus couldn't help but smile, too.

"Thraven's smarter than I gave him credit for," he said. "He angled this into a win-win for him. If Emily took you, then he would have you back under his control, and I would still be locked up here. Or maybe he would have just let me walk out. Since you killed her, he got to punish her for her mistake, and he gets to push me out of the picture."

"What do you mean, push you out of the picture?" Abbey asked. "I don't understand."

"Did you kill any Republic forces on the way in? Not the guards in here, I'm pretty sure they're all on Thraven's team. Planetary Defense? Republic Navy?"

Abbey's face flattened, and she glanced over at Bastion.

"You told me I could," he said.

"Yes," she replied.

Olus nodded. "You were already fugitives, but by killing Republic assets to rescue me? I'm going to be one, too. Thraven pulled me into this game because he wanted to keep me close. He knows I can't be bought. You don't become Director of the OSI without getting offers to look the other way that would make your head spin. He had to either allow me to operate, which he did by feeding me Mars while Emily was the real problem, or he had to discredit me."

"Which we're in the process of doing," Abbey said.

"Yes."

"You didn't give us much of a fragging choice," Benhil said. "According to Ruby, if you die, we die."

"I know. Ruby didn't know I set the timer to automatically reset before I came here. I couldn't risk losing you if something happened to me."

"What?" Bastion said. "We could have left your ass to rot, and we would have been in the clear after all?"

"Shut it," Abbey said, turning on Bastion. "We made our decision regardless."

"You made the decision," Benhil said.

"And I'm in charge, so it was all of us. Do you want to question it again?"

Benhil shook his head. "No, ma'am."

"What's done is done," Olus said. "We still have a chance to fix this mess."

"How?" Abbey asked.

"It's possible that PD doesn't know you came for me. For all they know, you're one of the bastards that took the *Fire* and *Brimstone*, and you circled back to finish the job with Mars."

"Mars isn't dead. At least, we didn't kill her."

Olus sighed. Sometimes he hated his job. "I don't like it, but we may have no choice but to change that."

"Are you serious?" Airi said. "We can't just kill an innocent woman. Especially if Emily Eagan was abusing her."

"Better her than us," Pik said.

"Captain, we have five minutes until Ruby brings the *Faust* back to Feru," Abbey said. "We're running out of time and options."

Olus stared at her for a moment, working out the problem. "Emily's terminal is right beside their bedroom upstairs. I can reach Ruby from there and tell her to hold off while you take care of Mars."

"Take care of her?" Airi said. "We can't kill her. I won't, and I won't let any of you."

"You can't stop us," Benhil said. "You especially can't stop Queenie."

"Queenie, you can't," Airi said. "It's not her fault. Captain, it doesn't matter if you get discredited. We can stop this from the outside.

How much have you been able to accomplish, anyway?"

"Thraven's pawns have control of the Committee," Olus said. "I don't think they control the Council yet, but it would only be a matter of time. I need to get back to Earth, to find out who's loyal to the Republic and who's loyal to the Gloritant. I need to see if I can shift the balance of power back in the right direction."

"We'll make the call when we get up there," Abbey said. "We need to keep Ruby away from Feru, or we're going to lose our ride."

"Agreed," Olus said.

"Let's move, Rejects," Abbey said, backing out into the hallway.

She took point, moving confidently ahead, while Olus remained behind the others. He was impressed with how well she had taken control of the fugitive misfits, bringing them in line through - he wasn't sure what. Respect? Fear? Most likely a bit of both. She had the Gift that Emily used to paralyze him, and he could see the difference in her demeanor, even compared to their first meeting. She was becoming more used to it, instead of trying to ignore it or fight it.

Whether that was a good thing or not would make itself apparent sooner or later.

For now, he needed to guide her to his ends, the one where the Rejects headed back onto the path of the *Fire* and *Brimstone*, and he made his way back to Earth, his purpose and presence here remaining secret and circumventing Thraven's trap. Hopefully, he could grab some data from Emily Eagan's terminal first. Data about the Covenant and the Nephilim, about what the ships were really made of and what they could really do. Ancient blueprints? Old technology somehow derived from God? The idea of it made his head spin.

Then again, he wasn't ready to believe any of it. Not without more proof. The Gift was compelling evidence, but it was also somewhat circumstantial.

"Jester, Fury, head toward the exit and see if you can get a bead on incoming PD forces," Abbey said when they reached the top of the steps. "And don't give me any shit about it, Fury. I'll do what needs to be done, and you'll like it."

Airi had opened her mouth to speak. Olus watched her shut it and nod.

"Yes, Queenie," she said.

"Lucifer, see if you can get on the rooftop and help them monitor the situation. Where'd you leave the *Imp*, anyway?"

"In the pool," Bastion replied.

"I didn't see a pool," Pik said.

"I ditched her in the lake," Bastion said. "May she rest in peace."

"Captain Mann, ideas on getting out of here after we deal with Mars?" Abbey said.

"The good thing about jungles is that they're easy to hide in."

"Even against sensor sweeps?"

"My jamming bot is still up in the office. It should come in handy for that. Unless there's another blood-sucking Gifter wandering around out there, I suppose."

"Roger," Abbey said.

"The bad thing about jungles is the spiders," Pik said. "I fragging hate spiders. There aren't any on Tro."

"Lucky," Benhil said.

"And unlucky," Pik said. "Have you ever seen a female Trover?"

"Come to think of it, no."

Pik laughed. "I'll take the spiders."

Olus followed Abbey, Pik, and Bastion up from the ground floor, while Benhil and Airi headed for the front of the mansion. There was no obvious sign of interference anywhere nearby, and he was sure it was because Abbey killed Emily Eagan. If the guards were all Thraven's, they knew better than to tangle with someone who could take out their boss.

Unfortunately, Planetary Defense wouldn't be as smart. He was hoping he could get them out without having to kill any of Feru's local militia or destroy any more of the Republic's assets. At least the Republic wouldn't drop any Marines unless things got really out of hand. It was his job to make sure they didn't.

Bastion split from them when they reached Emily's office, heading down the hallway in search of an access stairwell up to the roof. Abbey and Pik entered the office with Olus, and he immediately went over and grabbed his helmet from the floor, slipping it on and re-initializing his TCU. Then he picked up the jamming bot from where it had fallen, reconnecting with it and restarting its systems from the softsuit. When he tossed it into the air, it remained stationary there, active once more.

"Queenie," he said. "What's your identifier?"

She rattled it off to him, allowing him to connect to their short-range comm.

"Queenie, we've marked a dozen tangos incoming," Jester said. "Three squads of four. They're being pretty careful."

"Roger," Abbey said. "Secure the entrance. Don't engage with them unless they engage with you."

"Roger."

Olus turned his attention to Emily's terminal. It had locked itself when she had brought him down to the cells, but he stuck another extender to it and hacked in easily. A few seconds later, he groaned out loud. "Damn."

"What is it?" Abbey asked.

"It's been wiped. I was hopeful." He leaned back in the chair for a moment. "We need to make a decision on Mars." He looked at her.

"Are you asking my opinion?" Abbey said.

He nodded. "You have a lot of the same training I do. What do you think?"

"I hate to say anyone's life is less important than anything else," she said. "But in this case, I think we have to say it. She let the Venerant in; she's not completely innocent. I'll take care of it."

"Queenie, wait," Pik said. "I'll do it."

"No. I'm not going to ask you to do something I won't do myself."

"You aren't. I'm volunteering." He paused, introspective. "Won't be the first time I killed someone while they were sleeping."

The statement sent a shiver down Olus' spine, even though he already knew why Pik had been in the deepest pits of Hell.

Abbey responded by turning toward Olus. Pik grunted and headed for the door adjacent to the bedroom.

"Queenie, it looks like the skies are opening up," Bastion said. "But ground forces are heavy, heavy. Two more personnel carriers are en route, and it looks like they've got a Springer."

The Springer was a light mech, designed to maneuver through rough terrain. It wasn't common for planetary militias to have any, but the machine was manufactured by Eagan Heavyworks, making its presence less surprising.

"It doesn't matter what they have once we get away from the compound," Olus said. "I'm contacting Ruby now."

He switched comm channels, using the terminal's connection to send a long-range ping.

"Ruby," he said.

"Captain Mann?" the synth replied a moment later. "Are you well?"

"I've been better. I'm here with Lieutenant Cage and her team. We need to delay pickup."

"Roger," Ruby said. "How long?"

Olus considered. "We'll let you know. Is your position secure?"

"For now. I don't expect that to stay true forever."

"Neither do I. If you have to move, move. Just keep your comm lines clear."

"Roger."

Olus closed the link, turning as Pik re-entered the room. He looked confused.

"She was already dead," he said.

"What?" Abbey replied, a hint of disbelief in her voice. "Are you trying to make me feel better?"

"I swear, Queenie. No pulse. No movement. If I had to guess, I'd say she died the same time you popped the head off the bitch downstairs."

Olus and Abbey locked eyes. Emily had been drinking Mars' blood with regularity. It was an interesting outcome.

"At least I don't have to feel guilty," Abbey said.

"There's nothing to get here," Olus said, giving up on the terminal. If he had a few hours, he could try to restore something, but he didn't even have minutes. He would have to be satisfied with his memory of his first view of the so-called Covenant.

"Then it's time to evac," Abbey said.

"Agreed. We head into the jungle; we try to steal a ride back to Feru City. I'll get you on a transport hush-hush, and then I'll return to the *Driver*. Commander Usiari doesn't know I was here, or if he does, I'll make sure he won't be able to prove it. I just have to figure out what bullshit to feed General Omsala." He paused. "Actually, I can use that as a reason to go back to Earth."

Abbey nodded but looked concerned. "How do you plan to let us have our freedom once the whole fragging Republic is hunting us? It's one thing to escape from Hell. It's another thing to murder the Director of Eagan Heavyworks."

"I know. I'll figure it out. You had enough faith in me to come break me out. Trust that I'll do you right."

"I've heard that bullshit line before," Pik said. "What about the timer? You die, we die? That isn't going to work."

"You're right," Olus agreed. "Queenie, I'm going to give you the codes."

"What?" Abbey said.

"I'm assuming the virus wouldn't be able to kill you, anyway. I'm sure you considered the same."

"I did. I got shot at least a hundred times on Drune and came back. I don't think a superbug can knock me down. Not now."

"What?" Pik said. "If he can't off you, then why the frag are you still here? You could be on your way to Earth to get your kid."

Abbey turned toward him, but she sent her words over the team channel.

"Because this is bigger than me, Okay. Bigger than all of us. I swore an oath to defend the Republic, and it doesn't matter if I wound up in Hell. It doesn't matter that it wasn't my fault. Whoever Thraven is, whoever the Nephilim are, they threaten everything I've always believed in protecting. The same things you all believed in protecting at one time or another. If this asshole gets his way, there isn't going to be anywhere to go.

There isn't going to be anywhere to hide. We'll be as much a prisoner to his will as we are the Republic's. I want my daughter to live free."

"But you'll let us go, won't you Queenie?" Benhil asked. "You'll let us decide for ourselves?"

"Why the frag would I do that?" she replied. "You were in Hell the same as me. You're going to earn your freedom, just like I am."

Benhil was silent. Olus could imagine him cursing off the comm link.

"I'm with you, Queenie," Bastion said.

"You don't have a choice," Airi said. "None of us do."

"Then I'm choosing to pretend I have a choice," Bastion said. "This is still a lot more fun than Hell ever was. You can't deny that."

"Nope," Pik said. "I'm having a fragging blast. Except for that part where I got slammed into the wall and held there with magic. That kind of sucked."

"Lucifer, clear the rooftop, meet Okay and Killshot at the entrance."

"Killshot?"

"That's me," Olus said.

"Cool nick. Roger."

"What are you going to do?" Olus asked.

"I'm going to create a diversion." She looked at him, a devilish smile playing across her face. "I've got an idea."

CHAPTER THIRTEEN

ABBEY MOVED OUT ONTO THE rooftop of the Eagan mansion, quickly scanning the skies before making her way from the emergency access stairwell to the edge of the building. She didn't try to stay low or hide as she looked down at the area around them. Planetary Defense had taken a defensive position around the cleared area beyond the compound, a collection of vehicles lining the area, soldiers hiding behind them with rifles up and ready.

There were more soldiers closer in, hanging near the walls in the foliage that surrounded the property, waiting for the signal to close and engage. Just beyond the front gate, three squads of soldiers in battlesuits had lined the walls, prepared to go in hard and fast. They were the first and best line of offense the Feru defense forces could produce, not including the Springer.

The mech was hidden somewhere out of sight, ready to bounce into the fray at a moment's notice. Abbey had been on missions with Springers before. The mechs weren't that tough, but they could stand up to small arms fire and battlesuits just fine, and they were quick and powerful, their normal ordnance including a pair of light railguns, a heavy laser, and a handful of fragment munitions. Standard operating procedure was to hang back and catch enemy units by surprise, using their powerful jump jets to make high, fast arcs along the battlefield, firing down on targets from above. She had no doubt the pilot of the PD's Springer was hoping to do the same.

"This is Queenie," she said. "I'm in position. Prepare to engage on my mark."

"Roger," the other members of the Rejects, plus Olus, replied.

Abbey closed her hand into a fist. She could feel the Gift throbbing beneath her skin, still hyperactive after her fight against the Venerant. She had tasted the woman's blood, thick and metallic and gritty, taking it and swallowing before she could reconsider, and then questioning the decision when she felt the change in her system. It reminded her of a warrior's high, only more crisp and defined.

She knew she had made a mistake because she wanted more.

Emily had warned her that a taste would break her. She had laughed about it right before she died.

Then why had she tried it? Why had she been unable to resist? Did the individual control the Gift, or did the Gift control the individual?

She had to get her team out of here, away from the mansion, away from Feru. She needed to find the *Fire* and the *Brimstone*, and stop Thraven. Was it a mistake if it saved lives? She hadn't bitten Airi, as Emily suggested. She had taken the blood of a woman who was already dead. It was disgusting. Immoral. Reprehensible. It was also logical given the circumstances.

Wasn't it?

She looked down at the enemy forces again. She didn't want to kill them. Not if it could be avoided. Too many people were dying around her, enough that she was beginning to feel like a real demon. A real monster. Still, they needed the Gift. They needed the power. All of them would have been dead three times over without it.

She found the three squads near the front of the compound. The Gift was still active, but it wasn't as strong as before. She didn't hate those soldiers. She didn't hate what they were trying to do. She had a feeling that Emily's blood was the only thing keeping it awake.

She stepped back from the edge, took a few quick breaths, and then sprinted forward. She could feel the strength in her feet, enhanced by the Gift. Her steps were quick and light, and she reached the edge in no time, bouncing off as though she were in a battlesuit and letting the low arc carry her forward, from the sixth-floor rooftop of the mansion, over the front gates, and into the midst of the soldiers beyond.

She rolled when she hit the ground, tucking her shoulder and absorbing the impact, coming up and darting toward the first squad as its members turned to face her. They were hesitant, rattled by her sudden appearance within them, surprised by her bald head, her Hell brand, her deep red suit and the blood that marred her face.

She hit the first one quickly, batting his rifle aside and punching him in the helmet, hard enough that he spun and fell. She pivoted, swinging her leg up and out and kicking another under the chin, lifting him up and dropping him, turning again and punching a third soldier, hitting the armored chest with enough force that it cracked beneath her fist, pushing the man back and down. The last soldier caught up and tried to punch her, a suit-enhanced blow that would have crushed her if it connected. She ducked away from it, grabbing the outstretched hand in both of hers and pulling, tugging the soldier up and over and onto his back. He tried to get up, but she slammed her foot into his helmet. He fell back and didn't move again.

The other two squads had adjusted for her, and they swung their weapons her way. She bounced back and into the front line of foliage. One of the squads decided to follow.

"Mark," she said, calling the Rejects out. "Squad One is down. Two is giving chase. Squad Three is still manning the gate. Non-lethal if possible."

"What if it isn't possible?" Pik asked.

"Don't kill them unless they're about to kill you."

She moved deeper into the jungle, ducking behind a large tree. She could hear the motion of the soldiers entering the brush, their boots stomping heavily on the greenery around them. She could hear other motion in the trees further away, the defense forces already deployed around the perimeter being called back to find her.

She smiled. It was just what she wanted.

She stepped out from behind the tree, making sure the soldiers saw her, ducking back as they opened fire, their bullets striking the wood. Then she ran, racing ahead of them, leading them away, their attack at her back, bullets whizzing through the air around her. She felt something hit her leg, stumbled but stayed up, kept going as it healed. She felt another sting in her arm, brushed it off and kept going.

A soldier popped out of the trees in front of her, a young man who couldn't have been more than eighteen. He aimed his rifle at her but didn't fire, afraid to pull the trigger. She reached him, grabbing his weapon and pushing, throwing him to the ground. She turned back with the rifle and squeezed off a few rounds, her aim intentionally high.

"Killshot, sitrep," she said, ducking behind another tree and staying there for a moment.

"You pulled a lot of units away, but they're filling the gaps from the blockade," Olus said.

"Can you get to the trees?" Abbey asked.

"Affirmative. We're on the bounce."

"What's the range on the jamming bot?"

"Ninety meters."

"Don't get too close to me. I'm trying to find that fragging Springer."

"Roger."

Abbey moved again, running through the foliage, pushing through large leaves and hopping over mossy roots. The fire had lessened behind her, the militia losing her in the brush or becoming more cautious as they neared other friendly forces. There was still no sign of the mech, but she knew it had to be hiding somewhere nearby, waiting to make a grand entrance.

There. She caught sight of it out of the corner of her eye, a single glint of metal reflecting light through the trees. She adjusted course, heading toward it. If she could get to the cockpit and tear it open, she could stop it before it became a problem.

She was still ten meters away when it moved, its legs carrying it sideways like a crab, through a wider access point in the jungle and back the way she had come. She came to an abrupt stop.

"Killshot, Springer is incoming. They've made your jamming radius."

"Roger. I'll alter the bot for variable signal blocking. That should confuse him a bit."

Abbey didn't have the equipment to see the change, but the mech stopped moving almost immediately, pausing while Planetary Defense tried to adjust for the new dead zone. It would still allow them to get within two hundred meters, but in the dense cover that might as well be ten kilometers.

She sprinted after the mech again, nearly colliding with a squad of soldiers as they cleared the brush. She jumped toward the nearest one, bouncing into him with the force of the Gift, giving her the strength to knock him over in his armor. She wrenched the rifle from his hands, using it as a club and bringing the stock down to his chest. Then she dove to the ground, bullets passing overhead, pausing when she vanished behind the downed soldier. She shouted as she threw out her hand, in awe as the soldiers all toppled backward.

"Nice," she said, getting to her feet and running once more.

The Springer was moving again, too, headed toward the defensive line. Had Captain Mann led the Rejects into the thick of the defenses?

"Queenie," Olus said. "Turn left, one hundred meters."

She followed the directions, covering the distance, clearing a fallen tree and dropping into a ditch on the other side. The Rejects were all waiting for her there.

"What did you do?" she asked Olus.

"It's still trailing the jamming bot," he replied. "They'll have a bitch of a time sniffing us out down here."

"We still need a ride back to Feru City."

Olus nodded. "You were a Breaker. You know the value of patience."

"What are you suggesting?"

"I'm working on it."

She noticed his fingers tapping at the invisible pad embedded in his softsuit.

"That was your big plan?" Bastion said. "Jump into the middle of them and run?"

"It worked," Abbey said.

"So-so. I thought you had training?"

"Training to infiltrate. They don't give us much on escaping. Usually, if a Breaker gets caught, they get dead in a hurry."

"Good point."

"Queenie, get ready," Olus said. "I'm directing some big traffic."

Abbey grabbed the side of the tree and pulled herself up, peering over the top to the jungle ahead of her. The Springer was coming back again, trailed by a troop transport.

"How?" Abbey said.

"Little trick I picked up twenty, thirty years ago. Jamming bots are good for more than hiding you from scanners. If you shape the frequencies right, you can pretty much lead anyone who doesn't know any better anywhere you want them to go. And Planetary Defense on a planet like Feru is as unlikely to know any better as you can get."

"They think they're right behind us," Abbey said.

"The mech is yours, DQ," Olus said.

"DQ?"

"Demon Queen," Benhil said. "Sounds right to me. Shit, you'd have to be a demon to knock out a mech without a mech of your own."

"Or a suit, at least," Pik said.

"Is that a challenge?" Abbey asked.

"Call it whatever you want, Cage," Olus said. "That mech needs to go, or we aren't leaving this jungle."

"You're a Breaker," Benhil said. "Go break it."

"Airi, can I borrow your sword again?" Abbey asked.

"No," Airi replied.

"What?"

"You killed an innocent woman for no other reason than because it suited your selfish needs. You can go to Hell."

"She was already dead," Pik said.

"It doesn't matter. You were going to do it. You were ready to kill someone whose only crime was getting involved with someone false. Demon Queen is a good name for you."

Abbey stared at Airi, getting angry at her suggestion that her motives were selfish. She was trying to save the whole fragging Republic, maybe even the Outworlds, from Thraven's control. She didn't need to be chastised for having the guts to make the hard decision.

"We'll talk later," she said, furious. She turned and found the mech only twenty meters away. There was a chance it would spot them once it cleared the fallen tree.

She couldn't afford to let that happen.

She bounced up onto the tree. The Springer's torso turned immediately, spotting her and bringing its guns in line. She jumped as it fired, springing up high while the tree was blasted open by the heavy flechettes of the railgun. Her leap brought her over the cockpit, her arc leading her to the mech's shoulder. She landed on it, making eye contact with the pilot as he turned, eyes wide with surprise.

She ran along the top of the mech, managing to keep her balance as she cleared the shoulder and headed for him.

The Springer dipped, forward legs dropping. Abbey started to fall, reaching out with the gift to stay upright. The back legs crouched too, and then the mech's jump jets fired, sending it launching into the air. She looked up just in time to see a heavy branch approaching, and she threw herself from the top of the mech, reaching out and barely getting a hand on its back, her fingernails digging into the metal.

What?

She looked at her free hand. Her fingers had elongated into what looked like claws, holding her fast to the machine as it crashed into the branch, breaking it off before dropping back to the ground. She shook at the impact, her muscles wrenching, her shoulder threatening to dislocate. She pulled herself up, back to the top of the mech. It started firing, sending rounds into the brush at a target she couldn't see.

"Any day now, DQ," Olus shouted through the comm.

She growled as she dove forward, reaching out and getting her hands on the cockpit transparency, digging into the material and holding herself steady, inverted on top of the mech. The pilot looked terrified, and he reached for a sidearm, pointing it toward the shell.

She drew back her arm and punched, the force putting a crack in the cockpit glass. The pilot was shaking as he brought the sidearm up and started shooting.

The first three rounds were blocked by the transparency. The next three went into Abbey's stomach. She gasped at the pain, letting it make her more angry. Then she broke through, reaching down and grabbing the pilot by the collar, lifting him easily in one hand. She could smell his urine as she dropped him over the side of the mech.

She maneuvered herself into the cockpit, taking the controls and turning the torso back around. She didn't have the TCU to pick out targets, but she didn't need it. She fired the railguns, the rounds breaking through the trees too high to hit anyone on the ground but loud and messy enough to hopefully frighten them off. Branches shattered under the assault, and she kept shooting until the noise stopped, the internally loaded flechette cartridges empty.

"Ah, frag," she said, still feeling the pain in her stomach.

She looked down at the blood there. It was slightly thicker than normal human blood, but pitiful compared to Emily Eagan's. She was healing slowly. Too damn slowly.

"Queenie, we're clear," Olus said. "The transport is ours. I've convinced the pilot it's in his best interests not to mention this to the rest of PD. In fact, today may just be our lucky day."

"I don't feel that lucky right now," she replied.

She stood up in the cockpit, climbing back to the top of the mech and looking behind it. The transport was there, Bastion standing outside and waving to her. She hopped down, landing hard. She could feel the Gift calming inside her. She put her hand on her stomach. It was still bleeding. She wasn't invincible after all.

She stumbled over to Bastion, allowing him to take her arm and support her as they boarded the transport. Olus was telling the pilot what to tell Command to get clearance to head back to the city.

"Queenie," Pik said. "You get shot a lot, don't you?"

"I haven't learned to dodge bullets yet," Abbey replied.

"You're still bleeding."

"I know. It isn't healing like it should." She clenched her eyes, fighting the pain. "Food. I need food. Protein."

"Or human blood," Airi said.

"Frag off," Abbey replied. "Food bars. Anything like that."

The pilot turned in his seat, pointing to a storage locker on the side of the transport. "There are ration bars in there."

"I've got it," Bastion said, opening the locker. He found the bars and tore the packaging off, handing them over.

Abbey started eating, unable to chew as fast as she wanted to down the bars. No wonder blood was better. Liquid was a hell of a lot easier to ingest in a hurry. She pushed the thought away. A blender would do the same fragging thing.

The pain started to subside by the time she finished the fourth bar, and she sat in the transport in silence as it cleared the area and headed back toward the city. She wasn't quite sure what she felt, or what she should feel. She was losing herself to this thing that had been forced into her against her will. For all the power it gave her, what it took seemed so much greater.

Her soul hadn't been sold. It had been stolen.

Would she ever find a way to get it back?

CHAPTER FOURTEEN

"CAPTAIN MANN, WE'RE HERE."

"THANK you, Lieutenant," Olus said to the pilot of the transport. "You're sure about this, son?"

"Yes, sir," Erlan replied. "If you say there's something foul going on, I believe it. Heck, I believed it the second we found Ms. Eagan alive on that shuttle. I never expected it to be Emily, though. She was kind to me when we visited the estate with you."

"Snakes usually are," Olus said.

"Where are we?" Abbey asked. Her hunger was finally satiated, her wounds finally healed. It had taken nearly the entire stock of rations and the entire ride back to Feru City for her to recover from the damage.

Time she had spent trying to rediscover herself. Or at least, to not lose herself. She looked at her fingertips again. They had gone back to normal, leaving her wondering if she had imagined the claws that had sprouted from the ends. Except she had seen them on Trin and felt them during her fight with Thraven's assassin.

"Feru City," Erlan said. "Planetary Defense Depot N3."

"Planetary Defense?" Abbey said.

"Don't worry," Olus said. "We're making a short stop here for equipment, and then we're on our way."

"Equipment?"

"You need a new softsuit," Olus said. "And all of the supplies that come with it, among other things. Erlan's already cleared it with Major Tow, though Tow thinks the Lieutenant is going to bring it back to the Eagan estate. They're still looking for us there."

Abbey glanced at the young transport driver. "Why are you helping us?"

"I knew a lot of the people that died on the ring station. I want justice."

"How do you know you'll get it with us?"

"I trust Captain Mann."

"How do you know you can?"

Erlan looked at Olus. Then he shrugged. "The way I see it, Captain Mann has no skin in whatever happened to Eagan Heavyworks. Nothing to gain by its loss. Nothing to lose by getting at the truth. Director Eagan, Emily Eagan, they had something to gain or lose, depending on whose side they were on. As for you and yours?" He looked around the transport at the Rejects. "You all scare the shit out of me. But you didn't kill me. You didn't kill the Springer pilot when you could have. My gut tells me you're not exactly nice individuals, but you're fighting on the right side."

Abbey smiled. "Have you ever considered taking the RAMPY? You might make a good Breaker."

Erlan lit up at the compliment. "The military placement exams? Yes, ma'am. I've thought about it a lot. I haven't done it, mainly because I wasn't sure I wanted to leave Feru. Jesop's going to be pissed when she finds out I made my decision without her."

"You're saving all of our lives," Olus said. "And potentially the lives of thousands."

"Yes, sir."

The hatch on the side of the troop transport slid open. Erlan evacuated the driver's seat and headed toward it, greeting the other militia members at the base of the ramp.

"Jolip, Kerns," he said. "Did Major Tow call ahead?"

"Yeah," one of them said. "We've got a standard locker ready to load up."

"I need some other equipment. Didn't Tow tell you?"

"He said you asked for a softsuit. You pretending you're a hacker now?"

The other soldier laughed. "Yeah, just like he pretends he's a pilot."

"I am a pilot, asshole," Erlan said. "The suit is for Sergeant Barnes. She's the only one rated to use it, remember?"

"I'm just messing with you, Erlan. Geez. What the hell is going on over there, anyway?"

"Outworlders. They came back to finish the job. Ms. Eagan is dead."

"What? Are you kidding?"

"Nope. They're on the run in the jungle outside the estate, but we'll track them down. Barnes got her hands on one of their bots, and she wants the softsuit to try to open it up and see if there's anything it can tell us."

"Shouldn't we be getting the Republic military involved with this? They have ships in orbit right now. I'm sure they must have people more qualified for a job like this than we are."

"That's not my call," Erlan said. "Captain Oxix ordered me to come pick up the kit, so here I am. I already cleared it with Tow, remember? Can one or both of you go get me the Barnes' secondary loadout?"

"Yes, sir. I'll go. Kerns, you load up the locker."

"I've got the locker," Erlan said. "Why don't you both go?"

"Yes, sir."

Erlan left the transport, reappearing a moment later pulling a storage locker. He left it in the narrow aisle between the seats, removed the existing locker, and replaced it with the new one. He did it quickly, glancing back toward the hatch every few seconds. If either of the soldiers tried to come on board, they wouldn't like what they saw.

He got the old locker out of the transport only a few seconds before the two soldiers returned.

"Here you go," one of them said.

"Thank you," Erlan replied. "Dismissed."

He came back onto the transport carrying a large hardcase, which he placed in front of Abbey after closing the hatch.

"That went smoother than I expected," he said. "All of this action is new for us. You're benefitting from the confusion." He returned to the driver's seat and got the vehicle moving again.

"Let's just hope Major Tow doesn't decide to ask Captain Oxix about all of this," Olus said.

"He won't," Erlan replied. "Tow trusts me."

"How do you feel about betraying that trust?" Bastion asked.

He had been abnormally quiet for most of the ride. All of the Rejects had. Abbey didn't blame them. After what they had seen inside the Eagan estate? She was feeling out of sorts, too.

"For the good of the Republic, Lucifer," Olus said.

"We seem to need to do a lot of bad stuff for the good of the Republic, don't we, Captain?"

"We aren't demons for nothing," Benhil replied before Olus could answer. "We do the evil, so nobody else has to."

Bastion laughed. "That sounds like a good tagline." He put up his hands, spreading them as he spoke with a deep voice. "Hell's Rejects: We do the evil, so nobody else has to."

The comment drew a laugh from the others, all except Airi. Abbey could tell she was still sour about her decision to kill Mars Eagan, and who could blame her? She had been sent to Hell for doing something about the way her superior officer was treating her. She had suffered at his hands, and then because of her need to stop his hands. Mars had suffered, too, and her only reward was going to be death. Had been death. Maybe Pik hadn't pulled the trigger, but Airi was right about that. He had been willing, and Abbey had given the order.

She wasn't sorry about it. It was still the right call. Anyone in the HSOC with any combat experience would have agreed. Captain Mann agreed. They had a job to do, a shitty job that the Republic didn't want to touch, not that they could be trusted at this point, anyway. She wished it was a decision she never had to make, but wishing didn't make things different. Airi could learn to deal with it or not; it didn't matter. She would follow orders, or she would be removed from the team.

"Tow would have my hide if he could get his hands on it," Erlan said. "I expect to be off Feru before he knows he's been had." He looked at Olus. "That's what you promised."

"I did," Olus agreed.

"Wait a second," Bastion said. "You said you're heading back to the *Driver* with the pretense that you had nothing to do with any of this."

"I did," Olus repeated.

Bastion pointed at Erlan's back. "So what about him?"

"Lucifer, cool it," Abbey said. "Two ships, remember? The *Fire* and the *Brimstone*?"

"Uh, yeah, but-"

"Two ships, two pilots."

"Ruby's capable."

"And she needs to stay with the *Faust*. Besides, unlike you assholes, he actually wants to be part of this."

"Are you questioning my loyalty?"

"I don't know. If I promised not to drop you, would you still be here?"

Bastion hesitated.

"My point exactly," Abbey said.

"He doesn't have the same training," Bastion argued. "He doesn't have the same experience. We were hand-picked because of what we can do. He's just a Planetary Defense Grabber pilot on yet another Republic planet whose name I'll quickly forget."

"A puddle jumper pilot who's in the process of committing treason to save your lives," Erlan said. "I might not be on par with the lot of you, but if nothing else I'm an extra target for the bad guys to shoot at."

"He has a point," Pik said.

Abbey looked over at the Trover. She had thought he was sleeping. His eyes were still closed.

"Shut up," Bastion said, looking at Abbey. "I'm not going to win this argument, am I?"

"You lost it before it started," she replied.

Bastion grumbled as he leaned back in his seat.

"I know one thing," Pik said. "He isn't bunking with me."

CHAPTER FIFTEEN

THE TRANSPORT STOPPED A SECOND time a few minutes later.

"Feru Spaceport," Erlan announced. "I've already bypassed the security checkpoint and brought us to the shuttle floor. It's a little out of the ordinary, but not unheard of."

"What now, Captain?" Abbey said.

"Now we get off the planet," Olus replied. "Jester, find a shuttle pilot and see if you can make arrangements for a ride back to the *Faust*. Queenie, you and I need to talk. "

"Right," Abbey said. "Rejects, grab your gear. Jester, do what the man says. Pik, you're in charge of the locker."

"Okay, DQ," Pik said.

"Be quick about it," Olus said. "It won't take Major Tow long to realize the transport didn't go where it was supposed to."

The Rejects gathered themselves and piled out of the transport, leaving Olus and Abbey alone.

"Are you okay, Lieutenant?" Olus asked her.

Abbey shrugged. "I don't know yet. I'm changing. In a good way? I have a feeling the answer is no."

"Don't be too quick to judge. What seems wrong might turn out to be a blessing in disguise. The galaxy is changing, too, and the winners are the ones who change with it."

"That sounds like something you'd get in a fortune cookie."

"Where do you think I stole it from? In all seriousness, I've seen a lot over the years. What I've seen these last few weeks? I'm nervous about it. I'm also grateful that Gant convinced me I needed you."

"Me, too. I'd rather be here than under Thraven's control. Who knows what he would have made me into by now."

"We need what he tried to make you, Abbey. As uncomfortable as you may be with it. As crazy as it seems."

"Even if I have to resort to the same diet as Emily Eagan?"

Olus paused, his face hardening. "Yes. In the end, if that's what it takes." He tilted his head. "I'm volunteering if it makes you stronger."

Abbey looked at Olus' neck. She could feel the temptation. "No. Not yet. That's a dark road, Captain. One that I'm not convinced will leave me on the right side."

He straightened up. "Understood."

"Speaking of Emily Eagan," Abbey said. "She called herself a Nephilim. Do you know what that means?"

"How's your religious background?"

"My parents were atheists. Me? I'm more of an agnostic."

"Quick history lesson, then. The Nephilim, in a historical sense, are the the sons of God and the daughters of men."

"You mean angels?"

"Fallen angels. The ones who rebelled against God and were cast down from Heaven."

"You lost me at angels."

"Forget history, then. Emily Eagan claimed that she was part of a long-lost race of beings from another place in space-time. A parallel dimension. That her ancestors came to this one in a starship, and that the starship's Captain was God. Or at least, some portion of God."

Abbey opened her mouth to speak, but she couldn't come up with words to adequately describe the insanity of the statement.

"My original feelings, exactly," Olus said. "The Captain wasn't fully God, but a piece of God. Thraven called it a shard, as though God can make as many parts of himself as he needs to. I don't know. The point is, they went around and started spreading life in this universe until something happened and the crew rebelled. They killed the Captain, and then there was a war, and they vanished or something. I didn't get any of the details on that. I did speak directly to Thraven though. He was going on about a Covenant, and needing to conquer or destroy the Republic, and probably the Outworlds, too, in order to return home and finish the job."

"Finish killing God? Do you believe that bullshit?"

"I believe that Thraven believes it, and a lot of others do, too. I believe something exists that they call the Covenant. I saw part of it before Emily caught me. The *Fire* and *Brimstone* aren't normal ships. They're based on technology supposedly from the time of the rebellion against God. Why here? Why now? I don't know. And then there's the Gift. The Blood of Life, as you called it. That's nothing I've ever heard of or seen before, and I would think if there was a power like that in this part of the universe, there would at least be myths and legends about it."

"Maybe there are? Have you queried the WorldBrain?"

"Not yet. I intend to when I get back to Earth."

"Either way, that doesn't mean they're from a parallel universe if such a thing exists. There's plenty of unexplored space left out there."

"All beyond the range of our starships at the moment," Olus said. "Whether or not any of what they say is true, they still think it is. But even if they're from a distant part of the galaxy, there has to be a connection between them and us. It can't be a coincidence that our blood is valuable to them."

"You're suggesting that the Nephilim aren't new to our corner of the universe?"

Olus nodded. "I think they've been here in one form or another in the past. Whether they remained throughout history is questionable, but the link seems too strong to be an unhappy accident."

"Well, wherever they came from, however long they've been here, it seems they intend to do harm, regardless of the backstory."

"I can't argue with that assessment."

"If they want to harm us, then I want to harm them back."

"I can't argue with that either. At the same time, we need to know as much as we can about what we're up against."

"Sun-Tzu?"

"Know your enemy, yes."

"I'll add hacking Thraven's data storage to my to-do list."

"Thanks. I'll see if I can dig anything up from my end, too."

"What about the codes?"

"Codes?"

"To cancel the broadcast that will activate the virus you dumped in our heads."

Olus bit his lip.

"You said you would-" Abbey paused, staring at him. "You're fragging kidding me, right?"

"It's right out of the HSOC training manual," he replied, trying to fight off a smile. "I thought you would have caught on earlier."

"I've been a little busy. Besides, I felt the insertion."

Olus kept staring at her in silence.

"You're a piece of shit, aren't you, Captain?" she asked.

"I fight dirty if that's what you mean. I have to. You'll have to, also. The bright side is that you can physically make good on the threat if needed."

"How do you know I won't go out and tell them there's no implant? No virus?"

"Because you need them as much as I do. You know how this ends if we ignore it, Abbey. Also, I believe you."

"About what?"

"About your innocence. I believed you the second you told me. That means you're one of the good ones. The real good ones."

"Maybe once," Abbey said. "I'm with you in this, Captain, but I'm not good. Not anymore. I told you. I'm changing."

"I'll take what I can get. I'll stay in contact with Ruby. If anything else happens to me, don't come save me."

"Trust me; I won't."

Olus put his hand out. "Good hunting, DQ."

She took it. "Good hunting, Killshot."
Abbey turned and headed out of the transport, leaving Olus behind.

CHAPTER SIXTEEN

"QUEENIE," JESTER SAID.

ABBEY FOUND the Rejects assembled near one of the two dozen shuttles spread across a wide stretch of tarmac on the eastern end of Feru City. The settlement's skyline was visible to her right, an unimpressive arrangement of low-slung apartments and storefronts that surrounded Eagan Heavyworks' surface-based headquarters. She briefly wondered what would become of the corporation, and Feru, now that the Eagan family line had ended before settling her attention on a shorter than usual Atmo; a narrow, green-skinned female in a stylish jumpsuit with a high collar that accentuated the length of her slim neck. A crystal pin in the shape of a crescent moon was affixed to the inside of the collar, signaling her status as a member of the Crescent Haulers.

Had Olus already known there was a Hauler here? Is that why he had been so certain he could get them off Feru?

"This is Adjunct Captain Nilin," Jester said, "of the starship *Destructor*."

Destructor? That had to be a translator error.

"A pleasure," she said, looking at Nilin.

The Captain tried to mimic a human smile before noticing the brand on Abbey's neck. Her large, dark eyes grew larger, and she shifted her attention to Benhil. The rest of the Reject's brands were hidden beneath the collars of their suits, disguising their origins.

"Now I understand why your offer was so high," she said. "Please, hurry on board. I am taking a serious risk here."

"Serious risk for serious reward," Benhil said.

Nilin moved back to the shuttle, a standard Republic orbital lander with the Hauler's crescent moon painted on the side. She waved the Rejects in. "I'll request launch clearance immediately. Are you certain they don't know you're here?"

"So far, so good," Abbey said. "But you know how quickly things like that can change."

Nilin shook her fingers, a visual gesture Abbey knew was agreement. Then the Atmo vanished into the ship, leaving them to make their own way on.

"How much is this trip going to cost us?" Abbey said, moving in close to Benhil. She could guess, but she wanted to hear him say it.

"The disterium canisters," he replied.

"All of them?"

"Yeah."

"You could have gotten her to do it for one."

"If I wanted to haggle for an hour. I thought we were in a hurry?"

"Did you find out why she was here?"

"No. It didn't come up. What does it matter?"

"You know who the Crescent Haulers are?"

"Of course. That's why I booked with her. So?"

"The Republic wouldn't let a Hauler onto Feru unless they were hauling for the Republic."

"They've been here," Erlan said, catching the conversation. "Collecting the debris from the star dock and bringing it in for recycling."

Abbey was surprised. Space junk wasn't the type of collecting the Haulers normally did. "That's even more of a reason to worry. Who are they really picking the mess up for?"

"It doesn't matter," Benhil said. "You know the Haulers. They're neutral, and their lips are tight. Even if they're working with Thraven, they won't tell him about us."

"Not intentionally."

"I don't think we have much of a choice."

"That doesn't mean I have to like it."

"Sorry, Queenie." Benhil smiled. "Say, you got the codes from Captain Mann, right?"

Abbey kept his gaze, her face flat. She had no intention of telling any of them the virus was a ruse. "Yes. And no, I'm not going to let you leave."

He shrugged. "Just figured I'd ask."

The hatch closed behind Pik as he pulled the locker up and into the ship. Nilin reappeared, pointing to a maglock in the corner. "You can secure that thing over there," she said. "We have clearance to head out. There's going to be a short delay when we reach the *Destructor*. I'm the Adjunct Captain. Captain Trillisin is currently meeting with representatives from Eagan Heavyworks to negotiate another cargo transfer. I'm going to bring you up and then circle back to retrieve him. Once he's on board, we'll rendezvous with your ship, you'll make the payment, and we'll go our separate ways."

Abbey nodded. She wanted to ask what kind of cargo transfer they were negotiating, but she knew Nilin would never tell. Crescent Haulers had a long history of trust and a reputation to consider.

"Thank you, Adjunct," she said.

Nilin didn't respond, turning and heading back to the shuttle's cockpit. Abbey made her way to the seat beside Airi, claiming it and strapping herself in. Airi turned her head away, refusing to engage her. The hatch on the shuttle closed, and the reactor hummed to life.

"Airi," Abbey said.

She had decided to let the episode with the sword slide. It had worked out in the end, and she would rather forgive and forget than hold a grudge against one of her own.

"You've made your position clear already, Queenie," Airi said. "We have nothing to talk about."

The shuttle jerked slightly as it lifted into the air, the hiss of muffled thrusters increasing in amplitude before its anti-gravity coils reached full charge and eased some of the weight.

"Not in terms of an apology, no," Abbey said. "But I still want you to know that I understand why you don't agree with the decision, for whatever that's worth."

Airi didn't say anything and still didn't look at her. The shuttle continued to rise, rocking gently as it cut through the atmosphere.

"We're still a team," Abbey said. "We have to work together, like it or not."

"I know that," Airi said. "I'm not an idiot. I'm not a child. I've hated my CO before and still followed orders." She turned her head, looking at Abbey. "Just because you're in charge, just because you have the Gift, it doesn't mean you need to be arrogant and condescending. I know how to do my job. We're an uneven number now. I'd like to bunk with Erlan if that's acceptable to you."

Abbey tried to hold her anger. She had been accused of being arrogant before. She couldn't deny she was on occasion. But Airi's reaction was pissing her off. She couldn't stay quiet.

"You know how to do your job?" she hissed, keeping her voice low. "I came over here to make nice, even though there's no reason in the fragging galaxy why I should be. You refused to give your weapon to me. You failed to follow a direct order. You let your personal opinion and history affect the entire unit in the middle of a fight. You could have gotten all of us killed."

Airi opened her mouth to speak. Abbey shook her head.

"Don't even try," she snapped. "I'm sorry for what happened to you. I'm sorry you wound up in Hell. It's a shitty situation, but guess what? I'm in a shitty situation of my own. I didn't do anything to end up there, except be the idiot Breaker who grabbed one of General Kett's mainframes. The one that Thraven really, really wants to get into. Do you see me sitting here bitching and whining about it, or do you see me doing my damned job?"

Airi stared at her. Abbey could tell her words were only making Fury more furious, but so what? She needed to be put in her place, and she needed the other Rejects to hear it. She was getting sick of their bullshit.

"This is your one warning. The next time you pull a stunt like that, I will dig my teeth into your neck, and I won't let go until you're dead." She unstrapped herself from the seat and stood up. "If you don't want to be treated like a child, you should do your damnedest to stop acting like one."

She headed forward to an empty seat beside Bastion. The shuttle had cleared the planet's gravity and was vectoring smoothly toward a massive, flat starship a few thousand kilometers distant. A matching crescent moon logo was painted on the side of it, just below the bridge.

"I know it's been a bad day when I sit next to you on purpose," she said as she gained the seat.

Bastion looked at her and laughed. "You're full of compliments today, aren't you, Queenie?" He looked over his shoulder. "Nice chew-out."

"I never asked to be in charge of this outfit."

"You kind of did. You challenged me for command, remember?"

"Because you were going to frag everything up." She paused. "Do you think I'm arrogant?"

Bastion laughed again. "Sort of, yeah."

Abbey laughed, too. "Do you respect me?"

"Since when do you care what I think?"

"I don't know. Right now, I do. I feel like I'm losing myself."

"Just when I think you've lost the last vestiges of humanity, you hit me with a statement like that." Bastion smiled, putting his hand on hers. She decided not to yank it away. "I respect you. All of us respect you, even Fury. She's having a little temper tantrum right now, but she'll get through it. You're a badass and a hardass, and I know we're better off with you in command than we would have been with me at the helm."

Abbey smiled back at him. "You're not just saying that because I have the keys to the kill codes, are you?"

Bastion lifted his hands away, spreading them wide to feign innocence. "Would I do a thing like that?"

"Asshole."

CHAPTER SEVENTEEN

"ENGAGE CLOAKING," URSAN SAID, THE moment the *Brimstone* came out of FTL.

"Cloaking engaged," Dak replied.

Ursan stood, looking at the planet ahead of them. Anvil. Blue and green, with an abundance of verdant life and a population in the millions, orbited by nearly three dozen large Outworld military vessels drawn in from equally as many planets, a coalition of forces typical to the loosely affiliated system of the Governance. He knew from experience each of those ships would carry up to one hundred Shrikes. It was a force that was powerful enough to resist all but the most concentrated Republic attack.

"I could destroy them all if I wanted to," Ursan said softly. "Every last ship."

"Captain?" Dak said, overhearing him.

He wouldn't, though. They were Outworlders. His people. They had suffered the same way he had suffered. He wanted to help them.

"Bolar," Ursan said. "Prepare the shuttle."

"Aye, Captain," Bolar replied.

"The Triune just arrived in system, Captain," Dak said. "She's transmitting merchant status."

"Tell Otero to move in alongside us, so the conscripts don't get antsy."

"How are they going to do that, Boss? They can't see us."

Ursan felt the Gift beneath his skin, the statement making him angry. "Do you think I'm stupid?"

"What? No, Captain. It's easy to forget we're-"

"Give them relative coordinates," Ursan said gruffly. "I'm heading down to the shuttle."

"You want me to come with you?" Dak asked.

Ursan paused. He hadn't been thinking about it. "Yeah. That's a good idea. Lieutenant Iann, you have the bridge."

"Aye, Captain," Iann replied.

Ursan carried the satchel with him as he made his way toward the *Brimstone's* hangar until Dak put a large hand on his shoulder to stop him.

"Uh, Boss?" Dak said.

"What?" Ursan snapped.

"You might want to change your clothes. You don't want to draw attention, not with all of the soldiers here, being AWOL and everything."

Ursan blinked a few times. Why hadn't he thought of that? "Yeah. You're right. I'll meet you at the shuttle."

"Okay."

Ursan headed back to his quarters. He quickly stripped off the lightsuit and exchanged it for his standard dress. A fitted shirt, a pair of gray pants, a thicker jacket that would hide a sidearm. When he was done, he scooped up the satchel and put it over his shoulder, moving back toward the door. He noticed the terminal on his desk as he did. He paused, staring at it.

Something about it was wrong, but he wasn't sure what. He walked over to it but didn't turn it on. He blinked again. If he were going crazy, would he know it?

He moved away from the terminal, exiting the room. Everything would be better once he had Trin back.

He met Dak and Balor in the hangar. The Trover waved him onto the shuttle, and it lifted off as soon as he was seated.

"We've already got landing clearance, Captain," Balor said.

"And the Triune?"

"Waiting right outside. Unless they've got drones sitting up our ass they won't know we came from an invisible ship."

Ursan let himself relax in the seat. He cradled the satchel in his lap, resisting the urge to open it and look in at her. He glanced over at Dak instead, who was rubbing a cloth over his sidearm, an oversized blaster he had been carrying since the day they met.

"I can't believe you still have that thing," Ursan said. It felt like an effort to say something normal.

"Hix," Dak said, smiling. "Remember?"

"A better lover than any Trover woman," Ursan recalled. He forced a smile. "I'm not crazy, am I?"

"We're all crazy, Boss," Dak replied. "That's why we do this for a living, instead of staying planetside and waiting tables, or building bots, or whatever."

Ursan looked down again. Dak had given him a non-answer, and it was infuriating. He was desperate to stay under control after what he had done to Ligit. His officer was still in medical with a concussion and had already requested to be released from duty or transferred to another unit.

They made the rest of the shuttle ride in silence, touching down in the spaceport a few minutes later.

"Where do we find this bot builder of yours?" Ursan asked as they made their way to the loop station for transport from the spaceport. A decently sized crowd moved around them, having disembarked from a civilian transport that had arrived only a few minutes earlier than the *Brimstone*.

"Have you ever been here before?" Dak asked.

"No."

"Anvil's a funny place. You've got thousands and thousands of soldiers, both up there in those ships, and down here on the ground. Because of all the soldiers, part of the place is totally on the level. No dirty business. Squeaky clean. That's what you see from the spaceport." He waved his arm out at the city's profile. "Lots of financial institutions have headquarters here despite the relative distance from the meat of the

Outworlds, mainly because they feel safe. You get bankers; you get corps. You get corps; you get money. You talk protection, you talk serious firepower, even among the law enforcement. Yeah, and Anvil has a lot more laws than most other Outworlds. It's almost like being in the Republic." He laughed. "The Uplevel is where everything legal happens. The Downlevel is where everything illegal happens. The local government keeps it under tight control. Whatever happens Downlevel stays Downlevel, or you'll regret it. At the same time, that makes it a little wild."

"Your man is there?"

"Not a man. Gorix is Plixian. Anyway, you're carrying around a severed head, Boss. What do you think?"

Ursan glared at Dak, causing his friend to take a step away.

"Sorry," Dak said. "Yeah, we need to make our way Downlevel. It's early, so it might still be fairly quiet there. Easier to stay out of trouble."

"Whatever. I want to get this done as soon as possible. No matter what it costs. No matter what we have to give up. Do you understand?"

"I'm with you. Just remember, we're going to talk to him to see if he can do it. He's a whiz with machines, but it doesn't mean he can work magic."

"Maybe he can't," Ursan said. "But I can."

CHAPTER EIGHTEEN

GANT PAUSED AT THE JUNCTION between two of the crossing corridors, leaning over to glance around the corner before pulling his head back just in time to avoid notice from the incoming soldiers.

He growled softly, annoyed with how easy he had thought getting to the communications link would be, and how difficult it had become. The lower decks of the *Brimstone* were surprisingly populated and active, apparently having been turned over to the ground units to use as a training facility. More than one squad had gone jogging through the same hallways he was now attempting to traverse, and while most of them had been unarmed and unarmored, they were great enough in number that he was beginning to question whether or not he would be able to kill them all.

Especially since he had lost his gun back on Drune.

First things first. He was almost to the link, and he had managed to stay out of sight so far. It had just taken too damn long to get this far; long enough that the *Brimstone* had arrived off Anvil and he still hadn't gotten the fragging beacon activated or sent Abbey a fragging message.

He paused, clamping his jaw to keep himself from chittering in frustration. This wasn't the time to screw up and give himself away.

The soldiers moved past, heading along the adjacent corridor. Gant slipped out behind them, padding across the floor to the next corner. He scanned the area. Clear. Then he sprinted down the hallway to a door simply marked "Comm Service."

"Please let the link use computers and not brains in fragging jars," he whispered as he tapped the door control. It slid aside, revealing a small room surrounded by big, black metal boxes. "Praise Gantrian."

"What the frag?"

Gant froze, closing his eyes. "I take that back," he said as he opened them again, whirling around.

"A Gant?" the soldier said, staring at him. "Since when does Ursan have a Gant?"

"Have a Gant?" Gant replied. "What am I, a pet? I'm the ship's engineer, shithead." He stared down the soldier, hoping the retort would be enough to send him on his way.

"No. I've been with Ursan for two years. I would have known if there was a Gant on the crew. Where the hell did you come from? Wait a second. Balor mentioned some crazy ass Gant that attacked them -"

Gant threw himself at the soldier, his lightsuit giving him the power and speed he needed to reach the man's head. He twisted in the air, his foot stretching out and catching the soldier square in the jaw. He could feel the bones break beneath the blow as he altered his trajectory, bouncing off the side of the wall and landing smoothly while the grunt reeled from the attack. He didn't hesitate, moving in and grabbing the soldier's leg, his strong grip turning it and flipping the man over and onto the ground. He scrambled up and wrapped his hands around the crew member's head, pulling violently, rewarded with a quick snap.

"Have a Gant," Gant repeated, grabbing the soldier's feet and dragging him back toward the open door to the service room. "Have a fragging Gant. Are you kidding me?"

He got the soldier inside and closed the door, taking a moment to catch his breath. He was lucky the man hadn't been wearing a suit, or he might not have taken him down so easily.

He was still muttering to himself as he activated the service terminal. Like he had guessed, it had all been left unsecured. He could have turned all communications off if he wanted, but there wouldn't be much of a point. The bridge terminals would report the status, and they would simply flip the switch back on. It was the reason he had come in person instead of doing the job from Ursan's quarters. Once the beacon was active, he needed it to stay active.

He navigated through the interface and turned the beacon on. It might take some time for Ruby to notice it, but he was certain she would. He still wanted to send a separate message, but he had to keep the beacon lit first.

He moved to the rear of the room, where a small, bolted door blocked access to the inner workings of the link. He grabbed the bolts with his hands, his dexterity and the strength of the lightsuit allowing him to turn them without tools. He pulled them from the door and lifted it aside, and then ducked into the space.

Service lights activated at his presence, giving him a clean look at a narrow corridor that skirted around to the back of the black boxes. He followed it until he reached the smallest box. It was the only one marked with the Republic Armed Services logo. The rest was all tech purchased from contractors. He slid it out, careful not to disconnect the wires attached to it, and then unscrewed the outer shell that protected the electronics inside. A simple red light flashed every three seconds, indicating the beacon was active. He was going to make sure it stayed that way.

He reached down, finding the thin wire that connected the beacon to the network. He pinched it between his thumbnails, severing the line cleanly. A soft chitter of laughter, and he reassembled the box and put it back into place. Then he retreated from the service space, returning to the dead soldier.

"Why couldn't you have been carrying a knife or something?" he asked the man, grabbing his legs and pulling again, dragging him into the small corridor. Only then did he return the panel and the bolts to their proper position, hiding the rest of the evidence.

He returned to the terminal again, noting the beacon was still active. Someone on the bridge would notice at some point, and then they would know there was an infiltrator on the ship. How many would he be able to remove before then? Hopefully more than one.

He keyed into the Milnet, hopeful that Ruby was present on the standard military network. He knew it wasn't as secure as a direct link, but Thraven already knew about the *Brimstone*. What more could he do?

"Ruby," Gant said. He waited impatiently, glancing back at the door. "Ruby."

Nothing.

"Captain Mann," he said.

"Gant?" Olus replied a few seconds later. "Is that you?"

"Yeah. Captain, I'm-"

"Is everything working properly now?"

Gant paused. Olus was cluing him in that the channel could be dirty.

"Yes, sir," he replied. "I've made the adjustments to the comm link that you requested. How do I sound?"

"Loud and clear," Olus replied. "Thank you for taking care of things so quickly. I'll have my assistant get back to you as soon as possible."

"Roger, Captain. If I'm unavailable, they can come and speak to me in person."

"Of course. Mann out."

The link dropped. Hopefully, the short exchange wouldn't draw any undue scrutiny from the Republic's flagging algorithms, but it was equally possible someone was listening to every word Captain Mann said.

Oh, well. There wasn't anything he could do about that. He turned off the terminal and headed to the door. Abbey would be coming sooner or later.

He hoped to present her with a nice, undefended starship when she did.

He just needed to find a nice, sharp knife.

CHAPTER NINETEEN

GLORITANT THRAVEN WAS ANGRY.

IN a sense, he was always angry, but right now he was angrier than usual. He had felt the impact of Venerant Alloran's death. He knew Abigail Cage had killed her. That wasn't what was bothering him, though. Quite the opposite, in fact. He had been curious to see if the Terran would be able to stand up against a true Nephilim, a true child of the Gift. He had even gone as far as to presume she would survive, and that Alloran's long light in the universe would finally fade. He was pleased with the outcome, and even more pleased when he felt the lightest touch of the Gift spread away from the Venerant.

Abigail Cage had tasted.

What he wasn't pleased about was that Captain Mann had found a way around his design. He had circumvented the trap, saved by the fugitives from Hell without being associated with their attack. He had remained hidden and invisible, and had somehow broken away from Cage and the others and made it back to the *Driver* without any evidence he had been to the Eagan estate at all. According to his operatives, even the records from the hotel had been altered, the security streams erased. He had cleansed his tracks quickly and efficiently.

It wasn't all that surprising, but it was frustrating. He wasn't sure he could arrange the same sort of accident to befall the Director of the OSI as had befallen General Soto, but now he would be forced to try.

And then there was Ursan Gall. He had known by the way the man had responded to his orders that he had little intention of following them. The Outworlder had always struggled to stay under control, always whining, always complaining. He had suffered him for Evolent Trinity's sake, but now the Evolent was gone, and Cage had already proven she was stronger than Ursan could ever be, even with only half of the Gift inside her.

And Gall was losing his mind. He had taken Trinity's head. What was he planning to do with it? He had asked about reviving her. Just a head? It was unheard of. The Nephilim were no strangers to war or bloodshed. Their history was thick with conflict, continuing in one form or another for millennia after the defeat of the Shard. Their violence had meaning. Even the ancient technologies they had recovered served a higher purpose. This? This was pure madness.

Then again, Ursan was one of the Lesser, an evolutionary creature born from the essence of Elysium. He existed to be used, as the Father had promised all Lesser were to be used. It was to be expected that he would be unable to comprehend the fullness of the glory that was to come. It was to be anticipated that he would succumb to the Gift and go insane. Plenty of Potentials did. That was why the Converts existed.

Trinity had been a Lesser, a truth that he occasionally ignored. She had proven her usefulness.

Ursan was outliving his.

There was one other complication that was angering him, the implications of which he had yet to discern, but which had the potential to threaten all of his years of careful planning. He already knew the Watchers were out there, somewhere. He also knew Sylvan Kett had aligned with them, making him increasingly eager to crack the mainframe they had captured and hopefully uncover his, and by extension their, whereabouts.

What he hadn't expected was that they would get involved now and in such a direct way. That they had used the Focus to aid Abigail Cage? One one hand, they had done him a favor in saving Cage. On the other, it meant they knew of her as well. If they got to her first? There was no telling what might happen. Plus, they had cost him his flagship and a number of assets he had already allocated elsewhere.

At least he had a new flagship.

"Honorant Gizlan," Thraven said.

A projection appeared in the open space beside him. A tall, chiseled Outworlder in a crisp, dark uniform. He put his fingers up to Thraven in salute. "Gloritant Thraven," he snapped.

Thraven held back his smile. This was a true servant of the Nephilim. A human who could see past the simple destruction to the glory of the future.

"What is the status of our preparations?"

"Gloritant, we have completed the retrofit of four of the ships. They are converted, and their captains are awaiting orders."

"Only three?" Thraven said.

"There has been a minor setback with the fueling chambers, Gloritant. As you know, they can be difficult to prepare, and we've discovered that many of the cells are unsuitable. They have not been surviving the integration process."

"What is the failure rate?"

"Over sixty percent, Gloritant."

Thraven considered it. Venerant Alloran's reports had suggested a twenty percent failure rate on the integration of Lessers into the fueling chamber. Was it truly a surprise? They had been collecting cells from planets throughout the Outworlds, but their specimens were of questionable quality, necessitated by the need to remain hidden until the time to strike arrived. They didn't have the same resources to procure the higher quality material that Eagan Heavyworks did. It was part of the reason they had gained control of the company to begin with.

"Gloritant, stronger cells will improve overall systems performance," Honorant Gizlan said. "We have four ships, in addition to the *Fire* and the *Brimstone*. Perhaps a few exploratory strikes would be of value?"

"Perhaps," Thraven said, an idea beginning to form.

He couldn't argue that they needed better cells. Four ships laden with Shrikes, Converts, and standard infantry should be more than enough to seize a single planet, even one of formidable size. He had hoped to launch an organized offensive that would leave the galaxy trembling, but it seemed the Father was sending him on a slightly different path. He knew better than to question the will of his Father.

"Prepare the ships. We will launch a preliminary offensive, with the goal of collecting Lessers for integration."

"Yes, Gloritant," Gizlan replied, his eyes brightening with the order, his excitement obvious. "And who shall you name to lead this vanguard of the Great Return?"

Thraven knew Gizlan wanted the position for himself. In other circumstances, he might have even permitted it. His Nephilim brothers and sisters were committed to more important endeavors, and while Gizlan was a Lesser, he had proven himself loyal.

Not in these circumstances, however.

"I will lead the assault personally," Thraven said. "You will remain here and prepare for completion of the fleet."

Gizlan didn't miss a beat, snapping another salute even as he tried to hide his extreme disappointment. "Yes, Gloritant."

"You have done well, Honorant," Thraven said. "I expect you to earn much glory in the days and years to come."

Some of the disappointment vanished. "Yes, Gloritant."

"You are dismissed, Honorant."

Gizlen saluted once more, and then the projection vanished. Thraven turned his head, looking out the transparency to the field of starships beyond. The *Fire* was foremost among them, and already he could see the workers around it changing formation, shifting priorities to begin loading it with the full weapons of war.

He retreated away from the room, pausing when he reached the dark figures that stood motionless on either side of the door.

"Have the Font transferred to the *Fire*," he said to the one on the left.

There was no indication the guard had heard him, but he was

certain they did because as he moved away, one Immolent remained behind while the other followed dutifully.

He would go and clean up this mess, and then the real war could begin.

CHAPTER TWENTY

URSAN FOLLOWED DAK OFF THE loop transport that carried them into the city, keeping a wary eye on the individuals around them. He clutched the satchel defensively, holding it tight, nervous that someone might give it too much attention.

"Where to?" he asked, looking up. Vehicles crowded above them, skipping along designated lanes stacked six rows deep below the linked platforms that connected the Uplevel. It was more traffic than he would have expected judging by the activity at the spaceport.

"Not up there," Dak replied. "That territory is for the bankers." He pointed ahead. "That way."

"The station doesn't run through it?"

"And force the snobs to have to look at the likes of us?" Dak laughed. "It's bad enough for them when they have to ride the loop with us. Why do you think there are so many cars?"

Ursan redirected his eyes forward. The buildings were all massive, leaving this part of the city bathed in darkness despite the time of day. It felt hotter down here, too, and more moist. Like the wealthy were sweating on the poor. Or pissing on them.

"This part of the city reminds me of Caliban," he said. "I think I'd be worried if things were too clean."

"You and me both, Boss."

They walked for a while, following the flow of foot traffic through a number of alleys between buildings, the landscape becoming more industrial and aged as they did. Ursan noticed soon after that the composition of the individuals had slowly changed, the number of soldiers mingled in with the crowd increasing as they drew nearer to Central.

There was no sign announcing when they arrived, but it was clear all the same. Residences, storefronts, and eateries gave way to brothels and drug dens, clubs and Construct nodes, black market surgeons, and armories. They weren't advertised on signs or anything, but he knew how to identify them from his time frequenting similar locations on other planets. He was a career soldier after all.

"One second, Boss," Dak said, pausing in the middle of one of the streets.

Ursan stood with him, eying a pair of barely clothed human synths gyrating behind a large window. One of them caught his gaze, smiling and sticking her hips out provocatively before gesturing and causing the window to turn opaque.

"Recreation later, huh, Boss?" Dak joked.

Ursan glared at him, and he lowered his head. That kind of maneuver might have been tempting to him before Trin. Not now.

"What's the holdup?" he asked.

"I was just a little confused. Things have changed a bit. That pleasure house wasn't there before. It's this way."

Ursan followed him down an adjacent street. A vent from the upper levels was dumping steam out nearby, casting a haze on the entire area. He found his hand moving toward the blaster hidden under his coat as they walked. Something about this area didn't feel right.

He heard the clicking and smelled the salty brine before the Plixians appeared from a side alley, rushing toward them in a group, their legs tapping along the pavement. Ursan had the blaster out before he thought about it, but Dak's hand landed on top of it, pushing it down.

"Hold up, Captain," he said.

Five of the six Plixians remained back. The other one approached quickly, scuttling forward and reaching out toward Dak, putting a pair of three-fingered hands on his shoulders and clicking in a tight cadence.

"Dak, you meaty bag of putty. You're the last individual I expected to trip my trap." He hissed in laughter.

"Gorix, you cockroach," Dak replied. "How long has it been?"

"Four Earth standard?" Gorix guessed.

"Earth standard," Ursan said. "We're in the Outworlds, aren't we?"

Gorix's head turned, two beady eyes landing on Ursan while his antennae shivered. "Earth standard is an accepted and easily understood metric, even here on Anvil." He looked back at Dak. "Who's the hairless Curlatin?"

"Ursan Gall," Ursan said. "Captain Ursan Gall."

Gorix made a dismissive clatter. "Captain? Dak, you brought a soldier my way?"

"It isn't like you think," Dak said. "Captain Gall has funds. He can pay."

"Are you vouching for that?"

"Yeah."

Gorix's mandibles moved quickly in excitement. "In that case, follow me, Captain Ursan Gall. I've got a lot of good stuff I can show you."

"I'm not interested in it," Ursan said.

"No?"

"There's only one thing I need from you." He shifted the satchel so he could open it.

"Boss, maybe we should wait until we're inside," Dak said.

"We don't need to go inside if he can't help me," Ursan replied. He opened the bag, gently reaching in and wrapping Trin's hair in his hand.

Gorix sank from his thorax as he tried to see what Ursan had, snapping back in surprise when he lifted Trin's head and held it out.

"My wife," Ursan said. "Dak told me you make bots. I want you to make one that will allow her to walk again."

Gorix's head rotated toward Dak, whose expression told the Plixian that Ursan was serious and that he should respond seriously to the request.

"Captain," Gorix said hesitantly. "I am very skilled in bot repair and construction. Bots, Captain. Not Terrans. Even if I could rig a system that would mobilize the head, I mean your wife, I can't return life to dead things."

"The brain runs on oxygen and electricity," Ursan said. "It isn't that different from bots."

"Captain, I'm sorry if you came all of the way to Anvil for this, but this is beyond the limits of my abilities."

"So you can't do it?" Ursan asked. He could feel his skin beginning to burn. He was getting angrier by the second.

"No, Captain," Gorix said.

"Or you won't do it?"

"Captain Gall, if I could, I would."

"Liar," Ursan shouted. "It was Thraven, wasn't it? He got to you. He told you not to help me."

"What?" Gorix said. "I don't know who-"

"Lying again," Ursan said. He lifted his hand, throwing the Gift into Gorix. The force pushed the mechanic backward, sending him crashing into the other Plixians.

"Boss," Dak said.

"I came in good faith, and you attack me?" Gorix said angrily, twisting on the ground to get his legs back under him. "Kill them both."

"Gorix, wait," Dak said. "Ursan."

"Shut up, Dak," Ursan said.

The Plixians around Gorix produced sidearms from packs strapped close against their backs, wasting no time unloading the rounds within. Most of them were aimed at Ursan, but one of the Plixians had targeted Dak, and he dove to the ground as the slugs whipped past him, one of them grazing his shoulder.

"Gah," he shouted. "Mother fragger."

Ursan was burning with fury and despair. He held up his free hand, and the bullets headed his way all came to a stop, hanging uselessly in the air. He wanted more than anything to send them back to the individuals who had fired them, to watch their heads snap as the rounds struck them between the antennae with more force than their guns could manage. He held himself in check, shaking from the effort.

"I could kill all of your guards," Ursan said. "A thought. A gesture. They would all be dead. I don't want to kill right now. I want to save."

Gorix remained still, his mandibles dancing as he stared at the frozen bullets.

"I'll do what I can," he said at last. "I may be able to rig something up, but I'm going to need to call in a specialist on the organic to mechanical interchange. I can do larger work like muscle connectors, bionics, even implanted weapons, but what you want is at the near microscopic level."

"Bring whoever you need," Ursan replied. "I can pay. My starship, the Triune, is in orbit. That should cover it, shouldn't it?"

"Boss?" Dak said, getting back to his feet. "You can't sell your ship."

"Why not? I have the other one for now, and the only way I'm going to lose it is when I die. Probably at Thraven's hands."

"What about me? What about the rest of your crew?"

"Thraven won't blame you for following orders. He'll keep you on. This isn't your decision to make, Dak. She isn't your ship."

"That will cover it," Gorix said. "Assuming it's at least Castle class?"

"Castle? Frag that. She's way above Castle."

"Then we have a deal." Gorix hesitated. "I will require the head."

Ursan looked down at Trin's face. He didn't want to let go of her. "I'll stay with her."

"This work is going to take some time, Captain," Gorix said. "A week at the soonest. Most likely more."

"We can get a room nearby," Dak said. "You won't have to be far."

Ursan was motionless for a moment. Then he nodded and put Trin's head back in the satchel, zipping it closed. Only then did he allow the bullets to fall. They clattered to the ground as he stepped through them, holding out the bag to Gorix.

"If anything happens to it, I'll kill you slowly," he said.

Gorix clicked, his posture fearful when he took the satchel gingerly in one of his narrow hands. "Understood."

"No progress, no payment," Ursan said.

Gorix's head tilted as though he was going to complain. He nodded instead. "Dak knows where my workshop is located. Give me one local day to contact my specialist and do some preliminary research."

"Fine. One local day. Dak, let's go before I change my mind about leaving her."

"It'll be okay, Boss," Dak said.

Gorix turned his head and clacked something to the other Plixians, something Ursan's translator implant wasn't able to convert. He was about to question it when Dak put a hand on his shoulder.

"They're talking about what they want for dinner," Dak said.

"How do you know?"

"I spent some time with Gorix before I started running with you. I know the customs. Come on."

Dak started leading him away. The Plixians retreated as well, making their way back into the side street where they had appeared. Ursan paused, looking back, a sudden panic gripping him. "They're going to hurt her."

"Gorix can be trusted," Dak said. "Besides, you scared the hell out of him. Didn't you notice that line of green running down his foreleg?"

Ursan was confused for a second. Then he started to laugh. "No. I didn't notice."

"There's a shitty dive I know a couple streets from here. It's friendly to assholes like you and me, and it isn't a paradise, but the living's at least as good as it is on the Triune. We can wait there if you want?"

"Anywhere close," Ursan said, starting to rub his hands together. She had only been gone for a minute, and he was already losing it. He needed to get a grip. "I'm not crazy, am I, Dak?"

"You keep asking me that, Boss."

Another non-answer. "Never mind."

CHAPTER TWENTY-ONE

THERE WERE A FEW TENSE minutes during the shuttle ride when Abbey wasn't sure if the Haulers were as trustworthy as their reputation had led her to believe. After the craft had cleared the atmosphere, Nilin had adjusted course and put them on a direct heading toward one of the Republic battleships orbiting the planet. Not the *Driver*, Olus' ship, but another, older ship, whose tags were obscured by a smaller cruiser beside it.

She had felt herself tensing, only to feel like an idiot as the shuttle had passed over the top of the ship, the maneuver revealing the *Destructor* behind it. The cargo ship was nearly three times the size of the battleship, the bow facing toward them, the body stretching off almost endlessly into the black. Like the prison ship that had transferred her to Hell, it was composed of a fixed forward crew area and a detachable, and replaceable, aft where all the cargo was stored. It was essential both for quick transfer of big loads and for more effective escape in the event of an emergency. Not that there were many emergencies in Republic space. Not that a company like the Haulers needed to worry about it, anyway.

Everyone knew to leave the Crescent Haulers alone. Their founder had seen to that years ago, building the business on an uncanny ability to travel the universe safely. Doing that had meant some allegedly seedy deals with some allegedly seedy people, and the untimely deaths of more than a few government officials, military leaders, mercenary commanders, and heads of criminal enterprises that were thought otherwise untouchable. It was dirty business, but it also meant that the Republic had a source to handle their most precious cargo. One whose delivery percent had been at one hundred for nearly fifty years.

Which left Abbey wondering what the frag they were doing picking up useless space junk.

Unless it wasn't as useless as she thought?

Unless it wasn't the Republic that had hired them?

She was thinking like a Breaker, trying to untangle the knots in front of her eyes. While the questions were disconcerting, the activity was comforting. She had been questioning her sanity too often lately. She knew she was changing, and Olus had even suggested she embrace the change, but at the same time, it had seemed as though she was being replaced instead of altered.

She wished Captain Mann was still with them. She wanted to know what he thought of the situation. Were the Haulers working with Thraven? What if only some of them were? She knew the bastard had spies and operatives everywhere. Inside the Outworld Governance, the Republic Council, Hell, and the military. She still didn't know how long he had been moving his pieces into place, but she could guess it was a pretty long time.

Where did Sylvan Kett fit into that? She surprised herself with the question. She hadn't given Kett much thought since Mamma Oissi's. The Rudin had suggested Thraven was looking for Kett, desperate to find him because of what he knew.

What did he know? How had he learned it? She wished she still had her hands on the mainframe she had recovered. She wished she knew the whole story behind the small box that had been left behind on the *Nova*. Where had it come from? Had Kett lost it? Did the target on Grudin belong to the General? To Thraven? Or were they just a bunch of hapless idiots who got their hands on something they didn't understand?

She had seen the setup inside the compound. It wasn't the gear of hapless idiots.

Then whose gear was it?

"Queenie, you with us?" Bastion said, shaking her arm.

Abbey looked at him, snapping out of her internal monolog. "What?"

"Hail to the Demon Queen," he said, smiling. "We're here."

Abbey finally noticed the shuttle was inside the *Destructor's* hangar. The other Rejects were all on their feet, waiting for her to stand, too.

"If you'll disembark," Nilin said, moving into the back. "I will head back to retrieve the Captain. Once he's on board, we'll transfer you to your ship. Commander Pellem will meet you on the deck."

"Roger," Abbey said. "Pik, grab the locker."

"On it, Queenie."

"You can leave your weapons and gear outside," Nilin said. "I expect you'll have the courtesy not to bring it into the populated areas."

"Of course," Abbey said.

The shuttle's hatch opened, and they made their way off. A Skink was waiting for them there, a female dressed in intersecting layers of tightly wound and brightly colored cloth.

"Commander Pellem?" Abbey guessed.

A tri-forked tongue skipped out from the Skink's mouth, slipping along the lips to moisten them. "Confirmed," she replied. Her small eyes landed on the Hell brand. "Interesting."

"Pellem, show our guests to the mess," Nilin said. "They can wait for the Captain there."

"Aye, Adjunct," she said. She looked over at the rest of the Rejects, a hint of amusement rippling across her scaly face. "Quite a collection."

"We do our best," Abbey said.

"Follow me."

They dropped their equipment where Nilin had pointed and trailed behind Pellem, out of the hangar and into a wide corridor. There were other crew members present, moving from one place to another on the ship. It didn't take long for Abbey to notice that none of them were human.

"The Haulers don't like Terrans?" Abbey asked, curious.

"Excuse me?"

"I noticed there are no humans onboard. I admit we haven't seen much of the ship or the crew yet, but standard rosters are eighty percent homo sapiens or more."

"A keen eye. No Crescent humans on the *Destructor*. Captain doesn't approve."

"Why not?"

"Unreliable."

"What do you mean?"

"Terrans are unreliable. Accustomed to being above. Use status to do less."

"You tell it, sister," Pik said from the back.

Abbey looked back at him.

"What? You did notice I'm the one dragging the locker around, right?"

"You did notice you're three times the size of any of us, right?" Abbey replied.

"I'm just saying."

"Who saved your life on Drune?"

Pik laughed. "Yeah, but you aren't human. Not exactly. Not anymore."

Abbey paused. He was right, even if his presentation of the facts sucked.

"Not human?" Pellem asked.

"Long story," Abbey replied, matching the Skink's verbal pattern. "Rough week."

"That's the understatement of the eon," Benhil said. "If we can go ten hours without being shot at or nearly killed, I'll be a very happy man."

"Fugitives, yes," Pellem said. "Republic wants you. Saw it on the Milnet."

"Have access to the Milnet?" Abbey asked.

"Haulers have access to everything. A web of trust. Do not concern. Will not tell." She hissed and stuck out her tongue, a sound Abbey's translator told her was equivalent to a smile.

"I heard we're going to the mess. What kind of grub do you have on this boat?" Benhil asked. "Seeing as how there are no Terrans on board."

"Many good things," Pellem said. "Baked Skaluve Worms. Drugrum from Ganemant. Fizzig Al'kappa stew."

"I've never heard of any of that," Bastion said.

"Me neither," Benhil said. "Worms? Gross. Drugrum? Sounds like something that comes out of my backside."

"The stew might be decent," Airi said.

"I've had Al'kappa stew," Erlan said. "It isn't."

"Heh, you guys," Pik said. "Different papillae for different species."

"Papillae?" Bastion said.

"Taste buds," Abbey said.

"Where the hell did you learn a word like papillae?" Bastion asked.

"Just because I'm a Trover doesn't mean I'm uneducated."

"Yeah, it usually does. Your kind isn't known for its STEM aptitude."

"Frag you."

"I bet you saw it on a stream somewhere," Benhil said. "Didn't you?"

"No," Pik replied. Then he smiled. "Yes."

"Ha. I knew it."

"Do not worry," Pellem said. "Have cook synth."

They entered the *Destructor's* mess. There were seven or eight tables inside, most of them empty. A pair of Skinks were sitting in the center of the room, while a single Curlatin was at the table in the corner, his back to them.

"How may I serve you?" the synth asked, walking over to them. Like all synths, it had a human form. It appeared to be an older model, the synthetic flesh slightly worn and rubbery.

"Do you have anything good to eat?" Benhil asked.

"Something that won't repulse human papillae?" Bastion added.

"Our inventory of Terran sourced dishes is limited," the synth replied. "We do have a small supply of standard nutrient rations, if that is acceptable."

"It figures," Bastion said. "We've been off of Hell for what, four weeks now? I still haven't had anything to eat but fragging nutrient bars."

"They're good for you," Abbey said.

"Easy for you to say, Queenie," Benhil said. "You're eating them like you're preggers."

"Sometimes I feel like I'm eating for two million."

"Hey, Cookie," Pik said. "I'll take the Al'kappa."

"Of course, sir. Coming right up."

"Make it two," Airi said, drawing a look of curiosity from Pik. "What? My mother said never to say no to anything unless you've tried it."

"Have you ever been with a Trover?" Pik asked.

"No," Airi replied. "But I don't do everything my mother says."

"Smooth, Pik," Bastion said, laughing.

"Shut up. It's Queenie's fault anyway. She won't let us play with Ruby."

"She isn't a toy," Abbey said.

"She was made to be a toy," Benhil said. "She's programmed to like it."

"Forget it," Abbey said. "Not another word about Ruby, or I'll make sure that even if you could, you can't."

Abbey raised her eyebrow at Benhil, who put his hands up in submission.

"Lieutenant Cage?"

Abbey turned her head to the sound of her name, finding the Curlatin in the corner. He was on his feet, facing her way. Abbey stared at him. One of his large eyes was tinged with red and purple, like the entire thing was one massive bruise.

"Coli?"

The universe had never felt so fragging small.

CHAPTER TWENTY-TWO

"FUNNY YOU SHOULD BE HERE, Lieutenant," Coli said.

"Me?" Abbey replied. "You're supposed to be on Hell."

"So are you."

"You know this Curlatin?" Pik said.

"What are you doing here?" Abbey said, ignoring him. There was nothing good about Coli being here. Nothing.

"Overseeing the recovery," Coli said. "For General Thraven."

The name got the attention of all of the Rejects. They stiffened up, turning to face Coli.

"You work for Thraven?" Abbey said, not sure whether to laugh or just punch him in the other eye. "Seriously? What the frag was with the waterworks when they picked us up? You acted like the biggest pansy I've ever seen. How's your eye, by the way? It looks like shit."

Coli huffed. "I thought he was going to screw me after we made a deal. He never said anything about getting busted or Hell. Pick up the mainframe. That was the mission. But he got us out of there real quick. Some of us in one piece. Well, me. Mostly." He put his hand near his eye. "You fragging blinded me, you bitch. You have to know how sensitive a Curlatin's eyes are. Fragging low blow. The other members of the Fifth are here, though. Eighteenth Platoon, now." His big mouth spread in a toothy smile. "You want a reunion?"

Abbey glanced back at Pellem. The Skink was clearly confused.

"High-value cargo," she said. "Always send platoon to guard."

"It didn't seem odd to you that debris would be considered high-value?" Benhil said.

"Haulers don't ask. Don't tell."

"Yeah, right. Well, I highly recommend calling for whatever backup you have on this tug, right now."

The door to the mess opened. Five members of Fifth Platoon walked in. The good news was that they were in standard utilities instead of armor.

The bad news was that their eyes were all a dark, silvery-gray.

"Ah, frag me," Airi said, recognizing the look as she lifted her sword from her back. "Good thing I brought this along."

"I have a feeling I shouldn't have left the locker back in the hangar," Pik said.

Abbey looked back at Coli, her prior anger at the Sergeant exploding. It had been one thing when she thought the Fifth had gotten busted for smuggling. Knowing Coli was working with Thraven on the job?

She growled softly, ready to jump Coli and blind him in his other eye. There was no time for that, yet. She moved in front of the Rejects, putting up her hand, feeling the Gift flowing through her. The Fifth attacked, a line of plasma launching from their rifles, the bolts charging toward them and shattering against an invisible shield.

"Remember," Abbey said. "You need to take the heads."

"Fury, that means you," Bastion said.

Abbey bounced forward, launching herself into the lead soldier. Dis. She remembered the woman from Grudin as she slammed into her, knocking her back. She spun and caught an incoming fist, grunting as a plasma bolt struck her in the leg. She turned and kicked, catching another soldier in the hip and knocking them off-balance.

Then the Rejects were there with her. Pik grabbed Dis by the shoulders, throwing her against the wall. She hit it without complaint, bouncing off and coming back. Pik closed again, throwing a heavy punch at her head. She brought her hand up, and the fist hit an invisible wall, his arm bouncing off, the Gift throwing him to the ground.

"Frag," he shouted, rolling to his feet.

Bastion was on Abbey's other side. He had produced a knife from somewhere, and he used it to slash one of the Convert's arms, leaving a nasty gash at the wrist. He sidestepped one punch, ducked under a second, and stabbed the soldier in the chest before being thrown backward.

Red klaxons started flashing in the mess as the ship's alert system was triggered.

"What's happening?" Abbey said, throwing the Gift out and into Dis, slamming her into the bulkhead so hard she could hear her spine break.

"Soldiers attacking crew," Pellem replied. "Red alert."

Abbey turned back to Coli. "Thraven isn't going to like this."

"Some opportunities are too good to pass up."

"Worth starting a war with the Haulers?"

"Don't worry about that. The media will say the fugitives from Hell were responsible. After all, you were last seen in this area."

"You son of a bitch."

"So I've heard. Next time maybe you'll want to think twice before you punch a Curlatin in the eye."

"You're right. Next time I'll take both of them and save myself the trouble."

She burst toward him, the Gift burning beneath her skin.

He drew his sidearm; a simple pistol sized for his large hands. He aimed it at her, holding the shot as she approached. She lunged at him, noticing her fingers changing as she did, stretching into silvery claws.

He pulled the trigger.

The bullet hit between her breasts, the crack of her bones almost as loud as the shot itself. The force pushed her off course, and Coli ducked to the side as she fell to the ground and rolled to a stop, the pain almost unbearable.

"I don't understand why Thraven's been having so much trouble with you," he said.

Abbey pushed herself up on her hands, finding the Rejects on the other side of the room. Bastion was down. Dead? Pik was still fighting, but his left hand was a bloody mess. Airi was holding her own, her sword able to do what the others couldn't. Two headless Converts were nearby.

Pellem was on the ground, a pool of blood beneath her.

She picked herself up, getting to her feet. Her head was thumping in rhythm to her heart, the Gift moving to a matching beat. Her breath was steady, and she opened her mouth, snarling in fury and walking toward Coli. She didn't give a shit who or what Thraven had turned the Fifth into. She wasn't going to let her team die.

Coli pointed his sidearm and fired, the bullet hitting Abbey in the chest a second time. She felt the sting of it, but when she glanced down there was no damage. No wound. He shot her again, and again. She kept coming, kept moving, walking toward him.

His sidearm clicked as she reached him, the magazine empty. She reached out almost casually, grabbing him as he tried to back away and pulling him down to her height. She brought her other hand down and across, her fingers slashing across his good eye. He howled in pain for a second time as he crumbled to the ground.

She didn't kill him. Instead, she continued forward to where Pik was tangling with Sergeant Ray, trying to defend himself from the Convert's attacks. Each punch slammed hard into the Trover, and she could tell he was on the defensive as he tried to back away.

A plasma bolt caught Ray in the face, blasting half of it off. Ray froze for a moment, and Abbey watched as silver liquid filled the space, taking the place of the damage and allowing the Sergeant to move again.

What the frag?

Ray grabbed at Pik's bloody arm, hands wrapping around it and twisting. A sharp snap and Pik bellowed in pain, using his other hand to hit Ray and sending him flopping across the floor. Airi was on him in an instant, her sword dropping through Ray's neck.

"My eyes," Coli whined behind her. "My fragging eyes."

"Okay, are you okay?" Abbey said, ignoring him, heading over to her team.

"Hurts like a mother," he replied. "Arm's broken, and they shot my fragging hand." He held it up. Three of his four fingers were missing. He didn't seem to know it until then. "Fragging son of a bitch. Damn it."

"The ones in here are all dead, Queenie," Benhil said. "But the rest of the ship? If it's a platoon, there are at least ten more."

"Nine," Abbey said. "Illiard never made it out with them, probably because he got hurt. They're going to be killing the crew."

"And blaming it on you," Coli said between cries of pain.

"Lucifer," Abbey said, dropping next to the pilot. His eyes were open. Blinking. He looked dazed.

"I'll keep an eye on him," Pik said, grabbing Ray's rifle in his good hand. "Go take care of the rest of this trash."

Abbey looked over at Benhil, Erlan, and Airi. "Grab a rifle, let's go."

They picked up rifles from the downed soldiers, following Abbey out into the hall. She didn't know the layout of the ship beyond the path from the hangar to the mess, but it usually wasn't that hard to find the bridge.

"Trouble seems to follow you wherever you go, Queenie," Benhil said.

"Thraven seems to be wherever I go," Abbey replied. "It's okay. It only makes me want to kill him that much more."

"Roger that."

"Stay alert. They might not have armor, but they have some amount of the Gift."

"Not as much as you do," Airi said.

"I didn't see you getting tossed around back there, Fury," Benhil said.

"Anger and hate, Jester," Airi replied. "It's an effective counter."

"Even for regular humans?"

"It seems to be."

"Shut it," Abbey said. They were nearing an intersection in the corridors. "I'll take point, be ready to cover me."

"Roger."

She reached the corridor and stepped out into it. A few dead crew members were scattered along the length of it, most of them shot in the head.

"Damn it," she said. When Trillisin and Nilin came back, would they blame the Rejects for the attack? They had every reason to.

"Eww," Benhil said. "Dead Skinks smell worse than dead humans, I think."

"What does shut it mean to you, Jester?" Abbey asked.

"Sorry, ma'am."

They made their way past the corpses. Abbey listened for the sound of gunfire, but the ship was eerily quiet.

"How do you think they do it?" Airi said. "Soldiers that can't be killed I mean?"

"Olus said that they're using some kind of lost technology," Abbey replied. "Tech that predates humankind."

"What?" Benhil said. "As in, there were spacefaring races before Terrans?"

"Yes."

"Where the hell have they been hiding?"

"Good question."

"I don't mean so we can find them. I mean so we can stay the frag away. Things are already bad enough."

"You're going to be a hero, Jester."

"A hero? The Republic is after us. The Outworlds are after us. Thraven is after us, and within the next ten minutes, the damned Crescent Haulers will be after us, too. Correct me if I'm wrong, Queenie, but having half the galaxy trying to kill me is not my definition of a hero."

"No. But fighting to save the innocent is, and that's what we're doing."

"Not by choice. I'd rather be on Huli, swimming in the clear blue sea and sipping Rudin Brzlach."

Abbey put her hand up, registering the sound of boots ahead. She looked back at Airi, pointing to her sword. At first, Airi seemed reluctant to part with it, but an angry look convinced her. Abbey took the blade, closing her eyes. She breathed in. She could almost smell the soldiers. She could sense the Gift within them.

She waited until they were almost at the fork in the hallway, and then she turned the corner, leading with the sword. It slashed neatly through the head of one soldier, and she was saved from being shot by the other when Benhil popped out and blasted him, throwing his attack off enough that Abbey had time to decapitate him as well.

"Seven?" Benhil said.

"Hopefully," Abbey replied.

"The power of positive thinking."

They kept going, making their way through the *Destructor*. They came across more dead crew, most of them in the corridors, a few in private quarters. They killed three more members of the Fifth.

The red alert klaxons stopped wailing. The lights stopped flashing.

"They cleared the alert?" Airi said.

"They can't clear it," Abbey replied. "Only a senior officer has the codes. The Adjunct and her Captain must be back onboard."

"What do you think they'll do when they see the bodies?"

"Try to get to the bridge and contact the Republic," Abbey said. "Or their boss."

"We can't afford to have the Republic bearing down on us here. Did you see how many battleships were out there?"

"Three, counting the *Driver*," Abbey said. "Captain Mann's ship. I don't know if they would get involved."

"They might have to," Benhil said.

"We have to get to the bridge first. It's the only way."

They picked up the pace, running through the corridors, becoming more reckless. Abbey ranged ahead of them, feeling for the Gift, sensing it inthe Converts before coming upon them. She dispatched them efficiently, knocking them off balance before using the katana to remove their heads.

There should have been three remaining by the time they reached the bridge. They found one of the Fifth there, one of the other Curlatins. He was bigger and stronger than the others, but he was also unarmored and outnumbered, and they removed him without much trouble.

Abbey was still standing over his headless corpse when Trillisin and Nilin reached them, storming onto the bridge with heavy plasma rifles cradled in their thin arms.

"You," Nilin said, swinging her rifle Benhil's way. "I trusted you. We had a deal."

"Wait," Benhil said. "It's not what you think. We're the good guys."

"Your ship is under siege, Captain," Abbey said. "Not by us. By a man named Thraven. The same man who destroyed the station you've been collecting pieces of. The Eighteenth is under his control."

"Do you expect me to believe that?" Captain Trillisin, another Atmo, said. "I should kill you where you stand."

"You're free to try," Abbey said. "But I'm telling the truth. I kept their commander, Sergeant Coli, alive so you could hear it straight from the asshole's mouth."

"His word against yours?" Nilin said. "A soldier in the Republic Military versus a wanted fugitive? Put down your weapons. We'll let the Republic sort this out."

"Don't," Abbey said as they stepped forward.

"Why not? If you're innocent, you certainly aren't going to shoot us."

Trillisin moved for the command chair. Abbey stepped toward him, but Nilin turned her rifle in her direction.

"I can't let you contact the Republic," Abbey said.

"Then you'll have to stop me," Trillisin said. "You're free to try as well. But you know who we are and who we work for. Consider it carefully."

Abbey took another step before suddenly sensing the Gift, coming in fast.

"Get down," she shouted, turning toward the entrance to the bridge.

Nilin didn't listen. The bullets tore into her from behind, slamming her forward and onto the ground. Erlan and Benhil fired back as Abbey reached the hatch, catching up tothe Converts as they absorbed the

Rejects' attack.

She grabbed one of them, shoving him back as she brought the sword up and through the neck of the other, taking a hard punch to the ribs before countering with a blow of her own. She heard more gunfire behind her as she ran the soldier through, pinning him to the wall and ripping the rifle from his hands.

He writhed on the spike, reaching out for her, his face expressionless, his eyes gray. He didn't speak or show any signs of real intelligence. It was as though his consciousness had been replaced with simple instructions, like the kind loaded into bots.

Abbey left him there, walking back toward the front of the bridge. Airi was there; her face pained as she stared at the command station.

"I guess we're more alike than I wanted to admit," she said, dropping her rifle to the floor.

Abbey looked at the station. Trillisin was on the ground in front of it. He wasn't moving.

"You shot him?"

"He was going to contact the Republic."

"He was innocent."

Airi was silent for a few seconds. Then she shrugged. "I've decided you're right, Queenie. Nobody is innocent."

Abbey didn't remember having said that, but she couldn't disagree.

"Erlan, do you know how to fly this thing?" she asked. "Our regular pilot is indisposed at the moment."

"Uh. It's a little different than a Grabber, but I imagine the basics are the same, and I've read a few manuals and watched a few tutorials."

"Tutorials?" Benhil said. "If Lucifer were dead, he'd be rolling in his grave."

"Do your best," Abbey said. "Get us somewhere safe so we can rendezvous with the *Faust*. I want as much distance between us, Feru, and the Crescent Haulers as we can get."

"Aye, Captain," Erlan said, walking over to the command station. He paused at the sight of Trillisin's corpse. "Uh."

"It's a dead body," Benhil said. "If you're going to be a Reject, you'd better get used to it."

Erlan's face paled, but he managed to get himself seated around the body. He stared at the controls for a few seconds, and then tentatively began using the terminal.

Abbey stared at Airi until she returned the gaze, making eye contact. It wasn't necessarily a look of agreement, but it was one of understanding.

CHAPTER TWENTY-THREE

ABBEY STARED AT THE CONVERT pinned to the bulkhead. She had once known it as Private Lesko, an average looking Marine who had blended into the Platoon so well that she had rarely ever noticed him. While the body was his, there seemed to be no other hint of him now. He continued to reach out for her, trying to grab her from his position against the wall, held there by the katana that she had shoved so hard into him it had gone right through and into the alloy. She could feel the Gift pushing up against her as well, trying to knock her down or pull her forward, to affect her in some negative way. While Illiard had been able to use it to grab her back on Hell, it wasn't strong enough to do anything to her anymore.

"Why don't you just knock its block off and be done with it?" Benhil asked, standing nearby. "It's obvious there's no soul left in there."

"They came onto this ship. They didn't stand out enough to make the Haulers suspicious. Lesko had to be in there at some point."

Benhil stuck his hand in the Convert's face. It leaned forward, trying to bite him.

"Yeah well, he's gone now."

"Queenie," Erlan said. "I've got Ruby on the comm."

Abbey turned, looking to the front of the bridge. Ruby was projected there, sitting at the controls of the *Faust*.

"Queenie," the synthetic said. "I've been expecting you."

"We've had a minor setback," Abbey said.

"Minor?" Benhil said. "The Haulers are going to think we stole their ship. I wouldn't call that minor."

"There's nothing we can do about that now. Erlan, send Ruby the coordinates."

"Haulers?" Ruby said. "As in, Crescent Haulers?"

"Yes. Benhil bartered a ride to you, but there was a complication."

"Complication? Do you have to minimize everything?" Benhil asked.

"Do you have to catastrophize everything?" Abbey replied.

"I'm sorry, Queenie, but this is my definition of a catastrophe."

"We're still alive."

"For now. Wait until the Hauler's head honcho gets wind of this shit."

"I've sent the coordinates," Erlan said.

"Received," Ruby said. "I'll meet you there in twenty minutes."

"Any word from Captain Mann?" Abbey asked.

"Not yet."

"Gant?"

"Nothing."

Abbey frowned. "Roger. Queenie out." She motioned to Erlan to break the link. Ruby's projection vanished. "I'm ready to go to FTL when you are, Erlan."

"Aye, ma'am," Erlan said.

His hand moved across the control surface. A moment later, the cargo ship blinked away, leaving the support vessels that were collecting the remaining debris behind.

Abbey turned her attention back to Private Lesko. "Jester, do you have a knife?"

"Yeah, why?"

She held her hand out. He dropped the hilt into it. She took the knife and stabbed Lesko in the eye, pulling the blade out and watching. A line of blood started to run down the Convert's face, but only for a moment. The damaged eye was replaced with the same silvery material as she had seen replace Sergeant Ray's brain.

"Whatever it is, it keeps them alive," Abbey said.

"Alive, or just moving?" Benhil asked.

"Good point. Fury, I want you and Jester to head to the hangar and grab your gear. I want a full sweep of the ship. I'm pretty sure we got all of these things, but we need to be sure."

"Roger," Airi said.

"Erlan, you have the bridge. I want to go check on Bastion and Pik, and have a little talk with Coli."

"Aye, ma'am."

"By the way, we need to get you a call sign. No offense, but Erlan isn't doing it for me."

"My mother liked it, ma'am."

Abbey smiled. "You aren't officially one of us until you have a nick. And please stop calling me ma'am. You make me feel old."

"Aye, ma - Queenie."

Abbey left the bridge, making her way back the way they had come, able to navigate to the mess using their path of destruction. When she arrived, she found Bastion up and alert, sitting beside Pik against the wall, both of them keeping an eye on Coli. The synth was in pieces nearby, a nasty looking cooking knife in a dismembered hand.

"Bastard tried to stab me," Pik said when she entered. "Like I haven't been through enough already."

"How is your arm?" Abbey asked.

Pik shook his head. "My hand is wasted. My arm is broken. It hurts."

"Big baby," Bastion said.

"What about you, Lucifer? Are you okay?"

"I think I have a concussion. That Gift thing hits hard."

"It can. Okay, we'll see about getting you a prosthetic as soon as we can."

Pik smiled. "I've been looking for a reason to upgrade. This is going to handicap me until then."

"Hopefully we'll stay out of trouble for a little while."

"Famous last words," Bastion said. "You attract trouble like a pleasure bot attracts horny men."

"It isn't all bad," Abbey said. "We might be able to learn something from this turn of events."

"You should write a manual. How to Make Enemies Across the Galaxy. It'll be a bestseller."

Abbey smirked and walked over to where Coli was sitting, still and silent.

"Done whining?" she asked.

"Frag you, Lieutenant. I wish you had never found your way into my platoon."

"That makes two of us." She sat down at the table beside him. "Now, why don't you tell me all about Gloritant Thraven, and how you came to work for him?"

"Why would I do that? I'm as good as dead already."

"You can get implants to replace your eyes."

"I don't mean because I'm blind. Thraven will kill me when he can. Or he'll send someone to do it. You have no idea how deep into the Republic his influence goes. This isn't some two-bit idiot who crawled out of the ground to make trouble. He's been planning this for years."

"So I've heard. He also seems to be a man of his word. He made promises to you for getting the mainframe off Grudin."

"My family is taken care of. That's all I'm going to say. And he got me out of Hell."

"You don't care about what he did to the rest of the Fifth?"

"What did he do to them?"

"The way he changed them? Giving them the Gift. Making them harder to kill."

"Thraven surrounded me with a unit of super soldiers. Why the frag would I complain about that?"

"He took away their minds."

Coli shrugged.

"Do you know how he did it?"

"No. I didn't see the procedure. Only the results."

"Were they still able to speak at that point?"

"What do you mean? They can talk. They're the same crew. A little less free-spirited, maybe."

"They can't talk. I've got Lesko pinned to the wall on the bridge if you want a demonstration of what Thraven turned them into."

"What would be the point. I told you, I'm already dead, blind or not blind. Thraven will kill me."

"Not if I kill him first."

Coli began laughing, his gravelly growls echoing in the mess as he guffawed at her statement. "You? Thraven told me he's over five thousand years old, and I believe it. He told me he and his brothers and sisters killed God. But you think you can take him out? Watching him destroy you would be a good reason to see again."

"Did Thraven tell you anything about the Covenant? Or the Great Return?"

"Only that it was coming, and when it did only those that sided with him would be spared. I was loyal to the Republic, Lieutenant. But I had to be loyal to my family first. I want them to survive what comes next."

"And what's that?"

"Don't tell me you don't already know?"

"The *Fire* and the *Brimstone*, and a whole fleet of ships just like them."

Coli smiled. "That's just the start. The vanguard. Gloritant Thraven is clearing a path for the rest."

"The rest? Where are they coming from? How many?"

"I'm done talking, Lieutenant. You got all I'm going to give. Just enough to make you more worried than you already were."

"Okay," Abbey said. She grabbed Coli's wrist, standing and lifting him easily to his feet. "How badly do you want to live, Sergeant?"

"What do you mean?"

She pulled him over to Pik and Bastion. "Are you two well enough to help me drag this hairy piece of shit over to the nearest airlock?"

"Affirmative," Bastion said.

"Of course, DQ," Pik said.

They both stood.

"Airlock?" Coli said. "You wouldn't?"

"Why not? If you aren't going to talk, I don't need you."

"You're an Officer of the Republic."

"No, I'm not. I'm just a con, thanks to you. And do you know what I've discovered?"

"What's that?"

"I like not having to play by the rules."

Pik grabbed Coli's other arm, and they dragged him into the hallway.

"I wish you could see all of the dead Haulers out here," Abbey said. "I wish you could see the damage you've done, just so you could get back at me. Considering how badly you blew it."

"Did I?" Coli asked. "You're fragged, Cage. If not Thraven, then the Haulers. But it'll be Thraven. You're going to go after him even after what I said. That's the kind of individual you are. You crave the danger. Why else would someone with a kid drop into combat zones?"

"What did you say?" Abbey said, pausing. "How do you know I have a child?"

"Oh. Did I say that out loud?" Coli grunted. "Thraven's got your full record, warts and all. He shared it with me before the drop on Grudin, just in case I needed something to pull you in. You've barely been back to Earth the whole time she's been growing up. She probably thinks your sister, Liv, is her real mother. Like I said, it's clear you never wanted to be a parent. You put your life in danger like that all of the time, and for what? Where did it get you in the end?" He laughed again.

They came to one of the docking stations.

"Bastion, can you get that?" Abbey asked, pointing to the airlock controls.

"Sure," he replied, opening the inner door.

"You really want to die, don't you, Sergeant?"

"I told you. My family's taken care of. I'm as good as dead already.

Just vent me and get it over with. If you have the stomach for cold-blooded killing?"

Bastion and Pik looked at her, questioning her resolve. She squeezed Coli's arm harder, pulling him to the hatch and dumping him in. "I'll give you one more chance to spill what you know about Thraven and his plans."

"Go frag yourself, Abigail," Coli said.

Abbey hit the control on the side of the hatch, closing Coli in. He felt his way forward, standing and putting his mangled face to the transparency between them.

"Go ahead, Lieutenant," Coli shouted. "Do it."

Abbey stared at the Curlatin. She couldn't open the outer door until the *Destructor* was out of FTL. The computer wouldn't allow it. She had time to change her mind. To reconsider. It was one thing to kill an individual in self-defense. It was another to kill them like this. She had been heading down a dangerous path since she started using the Gift. A path Olus had urged her to take for the sake of the Republic. She could do more good if people were afraid of her. She would have more control.

At the same time, she could feel the anger and the hate permeating her soul, sinking in and sticking there, making it harder for her to let go of it. Did it make her stronger?

Yes. But at what cost?

"Do it," Coli shouted again.

She had already decided she would pay the price, whatever it was, if it kept Hayley safe. Thraven knew about her daughter, which meant she might not be. Abbey didn't have to like what she became. She just had to accept it.

"Do it," Coli shouted a third time. "Come on, Lieutenant. What are you waiting for? You don't have the guts?"

She felt the change in the rhythm of the ship's reactor as it dropped out of FTL, right when it was supposed to. Coli's face changed at that moment, his expression of defiance turning to one of fear.

"Wait," he said, his entire demeanor changing. "Lieutenant, wait. Don't do it. I'll tell you anything you want to know. I don't want to die.

Please."

Abbey stared at him. Her stomach had been churning, but now it began to settle, her whole body becoming numb despite the Gift.

"Abigail, please," Coli whined. "I don't want to die. I'm not ready. I have a wife. I have three young ones. We're so alike, you and me. We both have families."

"Queenie?" Bastion said beside her. "You don't have to do this. We can leave him here to rot until the Republic catches up and brings him in."

"Yeah, Queenie," Pik said. "I could do it if you want. This isn't the kind of person you want to become."

She turned her head, looking back at Pik and Bastion. Coli stopped whining, waiting for her to open the hatch and pull him back inside.

"You're right," Abbey said, still looking in at Coli. "It isn't the kind of person I want to become. It's the kind of person I have to become. Olus was right. You can't fight someone like Thraven unless you're willing to become someone like Thraven."

Then she hit the control. The outer door slid open, and Coli vanished before he even had a chance to scream.

"We can't let him win," she said, pushing past them.

CHAPTER TWENTY-FOUR

"THAT SURE IS A LOT of shit," Bastion said, his eyes wandering over the seemingly endless piles of debris the Haulers had recovered. "What do you think you're going to find in there?"

"I don't know," Abbey replied. "Thraven wanted this junk away from any interested eyes, which means my eyes are interested."

"Shouldn't we be getting out of the area? We left half of the Hauler's collectors in the lurch, and it won't take long for the Republic to track the disterium trail."

"I told you that you were free to wait for me on the *Faust*. I asked you to go to medical. I think that knock on the head you took made you dumber than you already were."

"Pik needs the medical bot more than I do right now." He laughed. "I know it's a machine, but it almost seemed relieved to get an injury it could do something with."

"It can't fix his hand."

"Replacements are better, anyway."

"It's my fault he got hurt."

"Don't go there, Queenie. You saved all of our asses again, but you can't do everything yourself. So where do we start?"

Abbey looked at the debris. It was separated into multiple piles, each of the piles nearly ten meters high and fifty meters wide, with a main drop station near the aft of the hold where a half dozen bots were busy sorting the remains by material. If the Republic, or in this case Thraven, had ordered it destroyed, it would be brought back to an orbital station and converted, recycled and then resold as base components, with any evidence of anything questionable burned in the process. If it had been collected for investigation, it would go to the closest OSI department for review by Captain Mann's agents.

It wasn't a stretch to think the former case was more likely than the latter.

"Terminals," she said. "Projectors. Mainframes. Access points. Anything that could possibly still have data stored on it. The components are going to be small, but that's why they may have survived. If Emily Eagan built the *Fire* and *Brimstone* for Thraven, then there has to be some record of their research and development. Records Thraven didn't want the Republic to find. That's why he ordered Ursan Gall to destroy the station, and why he sent the Haulers to clean up after him."

"Makes sense."

"The bots will have sorted any related debris into one these piles. That's the easy part. Finding a memory chip or an intact server in the pile, and doing it quickly? I may be wasting our time."

"Or you might find something useful."

"Since when did you become so positive?"

"Must be the blow to the head."

Abbey smiled. She had expected she might feel guilty after she had sent Sergeant Coli out of the airlock. She didn't. In fact, she felt as though she had turned a corner when she decided to embrace her situation.

They moved quickly through the hold, splitting up and running in the spaces between the stacks. The bots wound their way around them, making space as they continued their work unhindered and taking little notice of their presence.

They found the more delicate networking components stacked off to the side, close to the drop point. It was smaller than most of the other piles, but that didn't make it any less daunting. Most of the pieces were the size of a hand or smaller, the stack standing tall enough that it was obvious they would have to sort through thousands of parts. She wouldn't have even bothered trying, except she had an idea to speed up the process.

"Keep your eyes on the debris," she said. "Data chips are the size of a fingernail. Rectangular, and usually smooth. Mainframes are about this big." She motioned with her hand. "Square. Even if it looks damaged, we'll want to take it with us. You know what terminals look like."

Bastion kicked the base of the pile, sending smaller bits and pieces clattering away. "I'm done being positive. We're never going to find anything useful in this trash. It's like a mote in a galaxy."

"And how do you find a mote in a galaxy?" Abbey asked.

"You don't."

"You reduce the search area. There's an algorithm, but explaining it might make your head hurt."

"It already hurts."

"Then it might make it explode."

"I don't know if I would look on that unkindly."

"Are you ready?"

"For what?"

Abbey raised her hands. She could feel the Gift within her, moving beneath her skin. It wasn't burning like before. Could it be used for anything other than killing?

She stared at the debris, holding her hands out toward it. She started thinking about Thraven. He wanted to start a war. He wanted to kill innocent people. No. He already had. The Republic couldn't stop him. Not on their own. Nobody could stop him. Not without help. Not without more information. What were they up against? They had to know. They had to gather as much intel as they could, wherever they could find it. What was the Covenant? What was the Great Return? There had to be answers here. They had made the *Fire* and *Brimstone* from ancient blueprints. They had revived long lost tech. Tech that was going to kill them all, unless she could do something about it.

She felt the anger coming. It was getting easier now. The Gift responded to it, coming alive inside of her. She fought to hold onto it. To keep the anger in her heart. She could feel it thumping harder, the blood pumping stronger through her veins. She kept her eyes on the trash, imagining that it was lifting away and spreading apart, like a wave crashing against a rocky shore, converting the three-dimensional stack to a flat sheet, one that Bastion could quickly scan, the motion matching the algorithm.

"Oh, shit," Bastion said as the debris moved and parted.

"Anything?" Abbey asked. She scanned the first wave as well but didn't see anything they could use.

"Negative," Bastion replied.

The debris lifted, reaching higher toward the top of the hold, a new line spreading out ahead of them as it began to curl up and over, becoming a reel. Abbey couldn't hold back the smile over the control she had. The power. It didn't always have to be used to hurt.

"Wait," Bastion said, stepping forward and grabbing a half-slagged cube from the spread. He put it on the ground behind him.

"There," Abbey said, noticing a data chip. It looked like it was intact. He grabbed that, too.

"This has to be one of the coolest things I've ever seen," Bastion said as the debris continued to flow up and over, the pile shifting forward as it was replaced from behind.

Abbey's heart was pounding, a feeling of elation overcoming her. Benhil had told her she wasn't human anymore, and maybe he was right. At that moment, she felt more like a god.

No sooner had the thought arrived than the power of the Gift left her. The burning sensation turned to freezing cold, her arms prickling as all of the energy washed away. She fell to her knees, the scroll of debris collapsing suddenly, tumbling down in a storm of parts.

"Queenie?" Bastion said, moving to her side and kneeling beside her. "What's going on?"

"Cold," Abbey said. She could feel her body shivering. "Freezing."

"I don't know what you did, but we need to get you out of here. Erlan."

"Lucifer?" Erlan replied. "What's wrong?"

"I don't know. Queenie's in trouble. Prep the shuttle."

"I'm ready and waiting, sir."

Bastion reached down, collecting her in his arms and lifting her. She could see him flinch at the cold. "Frag. You're so cold. You feel like you're already dead."

"Data," she managed to say.

Bastion looked back at the few pieces they had collected. "Forget it. We need to get you back to the *Faust* and under some blankets or something."

"Data," she repeated.

He carried her over to it, bending to scoop up the parts and put them in her lap. "There you go, Queenie. Now we're leaving."

He carried her out of the cargo hold, all the way to the hangar. Erlan was waiting in front of the Hauler's shuttle.

"Oh, no," he said, following Bastion onto the ship. "What happened?"

"She was using her magic to move some of the debris when she collapsed."

"Why?"

"How the frag would I know?" Bastion snapped, lowering Abbey into one of the seats. "Latch her in, I've got the stick."

"Aye, sir," Erlan said.

He worked the straps, pulling them down over Abbey, swinging himself into the adjacent seat and securing himself just in time. The shuttle rocketed forward, bursting from the *Destructor* toward the *Faust*, waiting a few hundred kilometers away.

Abbey closed her eyes. Her head was pounding. She was still so cold. As soon as her lids met, the world behind them lit up, a single emotion forcing its way to the forefront.

Fear.

She opened her eyes, looking around, a feeling of panic overwhelming her. What the hell was going on?

"Queenie?" Erlan said, leaning toward her.

"Don't," she replied. Her body was tingling. She felt like she was dying. "I don't want to hurt you."

He leaned away from her. She felt the forward pull as the shuttle slowed to enter the *Faust's* hangar. Then she heard the landing skids clamp down on the floor.

"Queenie?" Bastion said, returning to her. The hatch opened. Ruby was the first to board. She had an injector in her hand.

"No," Abbey said, seeing it. The injector was torn from Ruby's grip, shattering against the side of the shuttle. "I don't want to sleep. I don't want to close my eyes."

"Okay," Ruby said. "What do you need?"

"Food. I'm hungry. So hungry." Her eyes fell on Bastion's neck. "No." She clenched her jaw.

Was that what this was? The Gift trying to take control? To make her do its bidding? Was that what happened to Private Illiard? To Private Lesko? Did the mind succumb if the will wasn't strong enough? If the Gift was trying to assert control, what would it make her do if it succeeded?

"No," she hissed through her teeth. She hadn't finally accepted the Gift to be challenged by it.

She had accepted it to use it.

For her needs.

For her desires.

For her goals.

For her strength.

Her hands gripped the edges of her seat. She could feel her fingers changing. She could feel them digging into the metal and bending it out of shape.

"Lucifer, Erlan, it isn't safe here," Ruby said.

"If she dies, we die," Bastion replied. "Well, the nerd here doesn't. And you don't. But I do."

"Why am I a nerd?" Erlan asked.

"Get. Out. Of. Here," Abbey said.

The Gift wanted to control her?

Frag that.

Ruby grabbed Bastion's arm, pulling him from the shuttle, with

Erlan close behind. They left her alone there. They couldn't help anyway. This was her fight. Her struggle. Her demons.

She pushed back against them, her eyelids slowly dropping, the Gift resisting the effort. Was it working for Thraven, too? A small laugh escaped her at the thought. Her eyelids continued to move, twitching as the action was resisted.

"This is my body," Abbey said. "My life. My fight. You aren't the master. You're the servant, and I'm the fragging Queen."

Her lids snapped closed, the resistance fading. Again, everything lit up behind them, a fullness of light that flashed and vanished as suddenly as it had come.

Her whole body tingled. She opened her eyes again. The interior of the shuttle was suddenly in crisp focus, as though it had always been veiled by something before that moment. Specks of dust floated in front of the lighting, and she followed each one. She could feel the Gift inside of her, at rest once more.

She raised her hands from the seat. The entire frame was bent and twisted. She looked at her fingertips. They were normal. Her lips were dry. She was still hungry. She unlatched herself and stood up. She felt warm again. Back to normal.

She found the computer components they had taken and picked them up. Then she made her way off the shuttle.

Ruby, Bastion, and Erlan were waiting for her there. They stared at her as she made her way down.

"I'm okay," she said.

"Are you sure?" Bastion asked.

She nodded. "I haven't felt this good since I made the drop on Grudin." She held up the data. "Let's see if we can get anything out of these. Lucifer, get us away from Feru, back to the Fringe. Erlan." She paused, smiling. "I think you have a new call sign."

"What?" Erlan replied. He shook his head. "No. No way."

"Ha," Bastion said. "Welcome to the Rejects, Nerd."

"I don't want to be Nerd," Erlan said.

"I never wanted to be Queenie," Abbey said. "You get used to it."

"There's nothing wrong with being Nerd," Bastion said. "Hell, if I didn't have a cool nick like Lucifer, I might take Nerd."

"Really?"

"No. But it suits you, kid."

"Queenie," Ruby said. "I was monitoring Milnet traffic while you were gone, keeping tabs on positioning to ensure we weren't about to be attacked. I picked up a beacon right before Lucifer pinged me about your condition."

"What kind of beacon?" Abbey asked.

"From the *Brimstone*," Ruby replied.

Abbey raised her eyebrows in surprise. "Gant?"

"I don't know who else would have activated it."

"Where?"

"Anvil."

"Interesting choice of destination," Bastion said.

"What's Anvil?" Erlan asked.

"An Outworld military base, mostly," Bastion said. "Why would Thraven send the *Brimstone* there?"

"I don't know," Abbey replied. "Let's go find out."

CHAPTER TWENTY-FIVE

ABBEY LED RUBY DOWN TO the belly of the *Faust*, into the small access space behind the Construct module where the virtual reality system's computer was located. It wasn't the best substitute for a Breaker's standard quantum mainframe, but it was the most powerful processor they had on board. It would have to do.

"I have to get the softsuit we picked up on Feru," Abbey said. "I'll be right back."

"Of course, Queenie," Ruby said. "Are you well?"

"You mean the episode in the shuttle?"

"Yes."

"I'm better now. The Gift. Whatever it is, it was trying to take control. To start bossing me around."

"I struggle to process that concept."

"Me, too. I think I beat it into submission."

Ruby smiled. "I'm glad. If you're tense, I'm programmed in over two hundred forms of massage."

"One of these days I might take you up on the offer. We don't have time right now. See if you can expose the interface port on this while I'm gone." She handed the half-melted mainframe to Ruby. "Hopefully we won't have to hack our own. I don't think we have the tools on board."

"We do," Ruby said. "I believe Gant has most of them in his quarters."

Abbey smiled. Gant was still alive, still out there, and still helping her. It was the best outcome she could have hoped for.

She wandered out of the Construct module and over to the armory, where Benhil and Airi had brought the equipment they picked up on Feru. She tried to remove the hellsuit, only then remembering that it was coded to Airi.

"Fury," she said. "Can you come down to the armory and help me out of your hellsuit?"

"Aye, Queenie," Airi said. "I'll be right there."

It only took a minute for her to arrive. She had already changed out of her lightsuit and into a light tank and pants.

"I heard about what happened on the shuttle," she said.

"News travels fast," Abbey replied.

"The ship isn't that big." She reached out, pressing her hands against either side of the hellsuit and pulling it apart. The material disconnected in response to her touch, the center slipping open. "Are you okay?"

"I'm fine," Abbey replied, shrugging out of the hellsuit. It dropped behind her, and she lifted her feet and pulled it down past her calves, leaving her naked.

Airi's eyes were lingering on her body again, but Abbey didn't let it bother her. She opened her locker, grabbing a pair of panties and a fitted shirt, putting them on before slipping the softsuit over it.

"Are you still planning to switch quarters and bunk with Erlan?" Abbey asked, flipping the more conventional clasps that held the armor on.

"No," Airi replied. "I'm sorry for the way I acted earlier. I don't envy what you've been asked to do. Or the burden you have to bear."

"Apology accepted. If you'll excuse me." She grabbed the helmet from her locker and moved to pass Airi.

Airi reached out, putting her hand on Abbey's arm. "Queenie," she said, hesitant. "I."

Abbey paused, looking at her. "You were checking me out that time?"

"What? No. I-" She paused again. "Never mind. It isn't important. Do you need anything else from me?"

"No. Thank you."

Airi bowed slightly and left the armory. Abbey watched her go, wondering what she had decided not to say. Then she left the armory as well, returning to the Construct module. Ruby had already disassembled the shell of the salvaged computer and hooked it into the Construct's server.

Abbey put on the softsuit's helmet, the data connectors snapping into place near her ear. She tapped her fingers on the thigh of the armor, bringing up a command line. Then she took a wire from one of the tightpacks and fed it from the helmet out to the computer.

"Do we have access to Milnet?" Abbey asked.

"Yes, Queenie."

"What clearance?"

"I have Captain Mann's credentials and full security clearance. What do you need?"

"Breaker tools. There's a standard package available on the HSOC network. Once we pull it in, I can update this suit's software and run diagnostics on the mainframe we recovered."

Ruby opened the server's main terminal, her hands working the projection. Abbey saw the raw source code move along her helmet's HUD, scrolling through the instructions as the synthetic opened Milnet and quickly navigated into HSOC, using Olus' clearance.

"The Republic will think Captain Mann accessed this data," Ruby said. "They'll be wondering why he downloaded Breaker software."

"He's a smart guy. He'll come up with a decent excuse. I can take it from here."

Abbey navigated the network, going directly to the package and initiating the download. It was done within a few seconds, and she quickly loaded it into the softsuit, her HUD going dark when the armor's operating system reset. When it came up again, she had a whole new suite of tools at her disposal, as well as direct access to the Heavyworks mainframe through the Construct server.

"Let's see what we've got," she said, transferring her activity to the projection so Ruby could see it as well.

She used the command line to try to access the mainframe, immediately running into a data corruption error. She ran a few more commands, trying to get a feel for the cause, before accessing one of the tools in the softsuit's system on a chip. It was a high-level tool, meant to try to replace missing data at the root, filling it in with random blocks in order to pull something out of the damage.

It took a few minutes to run, and then she was rewarded with a response from a directory request, uncovering a series of folders. Most of them had characters missing from the names here and there, replaced with question marks or exclamation points. She noticed one that read '?ro!ec! Co?en!nt.'

"Project Covenant?" Ruby asked, taking note of the same directory.

Abbey tried to access it. The command line spit out 'access denied.'

She wasn't surprised.

"Password protected," she said. "That's why we needed the Construct server."

She ran another tool, allowing her access to the server's powerful processing unit. It wasn't on par with the mainframes they had in the HSOC or even the machine she had been using on the *Nova*, but it was hearty enough that it wouldn't take overlong to brute force the security. She triggered the command, the lines a blur as it tried trillions of combinations of letters, numbers, and special characters per second.

"How long do you think it will-"

Ruby didn't get to finish her sentence. The lines stopped scrolling, the directory opening in front of them.

"About that long," Abbey said.

"Why does anyone bother password protecting anything when you have tools like that?"

"Normally a box like this one would be buried behind a biometrically secured armored hatch. Thraven already did us the favor of breaking it out into the open. Some data sources use layers of authentication, but I don't think Emily Eagan was all that concerned with this kind of security. She didn't believe Captain Mann would ever figure out it was her."

She stared at the contents of the directory. The damage to the data was worse here, and even her scrubbers didn't leave much of it discernible.

"That one," Ruby said, pointing to a subdirectory labelled 'E!y?!u? Gat?.'

"Why that one?" Abbey asked.

"The second word. G-A-T question mark. Replace the final letter with something that fits."

"Gate?" Abbey said, running through the letters. It seemed as good of a lead as any. She drilled down into the directory.

There were files in it. Dozens of files. Her tools could recognize they were there, but most of them were corrupted, only able to be displayed as solid lines taking up a row on her HUD.

"You retrieved the data chip as well," Ruby said.

"If I were back in HSOC HQ I could run deep forensics on this and try to pull something out. Out here? Not a chance."

"There's one file that isn't completely corrupted," Ruby said, pointing out a line near the center that read '----?---.'

"One character?" Abbey said. She didn't think it would give them much, but she executed the file.

The projection changed, giving them a half-composed three-dimensional view of something she didn't understand, but could easily infer into a complete shape. A loop of some kind. Or a gate.

"That isn't the *Fire* or the *Brimstone*," Abbey said.

"A gate," Ruby said. "A gate for what?"

Abbey tried to manipulate the schematic. The file crashed, her command line displaying a fatal error. She tried to open it again, and it refused.

"Damn it," she said. "I think that's the only look we're going to get."

"I'll get a snapshot of it from my memory banks," Ruby said.

"You'll have to hook into my diagnostic port to retrieve it."

"Where's the port?" Abbey asked, looking at Ruby.

Ruby reached up, digging a finger into the space behind her left eye and pushing it out. The motion revealed the mechanics behind the synthetic skin, and a small round hole a little off-center from the lens of the camera that was her eye.

"I almost forgot you aren't flesh and blood," Abbey said. She disconnected the softsuit from the Construct server and reconnected it to Ruby.

"You can remove the pleasure synth programming and reset me from here as well, but the restart will take hours."

"I need you with the team." She found the snapshots Ruby had taken and stored in her memory banks. Some of them surprised her. "You took pictures?"

"The clients requested them. Some of them enjoyed seeing themselves from my perspective, after."

Abbey found the schematic and transferred it to the suit.

"Did you like being in a pleasure house?"

"Like?" Ruby replied. "My emotions are simulated, Queenie. I don't understand the concept of like."

"Do you prefer being on the *Faust*?"

"I don't understand preference."

"What about loyalty?"

"I am programmed to be loyal to Captain Mann first, and to this crew second."

"Would you die for us?"

"I am not alive, and therefore I cannot die. However, I would gladly take critical damage to save any member of this crew."

"How can you do it gladly, if you don't have emotions?"

Ruby paused a moment. "They are simulated."

Abbey pulled the connecting wire. "Does that make them less real?"

"I don't know how to answer that," Ruby replied.

Abbey opened the image of the gate. It was impossible to get an idea of the scale or purpose from the schematic. Still, she would get it over to Olus when she had the chance.

"How long until we reach Anvil?" she asked.

"About an hour," Ruby replied.

"Have the Rejects assemble in the CIC in thirty minutes. We have a war to plan."

CHAPTER TWENTY-SIX

"GLORITANT, SENSORS ARE PICKING UP a disterium trail, and a full plume nearby," Agitant Sol said, keeping his head forward.

"Bring us out of FTL," Thraven said, his orders going out to all of the ships in his small fleet. "Adjust course to intercept. I want to see what my ships can do."

He was standing on the bridge of the *Fire*, in front of the command station, arms folded behind his back. A pair of Immolents flanked the station, still and silent, observing the activity on the bridge.

"Coming out of FTL," the Agitant said.

The universe came back into focus in a cloud of reddish gas, the disterium dispersing now that it was no longer being contained.

"Sensors are picking up a Republic border guard," Agitant Malt said. "Twenty ships. Mostly light cruisers. There's also an Outworld guard within a few AU of them."

Thraven looked at the projection in the front of the bridge, ahead of the viewport. He had expected a build up of assets this close to Anvil. Neither side had disappointed him. Then again, he had been hoping to test the *Fire* against something a little more dangerous than light cruisers.

It would have to do.

"Three and four, engage cloaking systems. One and two, you're with me."

He hadn't bothered to name his new ships. Not yet. Perhaps not ever. Their value was in their firepower, not in the souls who had perished in their making, or in the souls that were on board now, fighting his fight with him. They were all Lesser. They existed to serve.

"Yes, Gloritant," came the reply from the Honorants in command of the ships. He observed the projection, watching two of his warships vanish from their sensors.

"Gloritant, it appears the Republic has identified us," Agitant Sol said.

"And?"

"They are coming about, your Eminence."

"We're receiving a hail, Gloritant," Agitant Malt said.

Thraven smiled. He wasn't ready to reveal himself to the Republic. Not yet.

"Your Eminence, we have torpedo lock on the lead cruiser," Honorant Piselle said.

"Fire," Thraven said. "One and two, lock and fire."

"Yes, Gloritant."

The torpedoes from the ships were like streaks of light, crossing the distance so quickly the Republic ships had no option to evade them. They struck their targets within seconds, huge detonations causing quick flashes of burning air from the stricken ships before flaming out and leaving behind a new field of debris and a broken ship.

"Bring us in closer," Thraven said. "Give them a chance to fight back."

"Yes, Gloritant."

He had to put his hand back on the command station to hold himself as the *Fire* accelerated, crossing the gap between the two forces within seconds. Then the *Fire* slowed, leaving them in the midst of the Republic fleet.

"We're taking fire," Agitant Malt said.

Thraven could see the flashes from the cruisers' guns, along with the trails of their torpedos. The shields on the *Fire* flashed like lightning as they absorbed the impacts, taking the attack and shrugging it off.

"What is the status of the shields?" he asked.

"Shields are holding steady, your Eminence," Piselle replied.

"Return fire. Save the torpedos. They are costly to manufacture."

"Yes, Gloritant."

The *Fire* began to spew plasma and projectiles from around it, each of the weapons enhanced by the Blood of Life. They tore into the Republic ships' shields, reaching through and punching into the armor.

Thraven watched the projection, noting that one and two had taken a flanking position on either side of the fleet while the *Fire* traveled down the center. They were striking the outer formation, the Republic ships blinking off the screen one after another.

"Disterium plumes detected, Gloritant," Agitant Sol said. "They are retreating."

"Cease fire," Thraven said. "Let them run. There is nowhere for them to hide for long."

"Yes, Gloritant."

All three ships stopped firing on the Republic cruisers. Of the original twenty, only nine of them were able to blink away.

The rest were left hanging silently in space, venting atmosphere and equipment, lifeless and dead. The *Fire* sat in the center of the destruction, stationary as the debris hit the shields and evaporated.

"Have the Outworld ships reacted?" he asked.

"No, Gloritant. They have remained in position, observing the battle."

"This was no battle, Agitant," Thraven said. "It was a slaughter, as it was intended to be. As it was promised in the Covenant."

"Yes, Gloritant."

And this was with only three active ships. Once he had completed them all, there would be nothing that could stop the Great Return.

"Resume course to Anvil," Thraven said. "I will return when we have arrived."

"Yes, your Eminence."

Thraven turned and walked toward the exit to the bridge, the

Immolents moving in behind him. He couldn't wait to share the good news.

CHAPTER TWENTY-SEVEN

GORIX'S FACILITY WAS WELL-HIDDEN from prying eyes. After entering the alley in a fog of steam, Dak led Ursan through a worn metal door and into a warehouse. It was populated with the poorest residents in the city and smelled like urine, drugs, and cheap food. The sight and scent elicited an angry sigh from him.

"He brought Trin here?" he said.

"Through here," Dak replied. "Not to here."

"Damn roaches. They love the cool, dark places, don't they?"

Dak didn't answer him. Ursan knew his friend was getting tired of him. He knew he had been impossible the entire time he had been waiting to go and see the bot-maker. He couldn't help himself. He wanted her back. He needed her back. It was all he could think about. It was all he cared about.

They moved to a stairwell in the corner of the warehouse, descending five floors to a landing. Ursan moved to open the door at the bottom, but Dak put his hand out to stop him.

"Not through there, Boss," he said. "You don't want to go through there."

"Why not?"

"There are things that are illegal, and then there are things that are wrong. What happens through there is wrong."

A scream sounded from beyond the door, accenting his point.

"Why doesn't anyone stop it?"

"Because nobody cares about how clean the heels of their boots are."

Dak turned and knocked on the wall behind them. It slid aside a moment later. One of Gorix's guards was standing behind it.

"Dak," he said. "And the other one." He glanced at Ursan. "Gorix has been waiting for you."

They moved through the hatch, which immediately closed behind them.

The corridor had been roughly hewn into the bedrock that supported the city above, a three-meter diameter tunnel that traveled another fifty meters in before expanding into a complete network of tunnels and chambers. Ursan knew Plixians lived underground on their home world. He hadn't expected them to do the same on other planets.

"Captain Gall," Gorix said, meeting him at the entrance to one of the chambers.

A smaller creature the size of Ursan's hand sat on Gorix's top left shoulder. It was generally humanoid in shape, with thick, mottled skin that resembled stone and overly flat features.

"This is the associate I mentioned to you," Gorix said. "Villaueve."

Ursan nodded to the Lrug.

"You're a long way from home," he said.

"It's a small universe," Villaueve replied with a laugh. His voice was like tinkling bells.

"Villaueve is a nano-mechanical engineer," Gorix said. "His expertise is ninety percent of your expense."

"Is there anything you can do for her?"

"Come to my workshop," Gorix said.

Ursan followed the Plixian in. The workshop was spotless and neatly organized, with thousands of parts arranged in bins along the wall, and numerous works in progress resting at a half dozen stations situated across the floor. His eyes danced around the space, unable to rest until they found Trin, suspended in a liquid of some kind.

"What did you do to her?" he growled, pushing past Gorix and rushing to the station.

"It is an electrochemically charged preserving gel," Villaueve said. "The cranium was in the process of decomposition when I was brought in. The first order of business was to stop this loss of state before it did irreparable damage to the nerve endings. It is bad enough the brain was deprived of oxygen for days before I arrived. This gel should help undo some of that damage."

"You're saying you can help her?" Ursan asked.

"When did I say that?" Villaueve replied. "I said I am trying to undo some of the damage that was caused by improper handling. If you had placed her in a preservative when the accident occurred, her prognosis would be much better."

"You're saying this is my fault?" Ursan said, getting angry. "It wasn't a fragging accident. She was murdered by a Republic bitch."

"Boss," Dak said. "Calm down."

Ursan shook his head in an effort to clear it. "So, what's the status? Can you fix her, or can't you?"

Villaueve hopped off Gorix's shoulder and onto the table, walking over to a terminal and turning it on. He stared at a graph there for a second. "These are the readings from the sensors in the container. Synapse activity is increasing, which is good. She's responding well to the bath." He walked over to the container. He was half the size of Trin's head. "Connecting the organic wires to the mechanical ones isn't trivial, but it also isn't impossible. My work with augmentation is what brought me to Anvil. The Company wanted me to develop new enhancements for soldiers. Lucky for you, I hid a few of the prototypes when I was fired for bypassing standardized testing procedures in an effort to prove my work more efficiently."

"What do you mean?"

"I may have allegedly drugged a few of the soldiers and forcibly added the augmentations while they were unconscious," Villaueve said. "Those alleged soldiers may have accidentally perished. In retrospect, it wasn't the best idea, but my intentions were good."

He turned to Gorix, who lifted him in one of his hands. They walked across the workshop floor to a metal crate there. Gorix used two of his other hands to lift it open, revealing what looked like a suit of armor.

"It has the flexibility of a battlesuit, but the overlapping greaves double the protection and enhanced synthetic musculature greatly upgrades the overall strength. A centralized SOC handles all of the instruction processing, and also doubles as a Tactical Command Unit."

"It looks like an upgraded battlesuit. One that's meant to have a body inside."

"The original design is intended to be attached to a human body with bolts, screws, and wires. It's non-removable. As I mentioned, I had trouble finding volunteers willing to test it."

"I can't imagine why," Ursan said. The armor looked mean and impressive, but who in their right mind would agree to dedicate their entire life to wearing something like that?

"Gorix is going to create a mechanical skeleton to use inside the suit and a pump to send blood and oxygen into the organic part of the brain. We'll insert the head into the helmet and then solder it together so it can't be easily removed. Assuming we can return her brain operation to its prior condition, I think we can meet your goal of returning her to functional."

As a soldier inside of an advanced suit of armor. Ursan looked at Gorix and Villaueve, a smile spreading across his face. "You won't let me down. I know it. How long do you need?"

"Eight days," Gorix said.

"That's a long time."

"This is intricate work, Captain, despite the simple description."

"Yeah. I get it. Okay. However long it takes, it'll be worth it."

"There is the matter of payment."

"My ship? She's in orbit. Send a crew up to claim her. I'll sign whatever needs to be signed."

"Of course," Gorix said.

"I'll get out of your face now," Ursan said. "I know you have a lot of work to do."

"Vilix will escort you out."

Ursan followed the Plixian and Dak back through the workshop, into the tunnels and out to the secret door, and from the stairwell back to the warehouse.

"I told you it could be done," he said. "I told you she wasn't gone forever."

"You did, Boss," Dak said, his expression concerned.

"Then why so sour? We should go get a drink to celebrate."

"I just hope she comes back the way you want her to," Dak said. "Without any brain damage."

"She will. But even if she doesn't, once I return the Gift to her it'll heal."

"I hope you're right. It's good to see you happy again."

"Thank you, my friend."

They entered the warehouse, crossing it quickly. They were halfway across when Ursan noticed that all of the vagrants had vanished.

"Where is everybody?" he said.

Dak paused beside him, drawing his sidearm. "I don't like it."

"A double cross?" Ursan said, scanning the area. He didn't see anything or anyone.

"Gorix isn't that kind of bug," Dak said.

"Captain Ursan Gall," a voice said.

Ursan looked around. He still didn't see anything.

"Yeah?" he replied, less than confidently.

They appeared from the dark shadows of the ceiling above them, dropping twenty meters to the ground with apparent ease. They were creatures unlike anything he had seen before. Humanoid in shape, with muscular, mottled bodies, large heads and mouths full of sharp teeth, their feet ending in curled claws.

There were a dozen of the creatures surrounding them, crouched and compact and ready to attack.

"My name is Seth," the largest of them said.

He stood, and Ursan watched with fascinated curiosity as Seth changed, his body converting from monster to man.

"What the frag?" Dak said.

"I've been sent as an emissary for the Children of the Covenant. Gloritant Thraven sends his regards."

"Gloritant?" Ursan said.

He had never heard that title before and didn't understand it. Not that it mattered. There was only one reason for them to have come. His hands went up, the Gift flowing through him. He pushed out toward Seth, watching as the emissary was thrown backward and into the wall and smiling at the outcome. Whoever these assholes were, they were no match for his power.

"Not the best idea," Seth said, getting back to his feet.

Then he changed again, his form shifting within seconds to that of the beast. He clamped his jaws a few times, creating an echoing snap in the chamber. The rest of the creatures did the same.

"Uh, Boss," Dak said.

"Don't worry. I can take them."

The creatures pounced, all of them coming at once. Dak started shooting, hitting three of the Children and knocking them back, while Ursan swept the others up with the Gift.

Or tried to. The power washed into them. It slowed them, but they didn't react the way Seth had. They didn't go flying back.

"Boss?" Dak said again. He threw a big fist at one of the creatures, batting it aside, before two more were on him, tearing at him with sharp claws and reaching for his throat with their teeth. "Ahhhh."

"Dak," Ursan said.

He clenched his teeth and growled, his fingers elongating as he did. The first monster reached him, and he stepped toward it, ducking below its lunge and raking its stomach with his claws. It howled as it passed over him, but he barely noticed. He lunged at one of the beasts on Dak, delivering a Gift-enhanced punch to the temple that sent it rolling across the floor. Freed up, Dak grabbed the other, throwing it away. It landed on all fours, turning and rushing back.

"There are too many," Dak said. He shot another one, knocking it down. It rose a few seconds later, the wound healed.

"They have the Gift," Ursan said as one got its teeth on his arm and bit down, nearly severing his hand at the wrist. He jabbed his claws into the creature's eye, and it relaxed the hold. He punched it in the side, breaking its ribs, and it let go as it rolled away.

That one was replaced with another, who tackled him, pinning him to the ground. Seth. The large monster dug its claws into his shoulders and hips, keeping him in one place. Ursan looked past to Dak, suddenly surrounded by the creatures. They closed on him slowly, absorbing his slugs until he ran out of them. He turned, looking back at Ursan, who could see the fear on his friend's face.

"Don't kill him," Ursan said. "Please. It wasn't his fault. He was only following orders."

Seth looked back at the scene.

"We appreciate loyalty," he said. A sharp bark paused the attack. "Your man is free to go."

Dak continued to stand there. "Boss?"

"Dak, go. There's nothing you can do for me."

"But Boss."

"No. Go."

Dak lowered his head and started walking, heading toward the exit. The other creatures followed him all the way to the door.

"If you're going to kill me, kill me," Ursan said.

"Those weren't the instructions," Seth said. He backed away, standing and changing once more. "Thraven needs you."

"For what?" Ursan asked.

"Bait."

CHAPTER TWENTY-EIGHT

GANT WAITED BEHIND THE VENT cover he had dislodged from the bulkhead, watching and listening. He shifted from one foot to the other, growing impatient. Where the hell was everybody?

He came out of hiding, dropping the cover onto the ground. It clattered lightly. He paused to listen. No one had heard.

He had expected it to be easier to start killing the *Brimstone's* crew members. The problem was that they were so bunched together, it was tough to get them separated where he could hit them one on one. He wished for the millionth time that he hadn't lost his gun. Or that he could find another weapon. He would settle for a nice heavy pipe at this point.

He could wish all he wanted. That wasn't going to get the job done.

"You're an engineer, Prylshhharrnavramm," he barked to himself. "Figure something out."

He remained stationary for another minute or so, working through the problem. He needed to hit multiple targets at once. He couldn't hold a Terran gun.

But maybe a bot could.

Not a whole bot, but a piece of one? Now that would be stellar.

He picked up the vent and put it back in place. He had seen a pair of loader bots in the hangar when he arrived. He dropped onto his hands and started running on all fours. It was embarrassing and primitive to move this way, but it was also faster, and there was nobody around to see it.

He had to go up two decks to get to the hangar. He paused at the entrance to the emergency stairs to listen. Clear. He quickly opened the hatch, entered, and closed it behind him. Then he hopped onto the short railing that separated the declines. He made sure it was clear before he dropped down, catching the next railing like an acrobat, swinging around and dropping again, repeating the process twice more until he was on the right level. He shimmied up to the hatch and activated it. He leaned out, peering into the corridor. He was close to the hangar, and a soldier was walking away from him, in the same direction he needed to go.

Gant moved into the hallway, closing the hatch behind him again before dropping onto his hands and feet once more. It was faster. It was also quieter, and gave him a smaller profile. He scurried along the side of the wall behind the soldier, getting close but not too close. He needed to make it into the hangar without being noticed.

He trailed the soldier, following him along the corridor until they reached the larger, wider entrance leading into the hangar. He urged the soldier past it with his mind, hoping he would continue on and purring softly in response when he walked past the entry.

The hangar doors opened. A small Terran in a pilot's jumpsuit stepped through it.

"Lyso. Wait up."

The first soldier paused and turned around.

Gant cursed under his breath.

"Hey," the pilot said. "Where are you headed?"

"What's doing, Bol-" the soldier started to reply, until his eyes fell on Gant. "What the? That's the biggest damn rat I've ever seen."

"Huh?" Bolar said, shifting to look. "How can this thing have rats? She's brand new. And isn't that a lightsuit it's wearing?"

There was one other benefit to moving on four limbs. It made it easier to jump a longer distance.

Gant sprung up, launching through the air toward the two soldiers, growling as he did. He caught Bolar off-guard, using his face as a springboard, slamming it hard enough that he stumbled back a step. He bounced from there to the wall, pushing off and coming at the other soldier, spinning and kicking.

The soldier got his hands up, managing to block the kick but cursing at the pain of the impact, Gant's lightsuit giving him more force behind his blows. Gant let himself fall to the floor between them, noticing Bolar was going for his sidearm. He bounced up again, ramming his fist into Bolar's groin, causing him to shout in pain. Gant leveraged himself off the pilot's leg, pushing and springing back toward the soldier. A quick punch caught the soldier in the nose, breaking it and sending him reeling.

He turned back to Bolar, moving behind him, jumping up and getting his hands around his neck. The pilot reached back for him, trying to dislodge him. He held tight and pulled up and sideways, the strength of the lightsuit allowing him to break the pilot's neck.

Bolar dropped the the floor. Gant bounced off him, standing face to face with the soldier, who had enough time to grab a knife from his boot.

"Where the hell did you come from?" the soldier asked.

"Exactly," Gant replied.

Then he charged toward the soldier. The difference in size threw the man off at first. He wasn't used to something smaller than him being so aggressive. He held the knife out to intercept, but Gant shifted vectors, jumping and turning, hitting the wall beside the soldier, planting and pushing off. The soldier tried to adjust. Too slow. Gant grabbed his forearm, in his hands, opening his mouth and biting his wrist. He felt nauseous as his teeth sank into the flesh, reaching the muscles and tendons and going right through. The soldier cried out, his hand unable to hold the knife. He swung his arm into the wall, bashing Gant against it. Gant grunted, letting go, hitting the ground and rolling to where the knife had come to rest. He scooped it up, chittering with satisfaction as he did.

The soldier reached for him. Gant ducked beneath his legs, cutting into his left calf as he did, powering through to the tendons and forcing the soldier to fall. He rolled away from a heavy punch, and then jumped up and stabbed the soldier in the throat, wrenching the knife away and flipping back to the floor.

The soldier fell forward. Gant walked back to Balor, whose eyes were open, his mind aware.

"Nothing personal," Gant said. "You tried to kill Abbey." Then he finished the job.

He looked at the carnage. He wouldn't be able to hide that. Oh well. He just needed to move a little faster. He entered the hangar, hurrying to the corner where he had seen the loading bots. They were big and heavy, with numerous appendages intended to help lift, carry, and position all kinds of items, from crates to ordnance. These looked newer than the ones he was accustomed to. Their metal frames were still clean, and one of them even recognized he was approaching.

"Do you have work for me?" it asked.

"Not exactly," Gant replied. "Enter diagnostic mode for repairs."

"My systems do not report any existing anomalies."

"Excuse me. Enter diagnostic mode for upgrade."

"Entering diagnostic mode."

The bot's eyes went from blue to yellow. Gant examined the shell of the machine for a moment. Then he headed further into the corner, to a storage rack full of tools and supplies needed to maintain the bots. He found the tools he needed and quickly began disassembling the machine.

"Ten minutes," he said to himself. "All I need is ten minutes."

CHAPTER TWENTY-NINE

THE SOLDIERS ARRIVED EIGHT MINUTES later. Three of them, in plain black utilities. One of them had picked up Bolar's gun.

They entered like a special ops team, standing beside the open hatch, sweeping the room first with their eyes, and then with the gun.

"Head over to the shuttle," one of them said. "You can grab a gun in there."

The two soldiers started running that way.

"Do you need assistance?" one of the loader bots said, stepping out from its corner of the hangar.

The lead soldier was jumpy, and he turned and shot it, three times before he realized he wasn't being attacked.

"Shit on a quasar," he said. "Scared the crap out of me. Yeah, maybe you can help me. Has anyone else been in here recently?"

"Yes."

"Who?"

The other two soldiers emerged from the shuttle, each holding a rifle. They joined the first.

"It was a Gant. He came to upgrade my partner."

"We don't have a Gant on our crew. What kind of upgrade?"

"This kind," Gant said, dropping down from the back of the loader.

A thin rod of metal ran along his arm, bent at the elbow and heading up to a mount that wrapped across his shoulders. The appendage was attached there, along with one of the other rifles from the shuttle. He pulled the rod forward, which forced the pull on the appendage to move, which depressed the trigger on the rifle. Flechettes spewed from it, sweeping across the three soldiers as they tried to react. His aim was a little wild, but the rounds found their targets, cutting the soldiers down.

"Heh. It works." Gant shifted his shoulders, adjusting the weight. "I need to tighten the mount, though. The recoil is a bitch. Loader, can you lift this thing for me?"

The loader bot swiveled to face him, taking the mount and raising it.

"Thanks. Hold on one second."

He turned the bolts to tighten the contraption and then hurried over to the dead soldiers, ejecting the magazines from their rifles and bringing them back. He replaced the one in his weapon.

"Okay, give it to me."

The loader lowered the mount back onto his shoulders. He shrugged it into position. It was pinching his chest now, and pulling at the hair. He didn't have time to be a perfectionist. It would have to do.

"Thanks," he said.

"You are welcome," the loader replied.

Gant shifted his arms one more time and then began walking toward the hangar doors. There was no way the soldiers hadn't alerted the bridge of what they had found. Why weren't there any warning lights or sounds?

Maybe they didn't know how to turn them on?

He chittered in laughter at the thought as he crossed the threshold into the corridor. Let them try to stop him now.

He moved as fast as he could, thankful for the lightsuit's added strength. He would never have been able to carry the mount on his own. He reached an intersection without pause, nearly falling as he tried to navigate without adjusting for the added weight. He reached out and steadied himself on the wall. If there were soldiers coming, they would either take the emergency stairs or the lifts. He wanted to beat them there.

He reached another corner, coming to a quick stop when he heard the hatch to the stairs open, and muffled voices in tactical helmets. Did they have a response team just waiting for something bad to happen? He couldn't lean out to get a look without the whole weapon kit leaning out with him and making him a huge, obvious target. He also couldn't wait for them to get more organized.

He gnashed his teeth together, talking himself into the next round of craziness. Then he ran around the corner.

Four rifles were pointed his way. He activated his own, opening fire, using the element of surprise in his favor again. It didn't keep the soldiers from shooting back, but they had been expecting a Terran or larger, and so their shots were too high. They cried out in turn as the flechettes dug into and through them, the close quarters allowing the rounds to easily puncture their lightsuits.

They were dead before they could adjust their aim, leaving Gant alone in the corridor, his ears ringing from the noise.

"Bad design," Gant said, putting his hand to the ear closest the rifle. "I probably have hearing loss from that."

He opened the entrance to the stairs. They were clear. It would take a few minutes for the bridge to catch on that the team they had sent was already dead. He needed to make as much progress as he could in that time.

He made his way back up two decks, intent on returning to Ursan's quarters, knowing they were close to the bridge. He ran recklessly, not worrying too much about being seen or shot at or killed. He had already taken out ten of Gall's individuals, a good score by any account, and ten fewer than Abbey would have to worry about. He was hoping to claim the bridge, but anything at this point would be a bonus.

He ran into two more crew members on the way, shooting them before they had much time to react. He hated killing in cold-blood like that, but they had chosen their side. He just happened to be on the other one.

He slipped into Ursan's suite. It was empty. He threw himself onto the floor on his back, reaching up and working the screws to the makeshift rifle mount. He couldn't go onto the bridge with guns blazing. He'd wind up destroying half the terminals and Olus had told them to bring the *Brimstone* back, not destroy it. Even if he wanted nothing more than to turn it into dust after what he had seen.

At least he had kept the knife.

He grabbed it from its spot on his mount and moved back toward the door and then out into the hall. He headed forward, becoming more angry as he got closer to the bridge. If Gall wasn't in his quarters, he was probably there.

He reached the bridge unimpeded. There were still no alarms going off. No warnings. He knew there weren't that many crew members on the ship, but it seemed ridiculous to him. What the frag was going on?

He stood outside the hatch, listening. He didn't hear anything. It was as though the bridge had been deserted. He reached up to the door controls, tapping it and then backing away, knife up, ready to pounce on anyone who happened to be there.

A woman was standing in the doorway. She was young, with short, dark hair and a tired face.

She had her hands up.

"Wait," she said. "Don't kill me."

"What?" Gant said, confused.

"My name is Lieutenant JG Olain Iann. We surrender."

"What?" Gant repeated.

"I said we surrender."

Gant hesitated, unsure what to say. "What do you mean you surrender? Where's your Captain?"

"Captain Gall went down to the city. He's lost his mind, and taken us with him. He disobeyed General Thraven's orders. He nearly killed Ligit. I signed on to help him fight the Republic, not to get mixed up in this craziness or have him kill me because I looked at him funny. You'll tell the General that, won't you? "

Gant held back his laugh, finally starting to understand what was happening. "What about the rest of your crew? How many of you are there?"

"On the *Brimstone*? Thirty-two. No, that's wrong. Twenty-four, after Drune. Twenty-two, with the Captain and Commander Dak gone. There are fifteen more on the Triune."

"The Triune?"

"Our original ship. You can see it out the viewport from the front of the bridge."

"How many on the bridge?"

"Six."

Gant did the math. "There are still four of you out here somewhere. Are they mutinying, too?"

"I. I don't know. I didn't ask."

"If they want to stay alive, you need to get them here. The rest of my team is sweeping the ship right now."

"Aye, sir," Iann said.

"Can I trust you enough to put this thing away?" Gant asked, showing her the knife.

"Aye, sir. We're all in agreement. We never intended to cross General Thraven, but we're loyal, sir. We've known Ursan a long time. He isn't the same man, and I'm sure this ship is more valuable than he is."

Gant stared at her. Were these soldiers? They were acting more like mercenaries. He would never sell Abbey out, no matter how much she changed. No matter what she became. He would rather die than turn on her.

He lowered the knife. He wasn't ready to let go of it just yet. If these individuals could turn on someone they had worked with for years, they might turn on him. Especially if they realized he was here alone and he would sooner cut Thraven's throat and urinate down his neck than ever work for him.

"Surrender accepted," Gant said. "I'm assuming command of the *Brimstone* immediately."

"Aye, sir."

"See if you can get the others to turn themselves in to me. I would hate for the General to have to have them killed."

"Aye, sir."

"Don't just stand there, Lieutenant. Lead the way."

"Aye, sir."

Iann turned and moved into the bridge ahead of him, announcing him as they arrived. The six members of the bridge crew all saluted him. He acknowledged them with a return salute, and then sat at the command station, covering his face with his hand to hide his laughter.

Queenie was going to love this.

CHAPTER THIRTY

"WE'LL BE ARRIVING IN TEN minutes, Captain," Commander Usiari said.

"Thank you," Olus replied.

He closed his eyes and heaved a sigh. There was no part of him that was looking forward to his arrival on Earth. His conversation with General Omsala while en route had been anything but pleasant, and while he had managed to tie up his loose ends on Feru and claim innocence in the activity around the Eagan estate, he was certain that the General was one of Thraven's, and the Fizzig knew damn well that he had been there.

For the moment, Omsala and whoever else on the Committee was compromised were keeping things quiet, and trying not to disrupt the state of the galaxy. The media had blamed the fugitives from Hell for the attack and the murder of both Mars and Emily Eagan. They were claiming the Rejects were also behind the original theft of the ships and destruction of the ring station, and that there were links to the Outworld Governance that could potentially lead to the Republic declaring open war. Not that any of that was even remotely possible for a small crew to carry out, and ignoring the fact that they had 'escaped' after the original attack on Feru. Someone was pulling the strings on that one too, and he had a guess who they worked for.

The question was: where did that leave him? Thraven had to know the Rejects had escaped, and that he had escaped with them. Olus wasn't convinced the Gloritant hadn't wanted that very outcome. It was an unorthodox way to run a war. Then again, he had personally expressed his desire to Olus to kill God, which was as unorthodox a motivation as he had ever heard. Whoever or whatever God was to Thraven. Too much of the backstory was still a mystery to use it to build a profile and begin estimating what he might do next.

Except Olus already knew what Thraven was going to do next. Finish retrofitting the starships, and then begin attacking the galaxy.

Would he start with the Outworlds? Or would he move right through to the Republic, and keep playing the Governance for fools. How much awareness did the Governance even have of him? The Outworlds were all so loosely bound; it was easy to hide within them. It was easy to take advantage of them.

His instincts had been right when he had freed Gant. The Gant had somehow managed to get on board the *Brimstone*, and was trying to reach out to Abbey even now. He was sure Ruby would notice the beacon. She was programmed to observe things like that.

His instincts had been right when he had gone through the extra effort to break Abbey out of Hell, too. She was a natural leader, and had the strength and focus to see this thing through. The Gift Thraven had given her was taking her to the next level, turning her into something else. What? He wasn't sure yet. There was a risk there. A question. Would she be able to control the power without succumbing to it? He had urged her to embrace it, to claim it, to use it. Would she be able to do that without turning on them all? He hoped her daughter was enough of a motivation to keep her playing for the right team, but in the end it was all on her. If she submitted, if she failed? God help them all.

Where were those instincts leading him now? To Earth to deal with Omsala and the Committee, to find out what the hell happened to Iti, and to learn as much as he could about the so-called Covenant. What he needed more than anything right now was information. Intel he could use to out the crooked members of the Republic government. Intel he could pass on to Abbey, with the hope of finding something, anything that might be able to slow or stop Thraven's advance.

First things first. He was scheduled to meet with General Omsala in less than an hour. He had a feeling he knew what the General was going to say, and he had been doing his best to prepare for it. He expected that shortly after the meeting started, he wouldn't be the Director of the OSI anymore. He was working under the assumption that he might not make it out of there at all.

Thraven had maneuvered him in play to waste time on Mars Eagan while he stole the *Fire* and *Brimstone* and built his ships. Misdirection. Only he had a new scapegoat now. A new target. One that Olus had given him, and led right into his hands. At the same time, he didn't regret it. They would be worse off without the Rejects than they were with them. It was on him to work his own way out of his own mess. He wasn't some green cadet who didn't know how the Republic machine worked. He was an experienced intelligence agent, and an experienced killer, and he wasn't afraid to do what he had to do in order to protect the Republic and the citizens within.

Hell, he was even willing to help protect the Outworlds if it meant stopping a lunatic like Thraven kill innocents.

Olus opened the case he had brought onto the *Driver* with him. It wasn't a standard OSI operative kit, though that's what he had told Usiari's crew it was when they had brought it on board. Instead, it was an assassin's toolset. A list of equipment that the Republic would deny even existed if questioned. It was the kind of stuff most Directors of the OSI wouldn't even know about, let alone carry. But he wasn't most Directors of the OSI.

He pulled out the clothes first. Standard, generic, formal attire, suitable for wear both to meet General Omsala, or to wander pretty much anywhere in the galaxy where a wealthy target might be found. A fitted base layer containing synthetic musculature similar to a lightsuit but less powerful, adding twenty to thirty percent strength enhancement. Enough to overpower someone in a grapple, but not enough to crush their skull in his hands. A similar base layer for the legs. A collarless, formal merge-weave shirt, a pair of black pants, and a collarless black jacket with two columns of silver buttons across the front, all of it impact resistant, able to take rounds from most smaller arms.

He dressed himself in the clothes before digging deeper into the case, removing what looked like a pair of thin cards but were in truth flat-pack knives, nasty weapons that were easy to hide and would make it right through security in the Pentagon. They wouldn't get through a battlesuit. They would barely cut through a lightsuit, but most of his targets weren't wearing armor. He stuck one in each of his front pockets before reaching in and grabbing a more harmless looking device. A Republic identification card, a requirement to be permitted on Earth. Right now, it had his real name and information printed on it. With the right motion along the surface, it could scan nearby cards and 'borrow' the information from them, allowing him to steal the identity of anyone he was close enough to, useful for travel when the original cover was blown.

Finally, he removed a pair of eye lenses and a follicap from the case. The lenses would give him a basic terminal overlay to a tiny CPU embedded in one of the jacket's buttons, allowing him to use the setup as a simplified softsuit. The follicap was slightly different than the standard used for cosmetic alteration. There was also a fold at the bottom of the cap that could be brought down and stretched over the face and then programmed to alter the general shape. It couldn't mimic another person entirely, the tech for that was too bulky to alter on the fly, but it could add contours that made a huge difference in recognition. Those same updates would be automatically synced to the id card to prevent confusion.

He carried the follicap and the lenses into the bathroom, taking out a hair remover and quickly running it over his scalp. It had been a while since he had been completely bald. It made him look older and more frail. He didn't feel that way. He pulled the follicap on, leaving the mask portion tucked beneath it, taking his time getting it on properly and then using it to regrow the hair he had just abandoned. He also placed the lenses in his eyes, blinking a few times to get them positioned right. He had heard that they had augmentations nowadays that could replace the lenses, but he had never been a fan of the idea of permanently altering his natural state.

"Captain Mann," Usiari said, his voice coming out of the

communicator Olus had left with the case. "We've entered Earth orbit. A shuttle is standing by to bring you down."

Olus headed out of the bathroom. "Thank you, Commander," he said, lifting the communicator and sticking it to his chest. Then he closed and locked the now empty case.

He couldn't help but think of Abbey as he made his way to the hangar and boarded the waiting shuttle. Was she on her way to the *Brimstone* right now? Would they finally get their hands on one of the ships, and maybe discover where Thraven was hiding with the rest of them?

Or would Thraven have the last laugh once again?

CHAPTER THIRTY-ONE

"WE'RE DROPPING IN TWO MINUTES, Queenie," Bastion said. "You know this is crazy, right?"

"I'm moving shit with my mind, Lucifer," Abbey replied. "I'm so far beyond crazy; this almost feels normal."

"Roger that. I think what I meant to say is, you know this is suicide, right?"

"Either Gant is on board the *Brimstone* making life difficult for the Outworlders, or we're going to dump out of FTL right into a trap. What's suicidal about that?"

"Funny."

"You outmaneuvered the *Brimstone* before."

"I got lucky. What do you think the chances are I'll get that lucky again?"

"Fortunately for you, we aren't running from her."

He laughed sardonically. "Yeah. We're trying to board her. I feel great about our chances of doing that. How do we know she won't be cloaked?"

"If she's cloaked she can't attack us. I thought you were a badass drop-jock? You should be embracing the challenge. Unless you think Nerd should take over?"

Bastion glanced at Erlan in the co-pilot's seat. "This guy? He's not touching the controls of this baby until I'm dead."

"Stop bitching and start twitching," Abbey replied.

"You're not allowed to say that," Bastion said. "You were never a pilot."

"I can do it," Erlan said. "I'm pretty sure I've got all of the controls memorized."

"Pretty sure?" Bastion said. "Sorry, Queenie, I'm not that keen on dying today."

"Good. Fury, Jester, are you ready back there?"

"Locked and loaded, Queenie," Airi replied.

"I'll be ready in a minute, too, Queenie," Pik said. "Just have to get this suit on."

"You're supposed to be in Medical," Abbey said.

"Frag that," Pik replied. "They took my favorite hand. I want restitution."

"I don't want to know what favorite hand means," Benhil said.

"Can you carry a rifle?" Abbey asked.

"Affirmative."

"Fine, you're in. Stay in the rear and shoot over our heads."

"With pleasure."

"Ruby, any word from Gant?"

"No, Queenie."

"Trap," Bastion said again.

"So was Feru," Abbey said. "We made it out of that one."

"Not without casualties."

"You mean the *Imp*?"

"Yeah. That ride was sweet after the freak-monkey fixed it."

"Do you have to keep calling Gant that?"

Bastion laughed. "Whenever he isn't here to bust me for it."

"Hey," Erlan said. "What's that?" He pointed to one of the controls on the console between the two pilot seats, to a blinking red LED.

"We're being hailed," Bastion said.

"By who?" Abbey asked.

"The little red blinking light doesn't say," Bastion replied.

"Smart ass. Answer it."

"We're about to drop out of FTL."

"All the more reason."

Bastion reached over and tapped a physical button beneath the light.

"This is the *Faust*, Outworld identifier 12498166647," he said.

"Oh, it's you," Gant replied, sounding truly disappointed.

"Gant?" Abbey said.

A light chitter of excitement returned through the speakers. "Queenie," Gant said excitedly. "You're there. I mean, I knew you would be because I knew you were alive, but it's good to hear your voice."

"Gant, calm down," Abbey said. "Where are you?"

"The *Brimstone*."

"What?"

"Yeah, I know, right?"

"We're about to drop out of FTL near Anvil. What's your position."

"Geosynchronous orbit above the planet," he replied. "Queenie, you aren't going to believe this, but the crew of the ship surrendered to me."

"Surrendered?"

"I know. I had to duck off the bridge so they wouldn't hear me. They think I'm with Thraven, part of an elite unit that boarded and captured the ship. From what I've gathered, their Captain has gone a little insane. He brought the *Brimstone* here against Thraven's orders, sent one of the crew to Medical with a nasty blow to the head, and basically made everyone on the bridge terrified of him."

"You're talking about Ursan Gall?" Abbey said.

"Yeah."

"Where is he?"

"Planetside. Why?"

"He knows where Thraven is staging his war. He knows where the *Fire* is. We need him."

"It sounds like it. I was hoping you were close by. I tried to contact you earlier, but you must have been off the net. I could use a little backup here. Apparently, Gall also sold his starship to some Plixian traders or something. We just took delivery of fresh crew members, and it's only going to be a matter of time until they figure out I'm here alone."

"We're geared and ready. Are you visible?"

"Are you kidding? Can you guess how many questions the Outworld Planetary Defense would be asking if they knew the *Brimstone* was here? I'm sure they've seen the Republic streams. No, we're laying low, but I can give you a good positioning estimate. You can pass the *Imp* over when you get close."

"Uh," Bastion said. "Yeah. About that."

"I don't like the tone of your voice, Lucifer."

"I kind of crashed the *Imp* on Feru."

"What do you mean, kind of?"

"I was outnumbered ten to one. It's a miracle I lived to tell you about it."

"Lucky me."

"All right," Abbey said, cutting them off. "We've got a replacement shuttle. We stole it from the Crescent Haulers after Thraven's undead soldiers attacked us."

"Excuse me, Queenie," Gant said. "Did you just say you stole something from the Crescent Haulers?"

"I know. We didn't have a choice."

"Describe didn't have a choice."

"Forget it right now. Pass over the coordinates."

"I'll have to get them from the bridge. Hang tight off Feru. I'll be in touch. Gant, out."

The link closed. The red LED stopped flashing. Bastion looked back at Abbey. "Well, I'll be a freak-monkey's uncle."

"Shut up," Abbey replied. "All right, Rejects. Slight change of plans. We've got a line in from Gant on the *Brimstone*. He has the ship under control, but we have to be nimble to secure it. Okay, you, Jester and Nerd are going to take the shuttle over to the *Brimstone* and give Gant a hand. Lucifer, Fury, Ruby, and I are going to take the *Faust* to the surface to look for Ursan Gall. He knows where Thraven's been hiding, and I want to know, too."

"Aye, Queenie," they replied.

"Uh, Queenie," Erlan said.

"What is it?" Abbey said.

"You want me to go over to the *Brimstone*? As in, fly her?"

"You are a pilot, aren't you?"

"Well. Yeah, but. I mean. I've never."

"It's a prototype," Bastion said. "Almost nobody has ever."

"Aye, sir," Erlan said, smiling.

Another LED started blinking on the console. This one was green.

"We're here," Bastion said, reaching forward and hitting the toggle beneath it.

A sudden silence overcame them as the disterium reactors powered down, even though none of them had noticed the noise they made until it was gone. A blue haze of the crystalline material surrounded them as they came out of FTL, quickly passing through the cloud and clearing into Anvil's space.

"Lucifer, get clearance from Anvil's PD and bring us into geosync to wait for Gant."

"Aye, Queenie."

"Nerd, head on down to the shuttle with Okay and Jester. And don't let them give you any shit."

"Aye, Queenie," Erlan said, abandoning the co-pilot's seat and heading out of the cockpit.

Abbey moved into his place, leaning back into the worn chair. "See, it isn't always bad news. We're fifty percent mission complete."

"The last fifty percent is always the hardest," Bastion offered.

"Let's hope not."

CHAPTER THIRTY-TWO

"SHUTTLE'S AWAY," BASTION SAID.

HE didn't really need to. Abbey could see it through the canopy, making the short hop to the hangar of the *Brimstone*, which itself was a small point of light in what otherwise looked like completely empty space.

She could hardly believe the ship was there, and that Gant had single-handedly captured it for them. Well, not quite single-handedly. If Ursan Gall hadn't lost his mind, the crew of the ship wouldn't have been so willing to turn it over.

Still, she had a feeling he might have managed to get the starship away from them regardless.

"Queenie," Gant said, using short-range direct communication now that they were within close proximity. "There's something else you should know about this ship."

He sounded fearful, which surprised her. He had never struck her as being afraid of much of anything.

"What is it?"

"When I first got on board, I went to the engine room." He paused. "Well. I'm not sure how to say this other than, there's no engine."

"What do you mean there's no engine?"

Bastion turned his head, looking over at her, confused.

"I mean, it isn't a standard build. It isn't standard tech. Whatever the hell Thraven is, whatever the hell he did to you that let you survive the damage you took on Drune, he's using it to power the *Brimstone*. The main engine compartment is filled with people, all hooked up to a machine in the center. They're hanging from the walls. They're still alive. Still breathing. I'm shaking just telling you about it."

Abbey felt the chill herself. "Captain Mann told me they built the *Fire* and *Brimstone* from ancient blueprints that Emily Eagan claimed predated human civilization. I don't know what the Gift is, but it seems like it's a lot more versatile than we realized."

"And sick," Bastion said.

"I can't argue that," Abbey agreed. "There's nothing we can do about it right now. Gant, the others are entering the hangar now."

"I've got eyes on them," Gant replied. "Not a second too soon. Lieutenant Iann was starting to look a little squirrely to me."

"Funny you should say that," Bastion said.

"Bite me, thrusterhead."

"Lucifer, do we have clearance to land on Anvil?" Abbey asked.

"Yes, ma'am," Bastion replied.

"Good. Gant, you're in charge on the *Brimstone*. Be nice to Erlan."

"Erlan?"

"The new guy," Bastion said. "Call sign, Nerd."

Gant chittered in laughter. "I can't believe we have a new guy. What kind of moron signs up for this outfit on purpose?"

"He helped us get off Feru," Abbey said. "He deserves some respect."

"Ok, Queenie. You know I'll do what you say. Be careful down there."

"I will. You too. Queenie, out."

The link closed. Abbey glanced at Bastion. "Well?"

"On our way."

Bastion adjusted the throttle, and they began turning away from the *Brimstone* and adding velocity. Within a few seconds they were clear, and he adjusted course to get them headed toward the planet.

"I was out here once before," Bastion said. "We did a drop on a planet not too far from here, a little nothing colony. Some assholes there decided to make a quick jaunt into Republic space and attack one of our bases. They stole a handful of mechs, some guns, and ammo. Idiots."

He added more thrust, the *Faust* continuing to accelerate toward the planet.

"Anvil Proper, this is the *Faust*. We're headed in for a landing," he said, opening the line to Anvil's orbital control.

"Roger, *Faust*. We've got you on sensors. You're clear to land. Setting a marker for you."

The HUD at the front of the pilot's seat changed, showing a flashing beacon to indicate where the *Faust* was supposed to land.

"Roger, Anvil Proper. I have the ball.'

"That was easy," Abbey said once Bastion closed the link.

"You missed the details. Ruby passed them fifty thousand to keep things quiet. Unless they're on the take with Thraven, too, we should be going in clean."

Bastion adjusted the ship's vector and velocity, matching it up to the readings on the HUD. Abbey was sure this kind of landing was probably boring for him. Newer systems would have this kind of thing automated.

"What was I saying?" Bastion asked.

"Idiots," Abbey replied.

"Right. Idiots. So of course, the Republic retaliated. They sent my company over, dropped a couple of platoons on them. They didn't even know how to use the mechs they had stolen. Their plan was to strip them down planetside and then disappear into the stars and sell everything they had taken on the black market. You got a taste of that on Orunel."

"That's not the first time I was in a place like that."

"Yeah, I forgot, you like the action. Long story short, we dropped in and just decimated them. I mean, it was so unfair it was terrifying. I remember thinking at the time, how could anyone be so stupid?"

"Did you ever get an answer?"

He laughed. "No. But I'm kind of thinking the same thing about this guy, Gall. Every indication is that Thraven is stone-cold, but he just decided he wasn't going to follow orders anymore, and he came here for what?"

"According to Gant, he wasn't very happy I cut his wife's head off. He's trying to bring her back. It's kind of romantic, in a way."

Bastion laughed. "In the most fragged up way I can think of, maybe. But again, how can anyone be so stupid? Thraven is going to wipe the stars with him when he gets a hold of him."

"Not if we do it first."

"Roger."

The *Faust* shuddered slightly as it entered the atmosphere, the visual beyond the canopy turning orange from the heat of reentry.

"So, Queenie," Bastion said. "I think we're making a connection here. Good chemistry. What do you think?"

Abbey raised her eyebrow and looked over at him. "I think you should shut up and drive."

Bastion laughed again, falling into an amused silence as he guided the *Faust* downward. Within a minute they were cruising over the city, the volume of traffic amidst the tall buildings obvious below. A minute after that the ship was setting down gently between a number of orbital shuttles and smaller starhoppers like theirs.

"So, how do we find this asshole?" Bastion asked, powering down the ship and getting to his feet.

"I know we're called Breakers, but we don't just break into things," Abbey said. "We're pretty damn good at finding things, too."

"And when we do?"

"He's got the Gift, but so do I. If we work together, we should be able to take him clean. Just remember, we need him alive. Or at least, alive long enough to give us Thraven's address."

"Roger that."

Abbey moved out of the cockpit and into the CIC, where Ruby and the others were waiting.

"We're here," she said. "Ruby, keep the *Faust* warm for us."

"Yes, Queenie," Ruby replied.

"Fury, Lucifer, let's go."

CHAPTER THIRTY-THREE

"I WISH I HAD BEEN able to bring Jester with us," Abbey said as the Rejects made their way across the spaceport tarmac toward the loop. "He knows more about the Outworlds than all of us put together."

"Yes," Airi said. "And it's pretty much the only thing he's good for."

"That and whining," Bastion said.

"Olus wanted him, and I trust his instincts," Abbey said. "He just hasn't had any great opportunities yet. At least he knows how to shoot, and he hasn't run away yet."

"He wants to," Airi said.

"Olus?" Bastion said. "You're on a first-name basis now? Do I have competition?"

"Fury is competition relative to you," Abbey replied. "We aren't soldiers anymore, remember? Besides, he gave me the keys to your lives. I think that puts us on a more personal level."

"Yeah, sure. Of course, you have the hots for my arch nemesis."

"Captain Mann got you out of Hell," Airi said.

"Captain Mann put me in Hell," Bastion said.

"You beat the shit out of him," Abbey reminded him.

"Like that matters." Bastion smiled.

They reached the loop station, approaching a small kiosk.

"Cover me," Abbey said.

Bastion looked around. "We aren't under attack."

"I might be able to get into the city's data network from here. Make sure nobody sees what I'm doing."

"Roger."

Abbey reached under her coat to her softsuit, digging into a tightpack and retrieving a long, thin rectangle from within. She couldn't very well wear a helmet in the middle of a loop station, but while the standard TCU interface made things easier, it wasn't the only way to hack a machine.

She reached to the side of the kiosk, tapping the rectangle. A small needle extended from it, which she jabbed into the side of the box. An even smaller needle would extend from the first, reaching out and making a connection with the circuit board within. Her aim had to be relatively precise, but it was her job to be familiar with the make and model.

Abbey waited a few seconds while the disruption package did its work, injecting Breaker written malware into the device that forced it into diagnostic mode. A menu appeared on the projection, allowing her to access the command line. She was grateful the softsuit had included the piece of hardware. While it was standard Breaker kit, she hadn't expected to find it in a hand-me-down from Feru.

"Excuse me," someone said behind her. "I need to get a pass for the loop."

"This terminal's closed for repairs," Bastion said.

She assumed the individual moved on.

Abbey began typing in the air, her hands moving in quick, practiced motions that brought her deeper into the machine's systems.

"Is something wrong with the terminal?" someone asked.

"Just routine maintenance, sir," Airi replied.

Abbey spared a glance over her shoulder. An Outworld soldier in dress grays was standing there. Their eyes met for a moment, and then she returned to her work.

"Can I see some identification?" the soldier asked. "There have been reports of individuals trying to break into the terminals to get free passes. I just want to make sure your work is authorized."

Abbey cursed under her breath. It figured some other assholes were trying to hack the system, too. Thraven's?

"Are you on duty, sir?" Bastion asked.

"I don't see how that's relevant," the soldier replied.

Abbey kept digging into the system, moving as quickly as she could. She didn't let the soldier bother her. Focus was essential.

She reached the root network adapter for the service. Automated systems like these typically had a unique password and address that were passed to the control mainframes for authentication. If she could grab those, she could get back in at another terminal at another time. One that was as far away from Captain Do-gooder as they could get.

"With all due respect, sir," Bastion said. "I believe the question is highly relevant. After all, we're standing here in the open at one of the busiest terminals in the city, and yet you have the audacity to make an accusation that we're up to no good, like we're some kind of imbecilic thieves who are dumb enough to try to break into a secured system in the middle of a crowd of individuals?"

"I'm only asking you for identification," the soldier replied. "If you have it, why not just produce it so I can be on my way?"

Abbey entered the commands to request the machine's address, a twelve digit series of letters and numbers that she committed to memory when it appeared. Then she moved to another part of the system, using the address to try to uncover the password.

"The identification isn't the point, sir," Bastion said. "The point is your accusatory tone and stance. It's almost as though you're looking for trouble, even where there isn't any. If I had to guess, I'd say you've been on Anvil a little too long, and the pleasure bots and gambling isn't doing it for you anymore. Not when what you're really itching for is a good firefight."

Abbey tensed slightly, wondering how the soldier would react. She let herself relax when she heard him laugh.

"Yeah, maybe that's it exactly. I've been planetside for three months, and I still have three more to go. You aren't wearing a uniform. I assume you served?"

"Six years," Bastion said. "Right out of school. Dropship pilot. I fragged up my eyes. Now I'm working here helping fix this crappy hardware."

"A thrusterhead? Shit. Now I don't know why I'm talking to you at all."

"Army?" Bastion asked.

"Yup."

"Which planet?"

"Avalon."

"No shit?"

The soldier laughed. "Yup. This is my mandatory tour. I've heard rumors somebody on our side did a number on the Republic, so maybe I'll be getting some action after all."

"I've heard that, too. I wish I could still fly."

"You don't need to see to shoot," the soldier said. "At least not if you're a Republic soldier." He laughed. Bastion laughed with him.

Abbey entered a dozen commands in succession, rewarded a moment later when the password came back unencrypted. She stared at it for a moment, memorizing it. That was the other benefit to a full TCU. She wouldn't have to remember the details.

"Well," the soldier said. "Now that we're friends, will you please show me your identification so I can be on my way?"

"You just said we were friends," Bastion said.

Abbey quit the command line, quickly restarting the kiosk. She pulled the disruptor from the side of the box, retracting the needle and holding it in her fist.

"I've known plenty of good people who washed out of the military and had to turn to something less than legal to make ends meet," the soldier said. "Are you one of them?"

"I should kick your ass for even suggesting it," Bastion said. "You little groundfragger."

"Cool it," Abbey said, turning and putting her closed hand on the back of Bastion's shoulder. "We're all done here."

The soldier stared at her.

"What? You've never seen a bald woman before?" she asked. The softsuit's higher neck was covering her Hell brand.

"That's a military grade softsuit you have under your coat," the soldier replied. He leaned in a little closer. "Is that Republic made?"

Abbey stepped between Bastion and the soldier. "You just don't know when to mind your damn business, do you?" she said. She could feel the Gift reacting to her anger. "Fragging budget cuts. Yeah, it's a Republic suit. So what? The terminal's fixed, take a look. Move on or call for security."

The soldier's eyes flitted to the terminal. Abbey almost wanted him to make a move to contact security so she would have a good reason to smash his smug face.

He looked at her again, locking eyes. She was defiant, staring him down. He drew back, his eyes suddenly fearful.

"Uh. No. It's not a problem," he said, backing away. "Sorry for the interruption." He turned and walked hurriedly away.

"What the hell?" Abbey said, looking at Airi. She flinched, too.

"Your eyes, Queenie," she said. "They're. Oh. They're going back to normal."

"What do you mean going back to normal?"

"I don't know what you did, but they were red, and they changed shape. Like the eyes of a demon. I wasn't expecting that."

Abbey felt the Gift squirming under her skin. It had reacted almost subconsciously to her anger, as though overpowering it back on the shuttle had made it more eager to respond to her emotions. Had it really altered her eyes? She hadn't felt a change in them.

"Where to, Queenie?" Bastion asked, staring at her eyes in search of the change.

"I've got credentials to access the Anvil mainframe. I just need a terminal that won't get interrupted so I can dig in a little deeper."

"You did all that in five minutes?"

"That's what Breakers do."

"Is there anything you aren't good at?"

"Piloting starships, for one. I also suck at cooking."

"If we ever get anywhere that has a decent kitchen, I'll show you how it's done."

"You cook?" Airi asked.

"If it involves fire, I'm in," Bastion replied.

Abbey turned back to the kiosk, using the card Olus had given them to buy passes.

"Wait," Bastion said. "You hacked into that thing and didn't just take the passes?"

"That would be stealing. Stealing is wrong."

Bastion opened his mouth but didn't say anything.

"Wow," Airi said. "Someone finally shut you up."

Abbey pointed to a transport sliding into the station. "That's our ride. We can grab a hotel room downtown to get access to a terminal. Ursan's been here a few days already, which means he has to be staying somewhere. We find out where, we pay him a visit, and we get off this planet with the *Brimstone*."

"Now that's what I call progress," Bastion said.

CHAPTER THIRTY-FOUR

GANT WAS WAITING IMPATIENTLY IN the hangar of the *Brimstone* when the shuttle arrived. Lieutenant Iann was standing beside him, the former crew of the Triune nearby. He had nearly wet his lightsuit when the commander of the Triune, Otero, had called into the *Brimstone* to inform them that some Trover named Dak had informed him of the sale of the Triune to a bot-maker named Gorix, and that the entire crew was on its way over to the *Brimstone* to meet up with the rest of Ursan Gall's former mercenary associates.

And that's what Gant was sure this crew was. Mercenaries. Assholes for hire, whose loyalties only rested on the biggest paycheck, the next payday. Having figured that out, it was no surprise to him that Iann had turned on Gall. What good was a crazy Captain when you had money on your mind, not to mention your own person health? It also answered a few other questions for him. Namely, where the hell Thraven was getting his army from, figuratively and literally. He knew they couldn't all be guns for hire, not if he was going to use them to start a war, but how many were mercs, how many were those hard to kill, some-kind-of-dead former prisoners from Hell, and how many were whatever the frag Thraven was? Come to think of it; he was sure the Outworlds had a prison colony or two somewhere. Had he been filling his ranks from there, too?

Gall's people were experienced, but they weren't horribly organized. It seemed to him that they had gotten used to Ursan and his now-deceased wife doing most of the hard work, while they managed their assignments with all the enthusiasm of a clerk in a government office. It was a situation he could take advantage of, as long as he got the other Rejects on board before the crew worked up enough nerve to challenge the fact that they hadn't seen any other sign of Gant's Special Forces friends.

"General Thraven will be pleased with you for your assistance," Gant said.

He had been tossing platitudes like that out since he had entered the *Brimstone*'s bridge, glad to find it wasn't constructed of Terran remains. He hadn't mentioned the design of the engines to Lieutenant Iann. He was saving that for when he might need a few seconds of shock value and confusion.

"Thank you, sir," Iann replied.

She was the most stalwart of his allies, and so far had kept the others in line. But he could tell by the way Otero had been eyeing him that he wasn't convinced the Gant was one of Thraven's, or that he should be taken seriously at all. The only thing keeping him in check was the fact that he had undeniably slaughtered half the crew, even if he hadn't claimed sole responsibility for it yet.

The Crescent Haulers' shuttle touched lightly to the hangar floor, bouncing up once before settling. Gant could see the pilot through the canopy, the one Abbey had said was named Erlan. The one whose call sign was Nerd. He didn't look that much like a nerd to Gant, but maybe the nick was being lost in the translation to his own barking and chittering language.

"Is that the Crescent Hauler logo, sir?" Iann said, her voice a little weak at the sight.

"It is," Gant said. "Why?"

"Where. Where did you get it, sir?"

"Doesn't matter."

The Rejects exited the shuttle. Benhil was first, followed by Pik and Erlan. That made four of them to the twenty plus on Gall's crew.

"Hey, squirrel-man," Benhil said, leading the Rejects over.

They were fully geared in battlesuits, each carrying assault rifles. At least they looked professional.

"Jester," Gant said. "Okay." He noticed the right glove of the Trover's battlesuit was hanging limply. "What the hell happened to your hand?"

Pik just shook his head. "Fragging bastards."

"Nerd. Welcome aboard the *Brimstone*."

"Thank you, sir," Erlan replied shakily.

Gant could tell the kid was trying not to laugh at the sight of him. It was the biggest reason he hated going to small-time planets. Most of the locals had never seen a Gant before, and they tended to think of him as a damn pet or a cute, cuddly toy.

"Lieutenant Iann," Gant said. "I'd like your crew assembled here. They'll be disarmed and sectioned off to appropriate waiting areas within the ship."

"What?" Iann replied, confused. "You want to lock us up?"

"Not all of you. Only non-essential crew. I'm sure you understand, Lieutenant. We're outnumbered, and while I appreciate your surrender and loyalty to General Thraven, there's a web of trust that needs to be earned."

"I do understand, sir," Iann said. She tapped the communicator on her chest. "Iann to the bridge. We've been ordered to assemble in the hangar. All hands. Make a general announcement."

"Aye, Lieutenant."

A tone sounded a moment later, echoing across the hangar. "This is Ensign Calso. All hands to the hangar for general muster. I repeat, all hands to the hangar for general muster."

"This is bullshit," a voice shouted from the side of the space.

Gant turned his head slowly. He knew who had spoken without looking.

"Excuse me, Commander?" Iann said, looking at Otero.

"You heard me, Olain," Otero said. "There's no way this little rodent is one of Thraven's."

"How do you know?" Iann replied.

"You've seen how Thraven does things. You cross him; you die, plain and simple. He doesn't waste time with the likes of us."

"The General wants the *Brimstone*," Gant said. "And the *Brimstone* needs a crew."

"The *Brimstone* needs three people on the bridge," Otero said. "That's it. Thraven would have killed everyone else on board already. Who the frag are you really?"

"Maybe you're right," Gant said. "Maybe I don't need you."

Otero smiled, revealing a mouthful of gold teeth. He drew his sidearm, looking down at it. Gant hadn't been dumb enough to try to take away their guns alone.

"Maybe we don't need you."

"Otero," Iann said. "If you kill one of Thraven's men, you'll be signing all of our death certificates."

"Except he isn't with Thraven, you idiot. Where the hell would Thraven get a Crescent Hauler shuttle?"

"You know what?" Pik said, stepping toward Otero and pointing his rifle at him. "I think you should shut the frag up now."

The rest of the Triune's crew was assembled behind Otero, and they came to attention as one, brandishing their weapons.

"Why don't you shut the frag up?" Otero said. "You're outnumbered and outgunned."

"General Thraven will have your asses," Erlan said.

Gant glanced over at him, shaking his head lightly.

"Thraven will kill us anyway."

Gant cursed beneath his breath, backing toward the Rejects. He had been right to ask Abbey to expedite the reinforcements, but maybe he should have asked her to come before heading down to the planet? He had underestimated Otero.

The two sides stood opposite one another, weapons raised and pointed, the tension getting thicker with each second. The rest of the crew began filing in, freezing when they saw the standoff.

"We don't need more blood spilled," Iann said, moving slowly out of the crossfire. "Otero, what do you think you're going to accomplish?

Even if they aren't with General Thraven, do you really want to take that chance? One way we might live. The other we definitely die."

Otero looked at her, a fire in his eyes. "Yeah, I want -"

The *Brimstone* shuddered, shifting in space hard enough that everyone in the hangar was thrown off balance.

"What the hell?" Gant said.

"If I didn't know any better, I'd say something just hit the ship," Erlan said.

"Don't just sit there, kid," Gant replied, finding the knife he had taken. "They're off balance, and they aren't wearing battlesuits."

Erlan's face froze. Then Pik was up beside him, bouncing toward Otero and his men, spraying fire across the hangar. Benhil joined him an instant later, not hesitating to take advantage of the situation. The mercenaries had numbers, but they weren't as aggressive, and it cost them, a handful falling before they could regroup and start shooting back.

Gant bounced from the floor toward Lieutenant Iann, knife in hand. She put her hands up, still in the midst of surrender, and he returned the gesture with a smile before redirecting himself toward the fight.

Rounds filled the hangar, the volume of fire creating a near deafening echo as the two sides squared off. There was little enough cover, but Otero and a few of Gall's crew managed to get behind their shuttle, firing around the corner. A constant barrage of return fire kept their aim from being true, sending bullets ricocheting off the metal floor, some of them bouncing up and into the armored legs of Benhil and Pik's battlesuits.

"Okay, up and over," Gant said, bouncing away from a hail of slugs.

"Roger," Pik replied. He bent his legs and used the battlesuit's muscles to push himself into the air, rising twenty meters to the top of the enemy shuttle. Otero noticed, and he backed away from the edge of the craft, adjusting his aim overhead.

Erlan and Benhil moved in, crossing to either side of the ship, taking their time while the targets tried to figure out where to shoot. The shuttle had given them cover, but it had also limited their line of sight.

"Iann," Gant shouted. "Get your team back to the bridge. I want to know what just happened. I'll be there as soon as we finish up here."

"Aye, sir," Iann replied.

The Rejects were like cats hunting prey, closing in slowly while Otero and his remaining soldiers tried to defend themselves, taking pot shots to keep them honest. Gall's team had worked its way into a corner, and there was no way out.

"We surrender," Otero shouted. "Shit."

"You had your chance to surrender," Pik said. "And nobody tells me to shut the frag up."

"Okay," Gant said. "You aren't in charge here."

"Aw, come on, Gant. They're assholes. We should kill them and be done with it."

"We don't kill unarmed soldiers in cold blood," Gant said, loudly enough that Otero would hear.

"I do," Pik replied. "Queenie did."

"What?" Gant said, surprised.

"She dumped some ugly Curlatin out of an airlock. He deserved it."

Gant felt a chill run through him. Abbey was a soldier, not a killer. Wasn't she?

"Not today, Okay," Gant said through his communicator.

"They're still packing."

Gant sighed. "I said, we don't kill unarmed soldiers."

A few seconds later a handful of weapons slid across the floor from behind the shuttle.

"I really can't kill them?" Pik said.

"If Queenie were giving you the orders, would you keep asking?" Pik didn't reply. "Exactly. Go round them up."

Gant could see the huge Trover bounce down to the other side of the shuttle, and he held his breath while he waited to see if Pik would follow his orders. He had to know he would be answering to Abbey if he didn't.

Otero and his remaining crew moved out from behind the shuttle, with Pik at their backs. Erlan and Benhil moved into position in front of them, keeping them covered.

"What are you going to do with us?" Otero asked.

"Get on your shuttle," Gant said. "Get the hell out of here."

"You definitely aren't Thraven's."

"Nope. But I still want you off my ship. And don't think about heading to the surface to warn Ursan, either. What's coming to him down there is way worse than any of us. If you're smart, you'll make yourself scarce."

Otero nodded, defeated. He directed his men to the shuttle, boarding it quickly.

"Okay, make sure they get lost. Jester, Nerd, you're with me."

Gant hurried from the hangar with Erlan and Benhil behind him. The *Brimstone* was secure, but he had a bad feeling it might not matter.

CHAPTER THIRTY-FIVE

"WHAT'S OUR STATUS," GANT SAID, running onto the bridge.

Lieutenant Iann was sitting at the command station, but she stood and abandoned it as the Rejects entered.

"Officer on the bridge," she said sharply, saluting.

The rest of the crew stood and saluted with her.

"Yeah, whatever," Gant said, climbing into the seat. "Get back to work. Can I get a status report?"

"Sensors are reporting five unidentified ships have entered Anvil's orbit," Iann said. "They appear to be attacking the Outworld defenses."

"Visual?"

"Not yet."

"Bring us about."

The *Brimstone* began to shift in space, turning slowly. Gant didn't need to see the ships to know it they were Thraven's. Any Republic or Outworld ship in the universe would have been tagged by the *Brimstone's* identification system.

"We have to help them," Iann said.

"I'll give the orders, Lieutenant," Gant replied. "Jester, keep an eye on these clowns."

"Excuse me, sir?" Iann said.

Gant chittered softly, while Benhil positioned himself to the left of the bridge crew, his rifle up and ready for use.

The *Brimstone* continued to spin. Gant saw what had struck them a moment later. An Outworld cruiser. A starship. It had a gaping hole in its side and was floating dead in space; no doubt hit in the offensive. It had skimmed the *Brimstone's* shields, giving them a shove on the way past.

"We're being hailed, sir," one of the other crew members said.

"By who?" Gant asked.

"They're identifying as Captain Piselle of the warship *Fire*."

"Shit," Gant cursed under his breath. "Well, I guess the party's over. Nerd, take over at the pilot's station. Lieutenant Iann, have a seat over there. Anybody does anything I don't tell them to do, they die. Got it?"

The crew looked back at him, surprised. One of them started to stand until he saw Benhil watching and sat back down.

"Sorry to tell you, Lieutenant," Gant said. "Otero was right. We aren't with Thraven. We're called Hell's Rejects. We're special ops, but not the kind you were thinking of."

"Mercenaries?" Iann asked.

"Sort of. The bottom line is that Thraven is an asshole, and we hate him. You should too. He doesn't give a shit about the Outworlds, and he's been using you and your boss to position his rise to power."

"General Thraven is a decorated military officer with the Outworld Cooperative," Iann said.

"Really? How do you know that?"

"Captain Gall told us."

"How does he know that?"

Iann shrugged. "That's what he said. I had no reason not to believe him. What happened to Otero?"

"I sent him away in his shuttle. If you want to join him out there, be my guest."

"No thank you, sir," Iann said.

"We're being hailed again."

The *Brimstone* had turned nearly one hundred eighty degrees. Gant could see the *Fire* now, a few thousand kilometers distant and moving toward Anvil's orbital defense station. Streams of plasma and projectiles filled the space between them, the defenses firing full-bore. The *Fire* absorbed the attack, shield energy constantly visible as it took the brunt of the response. Four flashes of light followed, fired by ships further back and flanking the fire. They struck the station a moment later, each one creating a flare of detonating oxygen before the framework around the impact collapsed.

Within seconds, the station was gone.

"I don't understand," Iann said. "He's attacking his own soldiers."

Gant put his head in his palm. "Where did Gall find you?" he said softly. Then he lifted his head. "Iann, I want you to answer the hail. As far as the *Fire* is concerned everything is fine here, we're just waiting for Gall to return. If you try to warn them, you get shot. You don't want to get shot, do you?"

"No, sir," Iann said. "Gavash, open the link."

"Aye, ma'am."

"This is Lieutenant Olain Iann of the warship *Brimstone*."

"Lieutenant," a woman's voice said, filling the bridge. "Where is Captain Gall?"

"On the surface, Captain," Iann said. "He's been down there for a few days now."

"I assume you're cloaked. What is your position?"

"Captain, we're under attack, we-"

Gant didn't see who had spoken until after Pik's bullet had gone into the crew member's head and the body had slumped onto the floor.

"Ah, frag. Sorry, Piss-elle. Gall's mercs don't run this boat anymore."

"Who are you? Identify yourself."

"Gavash, close the link," Gant said.

"Aye, sir."

The link closed.

"Well, that idiot wanted to get shot," Gant said. "What about the rest of you?"

None of them moved.

"Forget the Outworlds. Forget the Republic. Thraven is a threat to everybody. You don't believe me? Keep watching."

He stared out the view screen with them. Smaller ships began to drop from the *Fire* and her escorts. Shrikes and dropships, all of them descending into the planet's atmosphere. More Outworld warships were closing in, one of them passing within ten klicks of the *Brimstone*. They fought back against Thraven's ships as bravely as they could and were destroyed just as bravely.

"Whatever you're doing down there, Queenie," Gant said. "Do it faster."

CHAPTER THIRTY-SIX

ABBEY, AIRI, AND BASTION WERE in the lobby of a downtown hotel when the warning tones began blaring out across the city, the resonance of the sound penetrating everywhere, from the tallest building rising into the clouds, to the deepest parts of the surface dwellings. None of them knew what it meant at first, but they watched as the individuals around them began lining up in a fascinatingly orderly method.

"What the hell?" Bastion said.

"Attention all citizens. Attention all citizens. Please report to the nearest protection facility immediately. This is not a drill. This is not a drill. All soldiers on leave are ordered to return to their assigned base immediately."

"That doesn't sound good," Airi said.

"Anvil is under attack?" Abbey said. "By who?"

"Two choices," Bastion replied.

"The Republic or Thraven," Airi said.

"Not good for us either way."

The message repeated, following the tone. It was obvious from the reactions of the other individuals that they had done this sort of thing before. Abbey was certain it normally was a drill.

She heard the sound of thrusters a moment later and turned to look out the transparent wall of the lobby to see a black Shrike rocket past, vibrating the building. A second later she heard the hiss of plasma fire, followed by the deeper repetition of projectiles and the muffled thuds of distant explosions.

"Excuse me," someone said, approaching them. He was wearing a tailored suit. A hotel employee. Maybe the manager? "We're evacuating the building. Please follow the line to the stairs. It will lead you down to the Protection Center."

"I don't need protection," Abbey said. "But thanks."

"It's illegal to remain on the streets during an emergency," the man said. "Punishable by twenty years imprisonment."

"We'll take our chances," Bastion said.

"Sir, I must-"

Bastion spread his coat, showing off his sidearm. "I said we'll take our chances."

The man eyed them for another second and then moved on to the next group of visitors who didn't understand protocol.

"We need to find Ursan Gall, right now," Abbey said.

"You wanted a terminal?" Airi replied. "How about that one?"

She was pointing to the hotel's reception desk, a white, spherical station in the center of the lobby. The employees behind it had already left their posts, joining the exodus.

"It'll do. Keep an eye out for soldiers."

Bastion and Airi both drew their sidearms, whatever good they might do against fully armed and armored grunts.

"I'm not sure which invader I would prefer," Airi said.

"I don't have a problem killing Thraven's soldiers," Bastion replied.

"But we might be able to talk our way out of it with a Republic platoon," Airi countered.

"True. Outworld Defense is going to be a problem."

"I think they'll be a little busy to start searching hotels to arrest us for loitering."

"Again, true."

Abbey vaulted the desk, tapping on the terminal and bringing up the projection. The receptionists had left in such a rush they hadn't bothered to shut anything down, making it easier for her to get deeper into the systems.

"How long do you need, Queenie?" Bastion asked.

"A few minutes," she replied. "Why?"

"A dropship is about to land on the platform across from this one."

"Can you identify it?"

"It's unmarked."

"Not Republic then."

"We should have taken bets."

Abbey's hands moved quickly, navigating through the menus of the system until she found the command line. It only took a dozen commands to get back to the city's network, and she closed her eyes when she did, recalling the address and password she had lifted from the terminal.

A nearby explosion rocked the building as she did.

"Whoa," Bastion said. "Outworld PD is on the scene. They just blasted the dropship. This place is turning into a war zone real fast."

"Then keep your fragging head down," Abbey said, entering the keys. A moment later she had an interface to the full network.

The sounds of fighting intensified. Shrikes zipped past in ragged dogfights, one against another, while more dropships could be heard descending on the city. Abbey moved through the network as quickly as she could, her mind running in multiple threads.

Why was Thraven attacking like this? There had to be a reason that went beyond Ursan Gall. Even if the man had disobeyed orders, it didn't make sense to assault an Outworld planet like Anvil to kill him. It couldn't be because he knew she was here, could it? He was revealing himself as an enemy to the part of the galaxy that had provided him succor while he built his army. For one person? She knew Thraven wanted her, but that didn't make any sense at all.

She navigated the network until she located the central visitor's database. The Outworlds and the Republic were similar in some ways, and one of them was the level of connectivity between loosely affiliated systems. Both governments wanted to know where visitors were moving to and from at any given time, and residency records were one of the best ways to do it, especially once they could be paired with payment cards and used to track every transaction. Fortunately, the machines like the loop kiosk needed direct access to insert records, and so the credentials she had gathered were viable to access the database directly.

"Uh oh," she heard Bastion say.

She glanced up. He and Airi were both running toward her. A squad of Outworld soldiers had bounced into view ahead of the hotel, taking whatever cover they could find as they squared off against approaching targets.

"Get down," Airi yelled, both of them vaulting the desk as the firefight started, the bullets smacking the hardened transparency of the building's face and pushing through.

Abbey ducked slightly but had to remain somewhat upright to work the terminal. She could see the bullets hitting the floor ahead of the desk through the projection, digging up tile and dust. She typed the database command in, running a query for Gall. The search only took a second, returning zero results. She wasn't all that surprised. She recalled the last command and changed the parameters, looking for Dak instead.

One result.

She copied the coordinates, backing out of the database to the Hotel's main interface. It had a mapping system there, used to direct visitors to their destinations. She put the location into the system. The projection changed, showing her a three-dimensional view of the city, lighting up a path from their position in the upper reaches all the way down to the surface.

"Lucifer, Fury, look at the map," Abbey said, committing it to memory. If she forgot any portion, hopefully someone else would be able to pick it up. "That's our target."

Airi and Bastion glanced up at it, almost at the same time a round passed through the projection and hit Abbey in the stomach. She felt like she had been sucker punched, and she cursed when she looked down and saw a hole in her softsuit. She had never been shot this much before she had been given the Gift. She was getting reckless.

She ducked down, a hail of bullets passing overhead and blowing pieces out of the desk above them. Then the destruction stopped, the firefight changing direction. Abbey stood, looking out to the fight. The blacksuits were closing in on the Outworld Planetary Defense unit, filled with holes but still up and attacking.

"We have to help them," she said.

"Help the Outworlders?" Bastion replied.

"I'm pretty sure it's better than helping Thraven."

"Ladies first."

"Fine. Fury, I'll knock them down, you take their heads."

"Roger."

"You have the map memorized?"

"As best I can," Bastion said. "I've never been that good with directions."

"You're a pilot."

He shrugged.

"Let's go."

Abbey stood, locking her eyes onthe Converts beyond the hotel. They had already decimated the first PD squad and looked to be targeting reinforcements from somewhere to the right. She could see a second dropship beyond them, which had landed near the first. That one was smoking heavily and had a huge, gaping hole in its side. Even so, there were still units coming out of it, damaged but not destroyed.

She felt the Gift responding to her anger, and she used it to bounce across the lobby, landing halfway and bouncing off again and throwing herself through the damaged transparency. It was so beaten it barely resisted, and she crossed over, slamming hard into one ofthe Converts and landing on top of it. It had been shot in the helmet, and half of its head was missing from the side, replaced with the silvery goop. She used the Gift to hold it down while she grabbed and broke both of its arms and pulled the gun from its hands.

Then Airi was beside her, Katana in hand. She brought the blade down in one quick slice, removingthe Converts head.

"One down," she said.

Abbey found the next target, taking up the rifle and firing, hitting it in the head, aiming for the eyes. The helmet's protective transparency shattered beneath the repeated rounds, andthe Convert stumbled, losing the ability to see. She turned and repeated the process on another, while Airi rushed over and decapitated the first.

Bastion emerged from the hotel, conservative with his attack, shootingthe Converts in vulnerable joints to disable them, reaching one and hitting it point-blank in the elbow, the force strong enough to dismember it and release the rifle it was carrying. He picked it up, ducking behind a column as a fresh contingent joined the fight.

"Queenie, incoming," he said. Abbey looked up. A pair of Shrikes were bearing down on the position, angling to strafe the platform. Airi was in their line of fire.

There was no time to reach her. She threw out her hand, desperate to move her out of the way. A moment later Airi was pushed forward, launched out of the area and back toward the hotel. The Shrikes released their rounds, peppering the platform, running bullets through both converts and Outworld PD alike.

"It doesn't look good up there either," Bastion said.

Abbey glanced further up, to space beyond. Streaks of flames suggested large forms losing orbit and burning up. Of course, if Thraven were assaulting the ground, he would be attacking the forces around the planet as well. Was the *Fire* here? Was the *Brimstone* secure?

"We can't waste time," she said, remembering the map. "There's a tube two blocks east of here."

"Roger," Airi said. "Thanks for the save, Queenie."

"Anytime."

CHAPTER THIRTY-SEVEN

"THIS IS IT," BASTION SAID. "Do you think he's in there?"

They were standing outside of a rusted hatch, located on the second subterranean level of a dirty hotel that rested below the formerly pristine skyline of Anvil city. Most of the fighting hadn't made it down this far yet, but many of the residents had vanished, making their way to nearby Protection Centers or holing up in hidden spaces.

It had been a challenge to make it down. Part of PD protocol was to disable civilian tube stations, leaving them inaccessible during attacks in the name of security. Abbey had been forced to return to the hotel terminal, to re-enter the network and re-activate the transport from the upper reaches of the city down to the base. It had wasted nearly five minutes, a damn lifetime in the middle of a battle. By the time they made it back to the tube they had to fight their way through another platoon of Thraven's soldiers, burning more time and energy.

They had gotten below, though. They had made it to the surface, to where Dak had used his identification to rent a room.

"Let's find out," Abbey replied.

She put her hand against the hatch, feeling the Gift moving beneath her fingers. It had been pulsing steadily, as though it was tuned not only to her own anger but to the fury of the fighting around her, the chaos and discord increasing its energy. She pushed it out into the hatch, the force wrenching it from its tracks and throwing it aside.

Bastion and Airi swept into the room, rifles ready. They covered it in seconds, both of their muzzles coming to rest aimed at the same spot.

"Who the frag are you?"

Abbey looked at the Trover sitting on the floor in the corner of the room. He had a massive pistol in his lap. His hand was resting on top of it.

"I'm looking for Ursan Gall," Abbey said.

"You aren't with Thraven."

It was a statement, not a question.

"No."

The Trover smiled. "He isn't here."

"I figured that much. Where is he?"

"They took him."

"Who?"

"They called themselves the Children of the Covenant. They took him for Thraven." He shook his head. "They weren't Terran. They weren't Trover. They weren't any damn thing I've ever heard of before." He paused, looking down at his gun. "They were monsters. Or animals. I'm not even sure which. I don't know what the frag is going on with anything, anymore. I thought Thraven was fighting for the Outworlds. Now he's attacking the Outworlds? I knew he had magic. Power, you know. He was going to help us conquer the Republic with it." He looked up at Abbey. "I should have known he wanted it all for himself. Isn't that the way assholes with power always do it? I just thought..." His voice trailed off.

"Why are you sitting there?" Bastion said. "There's a battle going on. You want to fight for the Outworlds? You're doing a shitty job."

Dak shrugged. "I didn't know what to do. Thraven let me live. He won't if I resist him. I've seen his work. You're her, aren't you? Abigail Cage?"

"How do you know my name?" Abbey asked.

"Thraven told it to Ursan. Ursan told it to me. You killed his wife. It's your fault we're here." His hand moved slightly on the gun.

"Don't," Airi said, pushing the rifle closer to him.

"Thraven's using you," Dak said. "Just like he's using all of us. Whatever you're here for, it's because he wants you to be."

"I came for the *Brimstone* and the *Fire*. The two stolen ships. The Republic wants them back."

Dak smiled. "Of course, you did. It doesn't matter if you take them. They were prototypes. Thraven's got more."

"What else do you know about the ships?" Abbey asked.

"Not much."

"Do you know about the engines?"

"What about them?"

Abbey took that as a no. "I know Thraven's building more ships. I need Ursan to tell me where."

"I know where."

"You do?"

"Yeah. But I'm not going to tell you."

"I'm not above torture," Abbey said. Maybe once, but not now. Not where Thraven was concerned.

"I have a high pain tolerance. It'll take a while. It's only a matter of time before his forces claim the city. Then what are you going to do?"

"So what is it you want?"

"I want you to help me save Ursan."

"You have to be kidding," Bastion said.

"Nope. Ursan's my friend. We've been running together a long time. He didn't know Thraven was going to do this. Trin talked him into signing up with the General. She convinced him it was his best chance at getting revenge for his parents. Once he can see it's not true, maybe he'll come back around."

"Or maybe he'll still want to kill me for killing his wife," Abbey said.

"Could be. But you were going to go after him anyway. If you two fight, whoever deserves to win will win. At least this way I'm doing the right thing, instead of nothing. Yeah, the more I think about it, the more sense it makes."

"Which could be exactly what Thraven wants," Bastion said.

"Queenie, you can't make a deal with this guy. He's a fragging mercenary."

"I have to eat."

Abbey stared at Dak. The options were clear. She could bring the Trover back with her and take her time getting him to talk, or she could agree to his deal and go find Ursan Gall. Getting out of a war zone as soon as possible certainly seemed like the safer course. And if Thraven really did want her to fight, wasn't it better that she didn't fall into his bidding?

On the other hand, how long would it take her to make Dak talk? Hours? Days? Ever? There was no guarantee, and every minute that passed meant another minute that Thraven had to bring another warship online. What was the bigger risk? Finding Ursan Gall in the middle of this shitstorm, or allowing the enemy to bring their full fleet to bear?

"You're a loyal friend," Abbey said.

"Not always. I let them take him. I ran away."

"It sounds like they would have killed you."

"Yeah. I should have fought, anyway."

"I find Ursan, you tell me where, no matter what happens after that. Deal?"

Dak nodded. "Deal."

"Queenie," Bastion said.

"It isn't your decision, Lucifer," Abbey replied. "I lead, you follow."

"Yes, ma'am."

"Let him up."

Airi and Bastion lowered their rifles. Dak got to his feet, clutching the pistol in his left hand.

"I can take you to Gorix's workshop. That's where the assholes grabbed him. It could be that Gorix knows where to find them. If I find out that cockroach set us up, I'm going to flip him on his damn back and leave him there to rot."

"Now that is cold," Bastion said.

"You aren't funny," Dak replied.

"How far is it?" Abbey asked.

"Not far. A couple of blocks. Ursan didn't want to be too far from the workshop."

"All right. Let's go."

CHAPTER THIRTY-EIGHT

IT ONLY TOOK A FEW minutes to cross the distance to the warehouse where Gorix's workshop was located. The surface of Anvil remained an as-yet unscathed dead zone, a place suddenly devoid of any signs of life. Abbey noticed a pair of deep red chairs in front of a large window in one of the buildings they passed. A pleasure house, where the synths had been removed from it to prevent them from being damaged. There were other shops around it in a similar condition, their most valuable goods removed from sight, their doors no doubt locked.

She could still hear the explosions coming from above, along with the constant vague echo of gunfire. A line of smoke was rising from a klick or two to the south, where a Shrike had apparently crashed. What size was Thraven's force, and would it be able to conquer the entire planet? In space, the modified starships would destroy the Outworld's lesser fleet. Shrikes were powerful against existing Republic tech but nearly useless against a ship like the *Fire* or the *Brimstone*. On the ground, The Outworld PD didn't know about his undying soldiers, and wouldn't know how to deal with them efficiently, especially when they used the Gift.

In other words, yes, he would be able to conquer the planet and the city with it.

It was only a matter of time.

"Ruby, what's your status," Abbey said as they moved into the warehouse. Like everything else, it was completely abandoned.

"There you are, Queenie," Ruby replied. "I was worried about you but didn't want to risk giving you away. I've been in contact with Gant. Thraven's forces are assaulting the planet, as I'm sure you've figured out. The *Fire* is here, along with four other starships featuring similar technology. The *Brimstone* is cloaked and safe for now, but the Outworld defenses are being torn apart. They tried to gang up on one of the ships and had some moderate success, but weren't able to destroy or disable it before they were obliterated. As for the *Faust*, the entire spaceport is on lockdown. No ships in or out under threat of being fired upon. Thraven's Shrikes are leaving it alone, though I don't know why. It is strategically illogical."

"I'm sure he has his reasons," Abbey said, considering Ruby's report.

They were in deep shit; their escape route pretty much cut off. Even if she did find Ursan Gall, what would it matter? There was no easy way off the planet or out of the system. Assuming Thraven took the spaceport and abandoned the weapons batteries there, they might be able to get the *Faust* in the air. Then what? Could they jump away before the *Fire* and her ilk caught up to them? She didn't know. She wasn't going to abandon Gant and the other Rejects, anyway.

"I want you and Gant to see what you can do about prepping for an emergency evac. I want vectors that limit the amount of time both the *Brimstone* and the *Faust* are exposed, and I want it ten minutes ago. Either all of us leave, or none of us leave."

"Yes, Queenie," Ruby said.

"We're tracking Gall now. I'll report back as soon as we have him. Queenie, out."

"This way," Dak said, leading them to a stairwell in the corner.

She knew something was wrong the moment she pushed the door open. The smell was horrible, like cooked meat and burned metal.

"Ugh," Bastion said. "What the hell is that?"

A dead Plixian was resting at the bottom of the steps. Its thorax was torn in half.

"Dead bug," Dak said. "I think the Children did this."

There was smoke still sneaking out through a hole in the wall, wafting up the stairwell toward them.

"They're all dead; I bet," Dak said.

Abbey led them down the stairs to the half-open secret door into the Plixian tunnels.

"What's through there?" Bastion asked, pointing at the other door. There was a horrible stench coming from that side as well.

"More death," Airi said.

Dak moved ahead of Abbey, grabbing the door and pushing it further into the wall, the thick muscles in his neck throbbing as he strained.

Abbey walked through in front of him. A sharp thump from behind gave her pause. It was followed by a number of smaller taps.

"Boots on the ground," Airi said.

"Yeah, but whose boots?" Bastion asked.

"Lucifer, watch our exit," Abbey said.

"Roger."

"Which way?" she asked.

"I know you have the Gift, but you should still follow me," Dak said, getting in front of her again, holding his pistol out ahead of him.

Abbey let him take the lead this time, following him through the many tunnels beneath the surface of the planet. They passed a number of dead Plixians, as well as a few Outworld humans. All of them were shredded as though they had been attacked by animals.

"What are these Children of the Covenant?" Abbey asked.

"I don't know," Dak replied. "First they looked like Terrans. Then they changed."

"What do you mean they changed?"

"They turned into monsters. Demons. They grew at least this much." He spread his hands. "Their faces elongated. Their teeth became fangs. Their hands became claws. I've never seen or heard of anything like it. Maybe it's common where Thraven is from?"

"Did Thraven ever say where he was from?"

"A planet in the Outworlds. He never mentioned it by name. He said that's where the Gift came from. That it's common on his world, though the effects aren't the same on his kind as they are on others. Ursan told me the Gift is poison to Trovers."

"And Gant seemed immune to it back on Drune," Airi said.

"Anger and hate," Abbey said. "You said it helps."

Airi nodded. "I think it does."

"Queenie," Bastion said through her comm. "Whatever you're doing, do it faster. The boots just made their way into the warehouse."

"It's right through here," Dak said.

They followed him out of the tunnels and into an open space. It had clearly been ransacked, with broken machines and hundreds of parts littering the floor along with more dead Plixians. There was blood everywhere. Dak pointed at one of the corpses.

"Gorix," he said sadly. "He was a friend of mine."

"We aren't going to find anything here, Queenie," Airi said. "We should go."

Abbey scanned the space. "You said Ursan brought his wife's head here?"

"Yeah." He looked out at the mess. "It was back there last time I saw it." He pointed to the corner of the workshop. There was nothing there. "It looks like they took it. There was armor, too. A special design. I don't see the box it was in. No sign of Villaueve either."

"Who?" Abbey said.

"Villaueve. He's a Lrug scientist. He said he could fix Trin."

"Fix a decapitated head?"

Dak shrugged. "That's what he said."

"Queenie," Airi said, pointing to a spot on the floor. "Look."

Abbey followed her finger. A dead Plixian was resting near the side of the room. His entrails had been spilled across the floor, the green blood from them used to scrawl out a simple message on the floor:

Prove yourself worthy.

"What the hell does that mean?" Abbey said.

"Queenie," Bastion said, his voice slightly shaky.

"What's wrong?" Abbey said.

"I think Dak owes you."

Abbey glanced over at Dak, confused. "Are you saying what I think you're saying?" she asked.

"Yeah. Ursan Gall is here. He's calling your name."

CHAPTER THIRTY-NINE

ABBEY LOOKED OVER AT DAK. The Trover seemed surprised, but at the same time amused.

"I told you," he said. "Thraven will get you to do what he wants. One way or another. He wants you to fight Ursan." He shook his head. "He wants Ursan dead, and you under his thumb."

"Frag that," Airi said. "Let's just shoot him and be done with it."

Dak glared at her.

"He isn't going to win," Airi added in her defense.

"You owe me the location," Abbey said.

"Kell," Dak replied. "You'll have to look it up for the coordinates. It used to belong to a narcotic cartel. It's got a good atmosphere for growing shit that will get you up. Thraven told Ursan the Outworld Cooperative discovered they were trying to frag up Outworlders to make them soft for the Republic. To make an invasion easier. I tried to tell him it wasn't true, but there was a paycheck involved, and a chance to go after the Republic, and Trin was pushing him to do it. I know now it was all bullshit. Too fragging late."

"Kell," Abbey repeated. The name didn't mean much to her, but Benhil probably knew about it. "Thank you."

Dak shrugged. "Sure. For whatever it's worth. I don't like the odds of any of us making it off this planet alive. The Children, they're immune to the magic. Even if you beat Ursan, you'll probably have to deal with them."

"Do bullets work?" Airi asked.

"Not that well."

"Damn."

"Whose side are you on, Dak?" Abbey asked.

"I told you, Ursan's my friend."

"So you're going to try to stop me?"

"No. That's not the way this is supposed to go down. But if Ursan wins, I'll back him up."

"What if he loses?"

"I'm against Thraven."

"Understood."

Abbey left the workshop, heading back through the network of tunnels to the warehouse. She could hear Ursan as she got closer.

"Lieutenant Cage," he was shouting. "Lieutenant Abigail Cage. I know you're here. I'm waiting."

She reached the steps. Bastion made his way down to her when he saw her.

"Is he alone?" she asked.

"Right now. But I wouldn't be surprised if there were more assholes nearby."

"Let's assume that much. Lucifer, Fury, wait here. Keep your eyes out for the creatures that Dak described. If they get hostile, our move is to retreat back to the tunnels and try to force them to come in one or two at a time, to wound them and cut them down just like Thraven's soldiers."

"I know you're close, Cage," Ursan shouted. "I can smell you."

"If Ursan kills me." She paused. The kill switch was bullshit, but they still didn't know it. If she told them now, how would they react? She needed their compliance to help Gant and the others. "If he kills me, Ruby can keep the reset running. Get back to the *Faust* and get out of here. The *Brimstone* should be ready to rendezvous by then. I can't say you'll survive, but at least you'll have a chance."

"Roger," Bastion said. "But Gall isn't going to kill you."

"Dak, if Ursan wants out of this bullshit," Abbey said.

He nodded. "I'll see what I can do. I won't kill yours if yours don't kill me."

"Deal," Airi said.

"Caagggeeee!"

Ursan screamed it at the top of his lungs, so loud and shrill that Abbey could feel the pain behind it. She didn't blame him for blaming her for Trin, even if his wife had picked the fight. She sure as hell wasn't going to roll over and die for him, either.

"Wait here another minute," Bastion suggested. "His head will explode, and we can sashay right out of here."

"Thraven's army is still out there," Airi said.

"Sashay," Bastion repeated.

"I'm going up," Abbey said.

She started up the steps without looking back.

"Good luck," Airi said behind her.

She reached the door at the top and stepped through. Ursan Gall was in the center of the room, his eyes already fixed on her. He looked wild, his hair half-shaven, his clothes dirty, his hands clenched in fists.

He laughed at the sight of her.

"You?" he said. He had tears in his eyes. "You're the one that killed my Trin? Look at you. What do you weigh, fifty-four kilograms soaking wet?"

"Ursan," Abbey said, taking a few steps toward him with her hands out. "I don't want to fight you."

He laughed harder. "What? That has to be the dumbest thing I've ever heard. Of course, you want to fight me. I want to kill you."

His last words came out as a hiss, and he sprang toward her, his fingers elongating into claws, the Gift reaching out ahead of him.

Abbey felt her Gift responding, rising to meet the attack. She bounced away, rolling and hopping to her feet, facing Ursan as he landed and slid, turning back her direction.

"Thraven wants me to kill you," Abbey said. "He knew I would find you. He set you up."

"No," Ursan said. "He knew you would find me because he wanted you to find me. He wants me to kill you. This is your trap, Cage. Your death. Not mine."

He sprang toward her again. She didn't move away this time. She met his Gift with her own, letting them cancel one another out. He landed ahead of her, leading with his claws, slashing wildly at her. She avoided the attacks easily, getting behind him and pushing him into the wall. He slammed it with his shoulder, the limb breaking under the force.

He bounced off and turned. His arm healed in seconds, and he rotated his shoulder a few times to test it.

"Ursan, Thraven isn't what you think he is. He isn't a friend to the Outworlds. He isn't a friend to anybody."

"I don't care," he shouted. "Do you think that matters? Do you think that makes any difference now? She's dead, Cage. She's dead because of you."

He threw his Gift out at her. She tried to block it, but this time it was too strong. She was thrown backward and then slammed down to the floor. She felt her body shatter as she hit, and she clenched her teeth in pain.

He was there before she could heal and get up, pouncing on top of her, putting his claws to her throat.

"You aren't so strong when you don't have someone to shoot your opponent in the back are you?" he asked.

"He's going to steal Trin from you," Abbey said. "He took her head."

"A good reason for me to kill you, then, isn't it?" he replied, almost calmly. "He'll forgive me for disobeying him. He'll let me stay with her when he brings her back to life. We'll be together again. A team."

Abbey felt her own fury rising. Not because of Ursan, but because of Thraven. He was using them all. Mars and Emily Eagan, Olus, Ursan, and Trin. Every life was a toy that he played with, a piece to be moved into position, manipulated into doing his will despite the illusion that the decisions were uniquely made.

Now she was going to have to kill Ursan Gall, even though she knew they weren't really enemies.

And that pissed her off more than anything else.

She didn't even move. One moment, Ursan was on top of her. The next, her Gift had pummeled him, blasting him away before he could react, knocking him back and into the wall of the warehouse.

He landed on his feet, looking at her, a smile spreading.

"I didn't want it to be that easy," he said.

He shouted and charged at her, coming so fast she could barely believe it.

It didn't matter. She put her hand up, and he hit it like he was hitting a wall. He stopped in his tracks, his body contorting against the sudden barrier, his bones breaking. He fell back.

She stood over him, holding out her hands. She had never seen it happen before, but now she watched as her fingers extended, the ends becoming a silvery gray that ended in slightly curved points. The anger was nearly overwhelming her. She could feel her heart thumping, and her face felt like it was on fire.

"Ursan," she said, fighting to keep control over it. "I don't want to kill you. We can work together against Thraven. We can stop him from destroying the Outworlds and the Republic both. He wants something, something he needs our planets, our individuals, to get. I have a vague idea from data I found."

"You can't kill me," Ursan said, his body healing. "You only have half."

He spread his hands, his body alighting in flame, the same way Trin's had. He pushed his palms out toward her. She was too close to avoid it.

She didn't need to. It washed over her, surrounding but not burning. She felt a tickle against her flesh, and she could see a shimmer of her Gift against her body, protecting her from the attack.

Ursan's eyes grew big as he stared up at her, and he shook his head. "What?" he said. "What are you? What are you?"

The flames died out. Tears streamed from his eyes. He moved

slowly, pulling himself to his hands and knees facing her. She watched and waited, confused by his sudden fear and weakness.

"What are you?" he said again.

"I don't know what-"

She didn't finish the sentence. He sprang toward her again, a gun appearing in his hand. He put it beneath her chin.

He never got to fire. Her hand finished its arc, her fingers digging in deep, slicing through the front of his neck. He stood directly ahead of her, frozen for a moment as his system tried to recover.

She didn't let it. She tore the gun away with one hand, placing the other behind his neck and pulling across. The motion finished the separation between his head and his body, and the two disconnected pieces fell to the ground.

Abbey stood over him, her chest heaving, her entire body burning.

She wasn't sure how long she stood like that, looking down at him. She stared at the blood that poured from his veins, dark and thick and full of the Gift. She remembered the taste of Emily Eagan's blood. The hint of incredible power. She wanted it. She wanted another taste. She wanted to drink it all. To add this power to hers.

No, she didn't. She stopped herself. She heard someone clapping. Clapping

"The Father writes that the true strength of God lies in his ruins. What has been, has been to fulfill the Covenant. Abigail Cage, you are the proof."

Abbey turned around, just in time to see the man step out of the shadows in the corner of the warehouse. He was wearing a plain gray cloak on top of a black uniform. He was old but handsome in a powerful way. Two soldiers flanked him on either side, all in black, their heads hidden behind dark helmets.

"My name is Selvig Thraven, Gloritant of the Nephilim," he said, approaching her. "It's an honor to meet you."

CHAPTER FORTY

"YOU'RE THRAVEN?" ABBEY SAID, TURNING to face him. She could still feel the Gift beneath her skin. She could still feel her fury. She hadn't wanted to kill Ursan Gall. This asshole had left her no choice. "I thought you would be taller."

The corner of his lip crinkled in a slightly amused smile. "You feel it, don't you, Abigail? The Blood of Life. The power of a god." He smiled more fully. "The power of a god."

There was movement near the stairs. Airi and Bastion, along with Dak. They came out with their weapons drawn, pointed at Thraven.

He barely reacted. A slight nod and their weapons were wrenched away, clattering to the ground ahead of them.

"Don't hurt them," Abbey said.

"Why not?" Thraven asked. He didn't bother to spare them a glance. "You don't understand yet, Abigail. To use a Terran expression, they are like unto sheep in a confused flock. They don't understand what is going to happen to them, so they don't know to be afraid. We were there when your kind was created, Abigail. We were there with the Shard. We created man, we created tro, we created lru and ganetan and atmin. We created all of the species. All of the intelligence. That means that they are ours to use as we will. As are you."

"Bullshit," Abbey said. "I don't know who or what you think you are, other than an asshole with some fragged up tech. I'm not going to let you trample your way across the Republic or the Outworlds."

"You can't stop me," Thraven said. "Not even you. Your power is impressive. It is so much more than I ever imagined it could be. The Gift overcomes most humans. Most, but not all. Some are special. Some have the potential to become Evolents, the true harbingers of the Return. Your anger makes you strong."

He lifted a finger. Abbey felt a sudden pressure at her neck. It was familiar to her. Clyo had tried to choke her the same way. She felt her neck burn, her body fighting to remain free to breathe. The Gift was reacting to whatever Thraven was doing. She felt as though it wanted to listen to him, to comply with his desire to choke her.

It had submitted to her once before, and it would submit to her again. She directed her energy inward, refusing to allow the reaction. She stared at Thraven, defiant.

"You've been challenged," he said, surprised. "And you've asserted."

"You can't just lift your finger and choke me to death if that's what you mean," she replied.

"What did you see when you closed your eyes?"

"A flash of light."

He smiled. "The honor and glory that you could possess, Abigail, if you were to accept what I can offer you. It can't be described in words alone. The light you saw, that was a symbol of that power. The Gift isn't darkness. It isn't evil. Come with me, and I will show you."

"How can you say it isn't evil when you're using it to destroy?" Abbey said.

"Do you call it destruction when you catch a fish?" Thraven said. "Do you call it murder when you slaughter a sheep for food? I'm preparing the harvest. I'm leading this place forward, to where it was always intended to be. It is written by the Father in the Covenant, and so it shall come to pass. The Great Return. The fall and the rise of the Nephilim and their children."

"It looks like killing to me," Bastion said. "If the battlesuit fits."

Thraven's eyes shifted to him, and Bastion fell to the ground.

"Don't," Abbey said. "Lucifer, shut it."

"Lucifer?" Thraven said. "Can you imagine all of the ways that you take the name of the Father in vain?" He curled his hand, and Bastion's body began to crumple in on itself. "Even the place where you came from. Hell? That's not the place of the Father. It's a twisted lie. The victorious should be remembered. The victorious should be revered. Not forgotten. Not waiting in the Extant for thousands of years." He lowered his hand, letting Bastion go. "But you don't know the truth. I can change your universe, Abigail. I can show you the truth, as I showed Trinity the truth. She joined me because she knew my cause is right. That it is just."

"She joined you because she was a power hungry bitch," Abbey replied. "You lied to Ursan. You told him you were a General, fighting for the Outworlds against the Republic. He had no idea what he was fighting for."

"Do you have any idea what you're fighting against?"

"I know you took people from Hell and turned them into monsters. I know you're making shitty analogies to justify murder."

"I gave purpose back to the purposeless. Power back to the powerless."

"What about the ships? The *Fire* and the *Brimstone*, and the technology that powers them?"

"Humans exist to be used. They were created to be used. But this isn't about that. This is about you. This is about your power. Your place in the universe. To think my original purpose for you was to capture a single mainframe. A simple task for someone like you. I didn't know what you were capable of. The speed and strength at which it has manifested is beyond anything I have encountered since I arrived here. There is more to you than simple tasks. More to you than these Lessers can ever understand. Haven't you ever wondered if there was more to life than what you know? If there was more to the universe than senseless conflicts over planets and resources so clearly in abundance?"

Abbey couldn't help but consider it. She had been content as a

Breaker, and she wanted to get back to her daughter. Outside of that? She had never thought about it. The Gift was forcing her to. She could feel it beneath her skin. She could sense the pull of it from the blood on the ground behind her. She could hear it in Thraven's voice. What if there was more to life? What if she were meant for bigger, grander things?

"You're thinking about it now," Thraven said. "You're wondering if there is some new, exciting purpose to your existence. One that escaped you until this very moment. That's why I came, Abigail. That's why I'm here in person. You are meant for better things. You are intended to share in the glory of the Great Return. It is promised by the Father in the Covenant. As a champion. As a High Evolent. As a Queen."

Abbey stared at Thraven. Her heart was racing, her blood thumping in her veins. "Ursan. He looked at me like I was something else. Something inhuman. What's happening to me?"

"The Blood of Life is in your veins," Thraven said. "You can control it somewhat. You cannot stop it. It is changing your DNA. Re-wiring your genetics. Making you into something more." He paused. "And something less."

"The other half of the Gift?" she asked.

"Eighty percent of those given the Gift either die or lose themselves almost immediately, their minds and bodies too weak to handle it. Those minds that are lost can be controlled, and they become part of my army. The other twenty percent have the same potential you do. Well, not the same potential. But without the other half, you will succumb to the changes sooner or later. You will become nothing more than a monster driven by violence and anger and lust and greed and hate. A demon, as the heroes of the Nephilim including the Father, eventually became. The other half allows you to control your change. It increases your ability in ways you can't imagine. It grants you true immortality and agelessness, so long as you keep your head."

Abbey stared at Thraven. Was he telling her the truth? Would she really become a monster if she refused him? Airi had seen her eyes change. Ursan Gall had been terrified of her at the end. Were those hints of what was to come? She knew something was happening to her, but she didn't feel angrier or more hateful than normal.

Or did she? Would she have jettisoned Coli from the airlock so callously two months ago? She wasn't sure.

"What if I've taken the blood of someone who has both parts?" she asked. "What if I tasted Venerant Alloran's blood?"

Thraven's eyes lit up in a way that terrified her. "Come with me, Abigail. Leave this simplicity behind. Accept the rest of the Gift. Allow yourself to evolve."

"You have to be kidding me," Bastion said. "Queenie, you can't possibly be considering this bullshit? He's lying to you."

Abbey looked back at the Rejects. What the hell was she supposed to do? They couldn't fight Thraven. Not like this. Maybe not ever. What was the choice then? Stay here and die, or go with him and live. It was the choice he knew she would have to make. The more she resisted the idea of his control, the more it became apparent that he had her right where he wanted her.

And he had done it so easily.

She needed power to stop this. Power only the Gift could give her. But if she went with him now, would she ever escape? Would she want to? If she were destined for something more, was it to be the one to destroy him, or to help him destroy everything else?

She had always believed destiny was what you made it, not some preordained bullshit. Olus had warned her about this in his own way. She knew what he would tell her to do.

But this was her life, damn it. Not Thraven's. Not Olus'. Not the Republic's. Hers.

Prove yourself worthy.

The Children had written it in blood on the floor of the workshop. Did they know how appropriate the statement was?

"I keep telling you assholes," she said, holding her eyes on Thraven's. "Go frag yourselves."

She was probably going to die. The Rejects were going to die with her. But she couldn't submit. Not to anyone. Not for any reason. Hayley would understand. If Thraven and his armies took Earth, she would fight him, and she would do it with every ounce of her soul, just like her mom.

Thraven's smile vanished. He didn't look angry or surprised. Only disappointed.

"I respect your decision, Abigail Cage. Now you must respect the consequences."

He put up his hand. Then she was airborne, launching back toward the wall again. She hit it so hard it cracked around her, and she nearly went straight through. She landed on the ground in time to see the other Rejects on their knees, choking.

"Wait," Airi said through it. "Gloritant Thraven. I. I want to go with you."

Immediately Airi got to her feet, once again able to breathe. Bastion and Dak were still choking, clutching their throats as though that would save them.

"Fury?" Abbey said through still-healing lungs. "What the frag?"

Airi ignored her. "I've tasted it. From the blood on my sword. Trinity's blood. I've tasted the Gift. I didn't die. I didn't go crazy. I don't know how to control it yet, but I want to learn. I may not be as strong as Abbey, but I'm smart enough not to pass up the opportunity."

Abbey's anger doubled, the burning heat of it inching toward the surface. Was that why Airi had been looking at her that way.? Was that why she was immune tothe Convert's power? Not because she was better at being furious than the others, but because she had bartered her soul for the Gift.

Thraven glanced over at her and nodded. "Very well. Take your sword and prove yourself worthy." He pointed at Bastion.

Airi looked over, pulling the katana from her back and walking over to the pilot. Bastion was suddenly able to breathe again, and his head tilted up toward Airi, his face twisted in anger.

"You traitorous bitch," he said.

"I'm not going to spend the rest of my life powerless to the universe around me," Airi said. "Not when I have a choice."

Then the blade came forward, the tip of it spearing Bastion in the chest and sinking all the way through. She yanked it out just as quickly, turning to face Thraven as Bastion dropped forward to the ground.

"No," Abbey said, the anger becoming too much to bear.

The Gift had never moved so quickly, had never felt so light and hot. She spread her hands out, rising to her feet as her entire body was engulfed in fire. It didn't burn her. It sat on top of her, and she pushed it out toward Airi, intent on turning her to ash for her betrayal.

The flames only made it halfway, dispersing into nothing before they could cross the full distance. She whipped her head toward Thraven, who was holding his hand up and steady, his power easily destroying hers.

"What you could have been, Abigail Cage," he said, shaking his head slightly, a flame of his own growing from his fingertips.

"Nephilim," someone said from the other side of the room.

Thraven and Abbey both looked at once, to the two individuals who had suddenly appeared as though out of thin air. A male and a female. The male was older, much older, with a white mohawk running down his head. He was wearing a silver lightsuit beneath a worn coat, a large ring on his finger, a gun in one hand and a strange kind of curved blade in the other. The woman was dressed in kind, but she was younger, her skin smooth and tight, her hair short and dark.

"Phanuel," Thraven said. "You survived?"

"No thanks to your Father," the man replied.

"You came for her?"

"I came for you."

"You cannot defeat me. I have bathed in the blood of our brothers and sisters. I have taken more power than you have ever tasted. And yet, I am but the tip of the spear."

"You and your kind took the One's Gift and turned it from something beautiful to something repugnant. We knew you would be back. We've been waiting for you."

"Then you've been waiting to die."

Phanuel shouted, bursting forward and firing the gun at Thraven at the same time he closed on him.

Thraven turned his flaming hand away from Abbey, directing it at the newcomer. It poured out toward him, but he dropped and rolled away, still shooting, his bullets hitting one of the guards standing beside the Gloritant.

"Lieutenant Cage," the woman said, suddenly standing beside Abbey. "I am Jequn. We have to go."

Abbey ignored her, finding Airi. She had backed away from Bastion, positioning herself closer to Thraven and his guards.

"I need to kill her first."

"There is no time. The Children will be coming, and Phanuel cannot win this battle."

"Then why is he fighting it?"

"To get you out."

"Bastion." She pointed to the downed pilot.

The woman looked at him. "He's still alive."

"I'm not leaving without him."

Jequn moved to him, leaning down over him. Abbey looked back toward Thraven and Phanuel. The other man had tried to close on the Gloritant, but one of his guards had intervened, blocking his path. They were tangled in a furious melee, blades flashing and striking against one another. Thraven noticed her, raising a hand toward her again, only to have a bullet hit it and blast it into shreds.

"Take that, shithead," Dak said, freed from the chokehold by the distraction.

Thraven started to turn his way, interrupted by Phanuel as he slipped past the guard and continued toward him.

"We can't help him," Jequn said, returning to her. Bastion was on his feet, a shocked look on his face.

"Lucifer, are you okay?"

"I want my mommy," he said.

"Dak," Abbey said. "Are you coming?"

The Trover nodded, rushing over to them. "I'm not staying here."

"This way," Jequn said. She tossed a puck-shaped device onto the floor. A beam of light spread upward from it. When she stepped into it, she vanished.

"Uh, I don't know," Dak said, looking at the device.

"Have it your way," Abbey said. She grabbed Bastion's shoulder and pushed him through, watching him vanish before he reached the other side.

Dak looked back as the doors to the warehouse flew open, the Children of the Covenant rushing into the space, growling as they bounded toward them. Phanuel was still locked in a duel with Thraven, his blade moving like a blur, met by the Gloritant motion for motion as though it were no effort at all.

"Frag you," Dak said, firing on the creatures. The lead target stumbled and fell, quickly replaced.

"Dak, come on," Abbey said.

The Trover turned back, extending his hand and scooping her forward as he crossed over the device.

CHAPTER FORTY-ONE

ONE MOMENT, THEY WERE IN the warehouse. The next, they were on the outside, in an alley nearly fifty meters away and still moving forward.

Jequn was standing directly in front of them, gun in hand, aimed right at them.

"Get down," she shouted.

Abbey ducked, pulling Dak with her. She smelled the creature behind her and then heard the sound of gunshots and the whistle of projectiles striking flesh over her head. The creature shrieked and fell to the ground beside them.

"Pick up the transporter," Jequn said.

Abbey scanned the ground for the disc, assuming that was what she meant. She found it, lifting it from the ground. Immediately, the light vanished.

"Wow," Dak said. "Nice trick."

"Where's your ship?" Abbey asked, getting to her feet as their savior knelt beside the downed Child, putting her blade through its neck.

"The dark side of the second moon," Jequn said.

"How the hell did you get here?"

Jequn pointed at the transporter. "We have a more powerful version. It delivered Phanuel and me here, but it only works one way. I assume you have a ship."

Abbey nodded. "Ruby."

"Yes, Queenie?"

"We're in trouble. Lucifer."

"Queenie?" Bastion said, still dazed.

"Pass the coordinates for the closest upper-level platform to Ruby. We need to go."

"Roger. Sending."

"Receiving," Ruby said. "What about the spaceport defenses?"

"Do something about them, or we're all dead."

"Yes, Queenie."

She could hear scraping on the ground, hurrying their way.

"We need to get to the upper platform," she said. "There's a tube that way."

Jequn nodded. "Take the lead. I'll protect the rear."

"Roger."

"I'll help you," Dak said.

"Your bullets won't keep them down for long."

"Yours will?"

"They're poisoned."

"Nice."

Abbey led them forward, racing through the streets toward the tube. She knew they couldn't outrun the Children for long. What about Thraven? Would Phanuel surprise Jequn and emerge victorious? She doubted it.

They crossed a wide street, nearing the tube. The fighting had intensified further, and she could feel vibrations on the ground and hear heavy fire a few blocks away. Mechs. By the sound of it, Thraven and Outworld Defense both had units crawling the downlevel streets and alleys.

Closer gunfire drew her attention back. The roar of Dak's pistol was impossible not to recognize, and she looked back to see the Trover shooting at a handful of oncoming Children. Jequn was ahead of him, having exchanged her gun for a second arced blade, which spread from her hand like a fan.

"Lucifer, get to the tube, make sure it's functional."

"Roger."

"Ruby, where are you?"

"On my way. I got clear of the fixed batteries, but the *Faust* sustained some damage."

"Can she make it to orbit?"

"Yes, Queenie. I think so. ETA forty-seven seconds."

It wasn't the best answer, but it would have to do. Abbey found Jequn as a silver blur amidst the Children, her blades flashing as she danced through their ranks, cutting into them while Dak knocked them down. She was impressive as she moved around them, jumping off the back of one, coming down on another, using her left weapon to block sharp teeth and the right to slice deep into a neck. More soldiers were coming behind them, converts in black lightsuits. Would they hold their fire until the Children were clear?

Abbey wasn't taking chances. The Gift was still flowing strongly through her, empowered by Airi's deceit. She put out her hands, grabbing one of the Children with it and dragging it down. Jequn saw it and bounced over to it, driving her blade through its neck. Abbey caught another, flipping it back, throwing it at the incoming soldiers. The creature knocked them down.

"Come on," Bastion shouted from the tube.

"Dak," Abbey said.

The Trover came running without hesitation. Jequn looked back, found one more of the Children to slaughter, and then jumped forward, landing easily beside them.

"Up," Abbey said, leading them to the tube.

They gathered in the module, Jequn regaining her gun and firing at the enemy as the clear doors closed and they began to rise. They had gone up nearly thirty meters when they suddenly jerked to a stop.

"What the frag?" Dak said.

"Thraven," Jequn replied.

Abbey looked to the surface. She could see him now, standing with

Airi on one side, and one of his guards beside him.

"Bitch," Abbey said, her anger renewed.

She knelt down, putting her hand to the bottom of the module. She could almost feel Thraven's power there, holding them in place. She pushed against it, fighting it.

It took a few seconds, but it gave way, the module released from the hold and continuing upward, quickly climbing beyond the sight of the surface, reaching toward the platform above it.

"Ruby?" Abbey said, watching a stream of fire from the sky pounding into something on the platform.

"A little messy out here," Ruby said.

The tube module reached the top. Abbey could see the remains of a mech on the platform, still burning and sparking from the *Faust's* attack. There were soldiers nearby, both Outworld Defense and Thraven's, separated on either side of the platform and passing attacks back and forth.

"How are we going to get up there?" Dak said.

"Jequn, do you have more of those transport discs?" Abbey asked.

She nodded, digging another a pair out of tightpacks on her suit. She handed one to Abbey. "Press this to activate it. It has to be flat on the ground to make a proper scan. It will flash blue when it's paired. It won't work before that."

"What's the range?" Abbey asked.

"Three hundred meters maximum," Jequn replied.

"You can't be thinking what I think you're thinking," Bastion said.

"The *Faust* can't land here," Abbey replied. "We need to get up higher."

"I'll carry the transporter up," Jequn said, pointing at one of the buildings. "It should reach."

"Go," Abbey said. "We'll cover you."

"I don't have a gun," Bastion said.

Jequn dashed across the platform toward one of the buildings. Abbey scanned the field, finding a pair of dead Outworld soldiers nearby. She reached out with the Gift, grabbing their rifles and pulling them to her, handing one of them to Bastion.

"It's almost cheating," Bastion said, tracking Jequn and shooting at Thraven's soldiers when they began to target her.

She reached the building, scaling the sheer face of it with hands and feet as though she had magnetic clamps on them, quickly rising toward the top. A Shrike streaked by, firing on the Outworld soldiers and blasting them from the platform.

"Let's go," Abbey said, leading them toward the building.

Bastion continued laying down cover fire as they crossed the gap, tossing the rifle aside when its magazine was empty.

"I hope this works," Abbey said, turning on the transporter and tossing it onto the ground.

The light flashed blue.

"Onward and upward," Bastion said, stepping into it and vanishing.

Dak was next, with Abbey right behind.

CHAPTER FORTY-TWO

"LET'S GO, NERD," GANT SAID, putting his hand on Erlan's shoulder.

Erlan looked back at the Gant. He still wasn't quite used to him, and he drew back slightly as their eyes met.

"Go ahead, say it," Gant said. "I look like a squirrel. Or a sloth. Or an ox, according to Jester over there."

"You're never going to let me forget that, are you?" Benhil said.

"Not a chance."

"Sorry, sir," Erlan said. "You're the first Gant I've ever seen. Then again, I've never seen any of those things you mentioned, either."

"You don't get out much, do you?"

"Feru is a small planet."

"I gathered. Now get us in motion."

"Aye, sir."

Erlan put his hand over the *Brimstone's* controls. Like he had told Bastion, he had watched tutorials on flying a starship before, but he had never actually done it. He thought he was doing pretty well so far. He had found the propulsion controls, the vectoring controls, and the emergency maneuvering controls, and he had them all laid out on the angled surface in front of him. He had also found a HUD that provided him information on the system's status, though it had taken a little help from the mercenary pilot whose position he had taken, a pretty woman named Waxaw, to get it all figured out.

"Are you sure you don't want Ensign Waxaw to do it?" he asked, having second thoughts.

He had been questioning his sanity since he had agreed to help Captain Mann get off the planet with his collection of former prisoners. What the hell was he thinking, abandoning the Planetary Defense to join a group of fugitives? Especially one that was being led by a woman who couldn't die and had claws. Fragging claws!

He was known on Feru for being a little bit impetuous. Like that time he had tried to kiss Jesop during that party after they had both had too much to drink. He could still feel the sting of it on his cheek when he thought about it too much.

"I want you to do it," Gant said. "I'm not ready to trust Queenie's life to a mercenary crew."

"You know I've never piloted a starship before, right?"

Gant chittered in laughter. "Then it'll be more interesting. Besides, we're cloaked. They can't see us. Any day now, kid."

Erlan began shifting the thrust controls and updating the vectors. The system itself was somewhat similar to the Grabber, only with a lot more individual adjustments. Maybe if he could keep things simple, limit himself to the main thrusters and a few vectoring changes, he wouldn't frag up too badly.

He should have stayed on Feru. He was out of his league here, with these individuals, on this ship. He had put on a good enough front during the stop at the depot, but that wasn't him. He was scared out of his mind. He wasn't a real Republic soldier. He was militia, trained just enough to pretend to be a warrior.

He was ready to go home.

The *Brimstone* started moving, sinking toward the planet at half thrust. Waxaw had already helped him enter the rendezvous coordinates, and now it was up to him to get them there at the precise time. The *Faust* would be on its way, and it was his job to catch them.

No pressure.

"Sir," the mercenary, Lieutenant Iann said. "We have a problem."

Erlan felt his rapidly beating heart somehow increase its pace.

"What is it?" Gant asked.

"The debris field. We're going to have to move right through it to reach the collection point."

"So?"

"Cloaked ships still leave an outline when they're surrounded by space dust. Piselle knows were out here. If she's watching for us."

Gant stood on top of the command station, looking out of the viewport and at the HUD. Erlan looked with him.

Thraven's ships were visible on the sensors, arranged further out of orbit. Anvil's Planetary Defense was gone. So was the Outworld garrison. In terms of controlling the space around the planet, the invading force had already won.

"What kind of firepower do we have on this thing?" Gant asked.

"Torpedoes, plasma, heavy railguns," Iann said. "I'm trained on the weapons station."

"You can't shoot at the *Brimstone* with the *Brimstone*, can you?" Gant said. "Fine. Sit there and be ready. If there's any sign they see us, we'll have to come out of hiding and try to dissuade them another way."

"Aye, sir," Iann said.

Erlan swallowed hard. He was enjoying not being shot at.

The *Brimstone* continued onward. Erlan adjusted the vectors a few times, checking coordinates and watching the clock on the HUD. There was no word from Ruby yet on the *Faust's* escape. He hoped it would come soon.

A blinding flash ahead of the station drew his attention. A moment later, another followed it, lighting up the space to the port side of the bridge as the *Brimstone's* shields discharged.

"We're taking fire," Iann said. "I think they've spotted us."

"Evasive maneuvers, Nerd," Gant said. "Iann, prepare to fire back. Gavash, turn off the cloaking system."

"Aye, sir," Gavash said.

There was no obvious change inside the ship. There wasn't much change outside either. They had already been made, the density of the debris from the destruction of the Outworld defenses creating a silhouette around them.

"Incoming," Iann said.

The HUD in front of Erlan lit up, showing him that the shields were being hit with torpedoes. Three of them. The system absorbed the blow, but not without complaining heavily.

"I said evasive," Gant shouted.

Erlan shook slightly in fear, and then set himself on the task. His hands moved across the controls, adjusting vectors and thrust to start turning the *Brimstone* over on her side, and angling her to give the attacking ships less of a profile.

"Iann, you can fire whenever you're ready," Gant added. "Hopefully before we're all dead.

"Aye, sir," Iann said. "Firing."

Erlan could see the two torpedoes launch away from the *Brimstone*, streaking forward, covering kilometers in less than a second and then redirecting and bursting toward one of the enemy ships. They struck its shields a moment later.

"Direct hit," Iann said. "No damage. The shields are too strong." She paused a moment. "More incoming fire. All of Thraven's ships are vectoring toward us."

"Not in the mood for dying right now," Benhil said.

"We can't outrun them," Gant said. "Nerd, get us in close to that one. As close as you can."

"Aye, sir," Erlan said, adjusting the controls.

He did it almost without thinking, watching the HUD as he made changes, the computer updating the projected path and time. He brought them on a direct course toward the port flanking ship, one of the large, dark-hulled vessels accompanying the *Fire*.

Its attack intensified as they drew closer to it. Torpedoes streaked their way, quick points of light that covered the distance in milliseconds, slamming into the shields. Railgun slugs were invisible to the eye, but all too visible to the sensors, and the space ahead of them filled with the munitions, peppering the bow.

"We can't take this kind of fire for long," Iann said. "Shields are down forty percent."

"What does the word evade mean to you, Nerd?" Gant asked.

"I'm trying, sir. I told you I'm new at this."

"Try something else."

Erlan looked back at the HUD. There was only one thing he could think to do.

He returned to the throttle, increasing the main thrusters to full power. The *Brimstone* accelerated quickly, the force pushing him back in his seat. The computer began to belch out collision warnings, as the enemy warship closed within seconds.

"What the frag are you doing?" Gant said.

Erlan looked back at him. The Gant's eyes were so big it was almost funny.

"He'll move," he heard himself say. Since when was he so confident? "Iann, get ready to fire everything we've got."

The ship was huge in front of the viewport. Erlan checked the projections on the HUD. The target's path was changing, the vector updating as it tried to avoid being rammed.

Erlan powered up the vectoring thrusters, cutting the mains. The *Brimstone* sank slightly and then began to rotate, drifting through space as it turned, moving into position at the back of the enemy ship.

"Fire," Gant said.

"Firing," Iann replied.

Plasma beams and railgun rounds reached out from the broadside of the *Brimstone*, slamming into the rear of the enemy ship. Its shields continued to flash, absorbing the energy while trying to change its path and get back in the fight.

"No you don't," Erlan said, adding more power to the starboard thrusters and pulling the *Brimstone* back so that it was facing the enemy's rear. "Fire torpedoes. Now."

Iann did, loosing a pair of torpedoes toward the stern. The first one was caught by the shields, but the second made it through. Erlan nearly pissed himself as he watched the projectile vanish into the ship's thrusters, detonating a moment later in a bright flash of light. The enemy ship fell silent, and then the back half of it started to come apart, spreading into a new field of debris.

"Target disabled," Iann said.

"Nerd, you are insane," Gant said.

"I didn't think that would work," Erlan replied, a sudden sense of pride sneaking up on him. He had tried a similar tactic in the Construct once and had been rewarded with a quick death.

"Don't get too comfortable," Gant said. "There are four more of the bastards, and we need to get back on course."

"Gant," Ruby's voice cut into the bridge. "I've got Queenie and the others on board. We're headed for orbit. ETA one minute, fifteen seconds."

"Out of time already," Gant said. "Get us there, kid."

"Aye, sir," Erlan said, checking the HUD again.

The other ships were getting close, but they were fortunate. The maneuvering had left the collection point closer to their side.

The race was on.

CHAPTER FORTY-THREE

THE TRANSPORTER BROUGHT THEM OUT on the top of one of the buildings, a flat surface high above the platform where they had started. Jequn was already there, and she lifted the device behind them before pointing to the sky. The *Faust* was out there, angling back with a pair of Shrikes behind her.

"We're only going to get one shot at this," Abbey said. "Ruby, disable the hangar force field and bring her in."

"Roger."

"How are we going to get up there?" Bastion asked.

"I'll make the jump," Abbey said. "I'll drop the transporter, and you come through. No hesitation."

"Lieutenant," Jequn said. "I should do it. I have more experience."

"Okay."

Abbey watched the *Faust* begin to drop, streaking toward them with Thraven's fighters on her tail. The wing-mounted turrets were firing backward, keeping them from getting the easiest attack vector, but also sending their rounds slamming into the rooftop nearby. Jequn handed Abbey one of the transporter devices, and then moved to the lip of the building, ignoring the hail of fire peppering the side of the structure. She put her hands up, her head turning to track the ship. They would have five seconds at most to make the transfer.

"Get ready," Abbey said, activating her puck and tossing it on the rooftop. It wasn't blinking blue yet.

Dak and Bastion stood close to it, prepared to walk into the light. She watched Jequn start to run along the edge of the rooftop as the *Faust* swooped in.

Her heart nearly stopped when the woman jumped, launching forward as the *Faust* reached them, at first appearing as though she would slam right into the side. She timed her leap perfectly, passing through the open hangar and into it, no doubt hitting hard as the opposing vectors brought the wall to her at speed.

It didn't matter. The puck lit up in blue. Dak and Bastion both jumped in. Abbey followed a moment later.

She stepped out into the hangar, the technology of the device handling the inertia and keeping them steady within. Jequn hadn't been as fortunate, and she lay in the rear of the space against the bulkhead.

"Ruby, we're in," Abbey said. "Re-enable the shields and get us out of here."

"Roger. Welcome aboard."

"Lucifer, how's your health?"

"I feel better than new," Bastion replied, putting a hand to the hole Airi's sword had left in his clothes. "Revenge will be sweet, I'm sure."

"Keep us alive long enough to get it."

"Yes, ma'am."

Bastion sprinted out of the hangar, heading for the cockpit.

"Nice ship," Dak said, looking around. "A little small."

"We've got a bigger one waiting upstairs. It's called the *Brimstone*. You might be familiar with it?"

Dak huffed and then was nearly knocked over when the *Faust* banked hard to the left.

Abbey kept her feet planted, holding on until they leveled out again.

"Queenie, best to buckle in somewhere," Bastion said. "It's going to get a lot worse."

"Give me twenty seconds."

"I'll try."

Abbey made her way to Jequn, leaning over her and picking her up. The woman gasped when she was lifted, her eyes opening, staring up at Abbey as she carried her away from the hangar.

"Did we make it?" she asked.

"Yes, thanks to you. Will you heal?"

"I will, but not quickly. I expended a lot of strength to repair your friend."

"Thank you."

Abbey brought her to the ladder. "Can you climb?"

Before she could answer, the *Faust* tilted again, dipping downward. Abbey grabbed the ladder, holding it tight to keep them from crashing into the wall again.

"Lucifer," she said.

"Would you rather be dead?" Bastion replied. "Hold tight."

The *Faust* bucked a few times before rising, the nose pointing steeply upward. Abbey continued to hold the ladder with one hand, getting her arm around Jequn's waist to keep them from being thrown back by the ascent.

"Queenie," Ruby said. "Gant and the *Brimstone* are decloaked and moving into intercept position. Gant reports that the *Fire* and three other ships are adjusting course to block."

"Fragging Thraven," Abbey said. "Don't worry about us. Do whatever you have to do to get there."

"I was planning on it," Bastion said.

The *Faust* continued its sharp climb, vibrating slightly as it hit the atmosphere, the gravity generators gradually easing her feet back to the floor. It was an odd adjustment from her angle, but she was grateful when she was able to stand again.

She helped Jequn up the ladder, showing her where to sit before rushing to the cockpit. Bastion was at the controls, while Ruby was managing the rotating turrets, firing back at the Shrikes still tailing them. She could see the *Brimstone* ahead, already in position and taking fire from the incoming ships. Shields flared around the starship, while streaks of light crossed the distance to the attackers, trading torpedo for torpedo.

Except the *Brimstone* was outnumbered four to one. There was no way she would survive for long.

"She should have a few docking rings underneath," Ruby said, her eyes closed while she studied the schematics Olus had provided. "We can clamp on there."

"What about the hangar?" Abbey asked.

"She won't fit," Bastion replied, eyeballing it. "Not with these long-ass wings."

"Ring it is."

"Bringing her in," Bastion said, increasing thrust and velocity.

The view in the cockpit started to rotate as he put the *Faust* into a corkscrew spin. Tracers streamed past the ship, the Shrike pilots trying to keep pace with the maneuver. The *Faust* was getting ever-closer to the *Brimstone*, approaching at speed.

"You need to slow down," Abbey said.

"I don't tell you how to grow claws, don't tell me how to fly."

Bastion's expression was intense as they drew near the *Brimstone*, passing underneath in the opposite direction of the warship's forward momentum.

"Where the hell are you going?" Abbey said.

"Relax. I've got this."

He hit the forward vectoring thrusters, sending the ship up and over, putting them back in the right direction and inverted compared to the bottom of the ship. Abbey was pushed back against the rear bank of electronics by the shift in force, feeling the pressure. Ruby kept the main cannons firing on the incoming Shrikes, hitting one of them while the other peeled away.

"See, now we aren't going too fast," Bastion said, increasing velocity to get back beneath the *Brimstone*. A torpedo flashed to their left, threatening to hit nearby, only to be absorbed by the shields.

"Gant," Ruby said. "We need shields down on the hull for docking."

"Roger," Gant said. "Give us a minute to find the switch."

"Are you kidding?" Bastion said.

He toggled the HUD, switching the view to show him his alignment against the opposite clamp.

"Okay, they should be off. We can't reactivate the shields down there while you're connected."

"Roger," Bastion said. "I already knew that."

Bastion guided the *Faust* forward, using the HUD to line things up. Flashes of light surrounded them, the shields taking the hits. But for how long?

"Queenie, we're getting blasted out here," Gant said.

"Are we ready for FTL?"

"We would be, but there's a group of warships in the way."

"The *Fire*?"

"Of course."

"Weapons?"

"Nearly out of torpedoes. Plasma is pretty much useless. We identified a weaker spot in their asses and took one of them out, but I don't think they're going to let us get back there to frag them again."

"They twisted the Gift to their needs," Jequn said. "We were never able to overcome the monstrosities they created. The ships are only one kind."

"You'll have to explain that to me later," Abbey said. "Right now, we need to get around those bastards and get out of here. Do you know of anything we can use? Any specific tactics that worked out for you?"

Jequn shook her head. "No. I'm sorry. We've been in hiding for a reason."

"Why the hell did you come out now?" Bastion asked.

"Because we had to. It isn't by choice."

Bastion adjusted the yoke, maneuvering the *Faust* into position. He hit a switch, and Abbey could hear the docking motor humming. The ship jerked slightly as the clamps connected, anchoring them to the underside of the *Brimstone*.

"Nerd," Abbey said. "Can you get us past those ships?"

"I'm trying, ma'am," Erlan said.

"I'm holding my breath here," Abbey said. "Don't make this the last one I take."

"Uh. Aye, ma'am."

"Get it up on sensors if you can," Abbey said, pointing to the inverted HUD. Their view was limited hanging from the warship's belly.

Bastion reached up, toggling controls to get the sensor view loaded. They could see the *Faust* inlaid on the larger icon of the *Brimstone*, with three other ships arranged in their path.

"I don't like the looks of that," Bastion said.

"Have a little faith," Abbey said.

"Our current pilot has less experience flying than our pleasure synth."

"I have the equivalent of four thousand hours in my memory stores," Ruby said.

"Vertical or horizontal?" Bastion said.

The *Brimstone* shook violently, and they shook with it, nearly getting knocked over.

"Maybe we shouldn't have connected," Bastion said.

"We all make it, or we all die," Abbey said.

"I'm putting my bets on die."

"You're always such a positive, cheerful individual."

"I do my best."

Abbey cringed when the *Brimstone* shook again. They were closing on the ships, and it was clear their exit point was in the center.

"Gant," Abbey said. "What the frag?"

"Shields are failing, Queenie," Gant said. "We're taking hits. Armor is absorbing a lot of it, but it won't last. Nerd's doing the best he can. Pretty damn good, all things considered."

"How long to FTL?"

"Ten seconds."

Abbey stared at the HUD as if she could will the position of the ships to change. The *Fire* was shifting in front of them, adjusting course to intercept, to block the egress. The *Brimstone* changed direction to match, trying to slip beneath.

"We aren't going to make it," Jequn said.

"Yes, we are," Abbey replied. "I didn't do all of this to die out of the fight. Bastion, give me full thrusters."

"What?" Bastion said. "Why? Oh." He smiled, pushing the throttle all the way open, and then grabbing the yoke. He shoved it forward, getting vectoring thrusters angling to help turn the *Brimstone* away from the *Fire*. "I think it's working."

The *Fire* was so close the icons were nearly touching, the *Brimstone* barely scraping by. Abbey looked up and out the viewport. The entire field was filled with debris and derelict Outworld ships, the remains of Anvil's orbital garrison.

It was gone. All gone. The planet was going to fall to Thraven, and they had no choice but to run.

But run where?

"We're clear," Bastion shouted. "Wooooo."

Abbey turned her head. She could see Thraven's warships on their flank, a pair of torpedoes angling in.

"Initiating FTL," Erlan announced.

The starfield shifted, filling almost instantly with the nebulous vapors of disterium gas. The torpedoes vanished into the field, rocking the *Brimstone* with one last heavy blow. If that one didn't destroy them, they would make it out.

Abbey froze, staring at the universe ahead.

Space bent around them.

Then they were free.

CHAPTER FORTY-FOUR

THE CREW OF THE *FIRE'S* bridge came to attention as Gloritant Thraven entered. He had an interesting look on his face, one that managed to meld anger, frustration, satisfaction, and amusement into one package.

His surviving Immolent entered behind him, flanked by a newcomer to the bridge, and to the *Fire*. A woman, but not the woman he had been after.

"Agitant Sol," Thraven said. "What is your report?"

Sol turned to face him, raising his hand in salute. "Gloritant. We tracked the *Brimstone* the moment she decloaked, trailing her toward the surface of the planet. At the same time, we began receiving reports from our Shrike pilots that a single Outworld ship had broken away from the spaceport cordon and was en route. Trajectory models suggested the two events were unrelated, but the *Brimstone* and the Outworld ship both made tight vector adjustments near the tail of their maneuvers to bring themselves in line. Your Eminence, we struck the *Brimstone* with six torpedoes and enough plasma fire to destroy an entire city. We believe she sustained heavy damage, but it wasn't enough. The ships were able to make their rendezvous and maneuver around our fleet and into FTL."

A silence fell over the bridge when the Agitant finished. Thraven didn't react. He stared out of the viewport into space.

"Your Eminence?" Sol said after a minute. "Are you well, Gloritant?"

Thraven's head turned slowly. He barely flicked his finger, and Sol fell over, dead.

"Am I well?" Thraven said softly.

He was considering it. Accounting for all of the sides. He had lost Abigail Cage. She had rebuked him. Even in the face of the loss of her mind and all that she was, she had denied him. He hated being refused. He also respected it. She had stood up to him when so many had not. It was an endearing trait in its own way. One that he could have looked back on fondly had he been given the chance to destroy her.

But he hadn't.

The Ophanim had intervened. The Watchers. The last of the followers. Phanuel himself had come to counter him, to challenge him, to save the life of the woman who had quickly grown from a needle under his foot to a powerful thorn in his side. He had sacrificed his life so that she could escape. And he had killed one of his Immolent.

Still, killing Phanuel had been a pleasure. An enjoyment he hadn't felt in years. Long had he desired to remove the head of a Seraphim once more, and he knew that day would come because the Father had promised it. The day was here, and it was good.

Abigail Cage had escaped. And that wasn't good. Not at all. The Ophanim clearly saw enough in her that they had given up their most experienced warrior for her. Why? Her control of the Gift was impressive, but she had refused to take the other half. She would be altered, and in that alteration become useless to them. Worthless. Did they think she could help them before that happened?

Did they think she could defeat him?

Never. He would see to it that she couldn't. Wherever she went, he would find her. He would hunt her. He would send out his Children. He would send out his Evolents. Perhaps he would even send out an Immolent. He'd like to see Cage deal with that. As for himself, he couldn't put any more of his personal energy into her. He had a harvest to plan. A mission to fulfill. He had taken a risk with the *Brimstone*, and he had ultimately come out ahead. Phanuel's death was worth more than Cage's life. So was Anvil and the crops he would reap here. So was the *Fire*, and all of the ships being integrated.

Right now he would focus on securing the planet and starting the process of rounding up the healthiest of the surviving soldiers to transfer back to Kell to be integrated into the systems of the waiting ships. They would need more than he had originally planned. He had taken one risk. He wasn't taking any more.

"Honorant Piselle," he said quietly.

"Yes, Gloritant?" Piselle replied.

"Contact the other commanders. Tell them to prepare to accept cargo. I want it delivered back to Kell as quickly as possible. Make sure they, as well as you, understand you have failed me in the simple task of destroying a single starship when you outnumbered it five to one. It is a failure that will not be permitted to happen again. A failure that I am only allowing now because I don't have the time or energy to replace you at the moment. A failure that has cost Agitant Sol his life on your behalf. I will not accept such failure again. Do you understand?"

"Yes, Gloritant," Piselle replied, clearly shaken.

"Gloritant Thraven?"

Thraven shifted his eyes until they landed on the woman who arrived with him. She was a poor excuse of a replacement for Cage, and while she had tasted the Blood of Life and survived, he could tell her potential was weak in comparison. Even so, she would make a fair Evolent given enough time.

"I'm sorry to bother you, sir," she said. "I took a big risk joining you. You see, when we were released from Hell, Captain Mann had something injected into our heads, to kill us if we tried to run. I thought with your power; you would be able to remove it or disarm it or something before Queenie had a chance to trigger it."

Thraven raised his eyebrow. "Interesting," he said, reaching out with the Gift. He connected it to hers, using it to scan her for anything out of the ordinary. Then he allowed himself a small smile.

"What is it?" Airi asked, confused.

"There is nothing in your head that isn't supposed to be there."

"What?"

"I'm afraid Captain Mann was playing you all for fools. You believed what you wanted to believe, based on his suggestions."

"But. But that means Queenie must know the truth. She's keeping it from the others. That bitch."

Thraven didn't react. His mind had already moved on, carrying the new information forward, calculating how he might use it to his advantage. Cage was strong, but would she be even half as strong without support?

It was a possibility he would have to consider further.

"Gloritant," Honorant Piselle said. "The commanders have been notified. Ground forces are beginning to collect specimens for testing."

"Very good," Thraven replied. "This is Noviant Airi. Show her to the quarters beside mine. She will be in training to carry out the will of the Father."

"Yes, Gloritant." Piselle looked at Airi, her jealousy obvious. "Follow me, Noviant."

Airi glanced at Thraven.

"Your training will begin when we return to Kell," he said. "I have no need of you until then."

He could see her become angry. Good. Anger was an essential fuel for the Gift. It would make her stronger if she could learn to harness it.

"What did you think you were coming to, Noviant?" he said. "Unlike others you may have served, I have no need or desire for your flesh. What I do require is complete obedience and devotion to the way of the Covenant. You will not survive here any other way. I can be a harsh master, but I will lead you and all of our kind to glory. I will fulfill the promise of the Father and herald the Great Return. That is my oath to you, and to all who serve." He glanced at Piselle. "Take her."

Piselle tried to grab Airi's arm, but she yanked it away. "I can take care of myself." She headed off the bridge ahead of the Honorant, leaving Thraven's presence without honor or respect.

Thraven watched her go for a moment. He would accept her lapse one time, and then he would be forced to teach her. He didn't think it would come to that. Trinity had once been equally angry and difficult to control, and he had brought her in line.

"Agitant Malt, the bridge is yours until Honorant Piselle returns," Thraven said.

"Yes, Gloritant," Malt replied.

Thraven left the bridge, trailed by his Immolent. He required time to recover in the Font, but there was one other thing he wanted to do first.

He crossed the corridors of the *Fire*, his servants moving hastily aside as he passed, kneeling or saluting, looking on him with respect and awe. He ignored them, singular in his pursuit.

He entered Medical soon after, making his way to an isolation room in the back corner. The hatch opened ahead of him.

A Lrug was sitting on the floor in the corner. He looked tired and beaten, his eyes heavy, his body bruised. Resting upright beside him was a closed case. A decapitated head in a gel solution was set on the table for treatment.

"Villaueve," Thraven said. "I am Gloritant Thraven."

The Lrug stood. "Gloritant?" Villaueve said. "Those things that took me work for you?"

Thraven nodded. "They are like children to me."

"They could have been a little more gentle. I didn't resist."

"You know how children can be."

"Right. If you don't mind me asking, sir, what am I doing here?"

"The same as you were before. No more. No less. And when you are done, perhaps you'll go free."

"Perhaps?"

"You're reliant on my magnanimity. Be careful."

Villaueve kept his eyes down. "You want me to integrate the head into the suit?"

"Yes."

"It isn't going to work. Not without Gorix to do the larger pieces. Your children killed him."

"Worry only about your part in this, Villaueve. I will take care of the rest."

"And then you'll let me go?"

"Perhaps."

"Perhaps. Right. What's so important about this woman that everyone wants her alive again?"

"Good help is hard to find."

Villaueve started to laugh, trailing off when he saw Thraven wasn't amused at all. "Yes, sir."

Thraven moved forward, leaning down in front of the head, looking into its dead eyes. Ursan Gall had been an idiot who ultimately needed to die. Trinity? She had still been one of his best, and thanks to the one misguided but intelligent thing her husband had done, perhaps she would be again.

He had need of a new Immolent. Maybe he would even give her a second chance with Cage. To convince her to join them? He still wanted her power under his control, especially now that he knew that she had asserted. On the other hand, she was a painful thorn, one that might be better off removed completely. No matter. He had time to decide.

"Am I well?" he said.

He paused a moment and then smiled. Cage was only one individual. The *Brimstone* was only one ship. Even with the aid of the Ophanim, it wouldn't be nearly enough to stop the harvest. It wouldn't be nearly enough to prevent him from leading the Nephilim to glory.

"Yes. I am. I'm very well, indeed."

CHAPTER FORTY-FIVE

ABBEY REACHED THE BRIDGE OF the *Brimstone*, with Bastion, Ruby, Dak, and Jequn following at her heels. She heard the unmistakable chitter of excitement before she even saw Gant, and she smiled widely when he came into view, standing on the arm of the command station to get himself closer to her height.

"Queenie!" he barked.

"Gant," she replied, leaning forward and hugging him. She could hear him purring as she did, and he shoved his arms against her to push himself away.

"Damn. Not in public." He was still purring. "Stop it." He closed his eyes. "Fragging larynx."

"Maybe I should be calling you freak-kitty instead?" Bastion said.

"Shut it," Gant replied. He backed away. "I wish I could be happier to have you here, Queenie, but we've got complications."

"What else is new?" Bastion said.

"What kind of complications?"

"Well." He waved his arm out at the bridge, where half a dozen crew members she didn't recognize were stationed. "That's one."

One of the crew members was standing, and she came forward. "Lieutenant Olain Iann," she said, introducing herself. Her attention shifted to Dak, her expression turning fearful. "Sir?"

"Lieutenant Iann," Dak replied. "This ship is under Republic control, and you're still alive. Why is that?"

"Sir, we were led to believe we were boarded by General Thraven's forces. We didn't come to realize we were misled until it was too late."

"Led to believe?" Gant said. "Misled? Bullshit. You said it first, I just went along with it." He looked at Dak. "Wow. You're bigger than Pik. Where's Fury?"

Abbey felt her hands clench at the question.

"Gone," Bastion said. "She turned traitor on us."

Benhil appeared from the side of the space. He was still armed and armored, keeping an eye on the bridge crew. "Shit. Are you going to send the signal, Queenie?"

Abbey shook her head. "It won't do any good. Thraven will have disabled it by now."

"Maybe we should all go-" Benhil stopped talking when Abbey glared at him. "Nevermind."

"Dak," Abbey said. "Are you willing to take responsibility for this crew?"

"I don't know." He eyed Iann. "Mutiny? After all these years?"

"Sir, you can't argue that the Captain was losing it. You saw what he did to Ligit."

"Besides," Gant said. "They didn't have that much of a choice. Not really. I mean, I did kill half your crew."

"You?" Dak said, surprised. "Alone?"

Gant nodded in reply.

"If you don't mind me asking, sir," Iann said. "Why are you here with these individuals?"

"She's got you there," Benhil said.

"I'm loyal to Ursan," Dak said. "But I can't say his mind was right, and he did lose fair. Queenie even tried to let him off the hook. And then there's Thraven. You've seen he's no friend to the Outworlds. We got him these ships, and now he's using them to attack our planets. He lied to us. He tricked us. Trin and Ursan are both dead because of it. I don't know who he is or where he came from yet, but I know this universe is going to suffer if he gets what he wants, and the enemy of my enemy is my friend."

"Well said," Abbey said. "This isn't about Republic or Outworld. What's happening here is bigger than all of that, and it's been cooking for a long, long time. We aren't many, not yet, but we're the only ones who can do anything about it right now."

"At least we captured the *Brimstone*," Bastion said. "Halfway there, right?"

"Yeah, about that," Gant said. "Remember I said complications? Plural. As in more than one."

"What's wrong with the *Brimstone*?" Abbey asked.

"Those last two torpedoes did a number on her. Somehow she's still holding together, but I'm not sure what we're going to have left when we come out of FTL. Not to mention, we expended almost eighty percent of her munitions shooting back at the *Fire*."

"Severely damaged and unarmed?" Bastion said. "That's more like us."

"Where are we retreating to?" Abbey asked.

"An Outworld system Jester recommended," Gant said. "Machina Four?"

"Never heard of it."

"It's not on standard maps," Benhil said. "But we can trade our disterium to resupply there, and if we need any repairs, that's the place to do it."

"How far is it from Kell?"

"Kell?" Benhil said. "As in the cartel?"

"That's where Thraven's building his fleet," Dak said.

"We need to get to Kell and stop him before he can launch any more ships," Abbey said.

"Good plan in theory, Queenie," Bastion said. "But in case you missed it, we just got our asses kicked. So did you, as surprising as that is. We can't go to Kell. Not if Thraven is going to be there. Not unless you want to die."

"I don't intend to just go to Kell." Abbey turned to face Jequn.

"You came to Anvil for a reason. You saved my life for a reason. Your friend sacrificed himself for a reason. I think now is a good time to tell us who you are, where you came from, and what you know."

Jequn met Abbey's gaze. Then she nodded, took a deep, strong breath, and began to speak.

81446620R00151

Made in the USA
San Bernardino, CA
07 July 2018